The Immortals

The Immortals

TORI EVERSMANN

2MUDDYLABS
2MUDDY LABS PRESS
WEST PALM BEACH
2015

Published by 2Muddy Labs Press
West Palm Beach, FL
www.2MuddyLabs.com
Cover design by Katie Campbell

Manufactured in the United States of America
First Edition 2015

ISBN: 978-09965-66-7-04 (hardcover edition)
ISBN: 978-09965-66-7-28 (trade paperback edition)

For
The Diva War Brides
and for
the other Immortal Wives and Mothers
of Operation Iraqi Freedom

The minute I heard my first love story,
I started looking for you, not knowing
how blind that was.
Lovers don't finally meet somewhere.
They're in each other all along.

—Rumi

Embrace the change no matter what it is; once you
do, you can learn about the new world you're in and
take advantage of it.

—Nikki Giovanni

1

2006

The car shimmied as Calli Coleman gripped the wheel. Even in June, the wind off Lake Ontario nudged them from side to side, blowing her small family and her toward a future she could not imagine. Clouds wandered across the northern New York sky, seeking a place to settle. The silos, farms, and pastures tucked right up to the edge of the highway, boxing her in.

Behind her in the Land Rover, Audrey, already three, watched a movie on the portable DVD player. Giggling and watching intently, Audrey was truly a little girl now, and getting so big. Calli was finally starting to trust herself as a mother, but it hadn't been an easy road. For the first two years of Audrey's life, a maternal alarm had buzzed Calli from sleep almost every night. She had to make sure Audrey was still breathing; she'd read so many articles about crib death. Babies suffocated in their own beds by blankets or stuffed animals. But every night, there she was, her chest gently rising and falling without fail.

Even now, Calli wasn't sure she was a *good* mother. Was she? When Calli was a child, her own mother had screamed, unprovoked, at her and her sister that she was a bad mother, that she couldn't take the stress of motherhood. Yes, the girls had told her. You are a good mother. The best mother ever. Calli was never sure if what they were saying was true, but it seemed to be what their mother wanted to hear.

"Mama," Audrey shouted, huge earphones covering her ears and most of her cheeks like a pilot readying her jumbo jet, "the player isn't working." Calli twisted her right arm back and felt the DVD buttons like braille to figure out the problem, balancing the steering wheel with her knee and one hand, ensuring that she wouldn't veer out of her lane. She just wanted to get there. Their new house. Their new life.

Luke, Satchmo, and Charlemagne were in the SUV, behind Calli and Audrey. Luke had offered to take their dog and cat in the truck. As soon as they left Baltimore, Satchmo would settle into the passenger seat, snoring and farting, but Charlemagne's incessant meowing—now *that* would have driven Calli off the road.

The Army had contracted a moving company to pack and bring their things to Sackets Harbor, but necessaries—bottles of Merlot and Chardonnay, vodka, bourbon; bags of pasta and boxes of couscous; a small library of cookbooks and recipes; novels, videos, and toys for Audrey; olive oils and three different vinegars, some kitchen utensils and camping gear, tailgating chairs, Calli's untuned guitar, and clothes—were tucked where they could fit in the cars. Though the Army guaranteed their things would arrive safely at their destination, delivery could take anywhere from ten days to three weeks.

Three weeks on an inflatable mattress in sleeping bags.

Victorian homes and dilapidated barns lined the road as they entered Jefferson County on Interstate 81. Calli took it all in: the crumbling gingerbread lattice, the nineteenth-century hay rake in an overgrown pasture, roadside creameries selling cheese curd and homemade ice cream, a storage facility emerging out of a plot where a house had been razed. But hey, Calli thought, it was better than Watertown or Carthage or living on post at Fort Drum.

One month ago. Had it really been a month? One month ago, she and Luke had been on Nantucket at her parents' summer house, a circa-1800 residence with weathered shingles, blue shutters, and big hydrangeas on the eastern end of the island, where Calli had spent most of her childhood summers. It was there she'd learned to ride a bike and sail at the yacht club, to cast for bluefish off the wide beaches in the roiling Atlantic waves, to bodysurf, drink beer, and smoke bongs; to know when a boiled lobster was ready. It was there she'd lost her virginity on a very sandy beach after her senior year of high school to the cute, tan lifeguard from Harvard. Calli had always dreamed that one day she and Luke might own their own place there instead of leeching off her parents' generosity. That would have to be after the Army now. At least two and a half years away.

One month ago, they'd been drinking age-worthy wines at the Nantucket Wine Festival. When they rolled off the ferry in Hyannis, they'd driven straight from Cape Cod to northern New York. All the way up to Fort Drum. The Army had given them options: Fort Polk in Vernon Parish, Louisiana; Fort Richardson in Anchorage; or Fort Drum, in Nowheresville, New York.

Today as she drove north with the drone of the car humming and stale gum grinding between her teeth, Calli's mind wandered back to that initial, dreadful visit.

Last month, exiting the interstate had been a relief after eight empty hours on the road, but the place depressed her instantly. It was one of those places she used to see in movies about war, one of those places where the people who were left behind lived. She couldn't stand the idea of living on an Army post, especially not in the enlisted soldiers' housing. There were no sidewalks. No parks. Just gravelly parking lots with American-made pickup trucks and Japanese compacts with a barrage of bumper stickers and decals: HEROES DON'T WEAR CAPES—THEY WEAR DOG TAGS; IF YOU CAN'T GET BEHIND OUR TROOPS, FEEL FREE TO STAND IN FRONT OF THEM; FREEDOM IS NOT FREE; ARMY WIFE; NO I'M NOT SINGLE—HE'S DEPLOYED; GOD AND GUNS: TWO THINGS YOU CAN STILL BELIEVE IN. And everywhere, yellow ribbon magnets. At one intersection, there was a drive-through car wash with seven stalls, a McDonalds, Ting Lings' Chinese To-Go, Burger King, and a dilapidated bank building of crumbling stone. Every other mile, a commercial real-estate sign hawked cheap land zoned for big-box stores and fast-food chain restaurants. *BUILD TO SUIT. 20+ ACRES. ZONED COMMERCIAL. 45 ACRES PRIME.* Scattered at the edges of the sprawl were what must have at one time been beautiful—now abandoned—farmhouses. These days, they were decrepit heaps of clapboards, with broken glass or missing windows, the trim nibbled away by termites. A sagging chimney or two.

At the entrance to Fort Drum, long lines of vehicles sat waiting to go through the barricades at the front gate. The sign to her right proudly read, WELCOME TO FORT DRUM. HOME OF THE 10TH MOUNTAIN DIVISION. The unit patch—red, white, and blue, of course—stood off to the left of the words. Just beyond the campy welcome rose an enormous digital sign with bold red letters: STOP! Everyone had to stop and show a government-issued ID or pull over and prove their intent before entering the post.

"Wow, this is pretty insane," Calli said, watching the line creep ahead. "Will it be like this all the time?"

"I think so," Luke replied.

"Right. That's just great. Lovely."

"What am I supposed to do, Cal? I can't make this line go faster. I'm sorry."

Calli stared out the window.

"You act like I orchestrated this whole move just to ruin your life," Luke said. "Seriously, can you imagine if we'd moved to Alaska?"

"I know. I'm a snob. You married a snob. I can't help it. It's just . . . just not what I expected." She shook her head, trying to shake off her dark mood. She knew she was acting childish. They'd discussed their options—together—for weeks, before finally arriving at what seemed like the best choice for the three of them. This wasn't the time to make Luke feel bad.

Ten minutes and one car inspection later, a soldier waved them through.

"Have a good day, Master Sergeant," he said.

"Thanks, Corporal."

"How can you tell he's a corporal?" Calli asked once they'd driven off.

"It's on his uniform," Luke said.

Despite being married to a soldier, Calli had realized more and more in recent weeks that she knew next to nothing about the military or how Luke spent his days. Back when they'd first met, he'd shielded her from the details of his time in the infantry, with the Ranger Battalion in Panama. It was ancient history anyway, he'd tell her. Since then, he'd taken a position at the Army War College for three years and then as an instructor teaching ROTC at Johns Hopkins. For a long time, it was easy for Calli to forget, given Luke's nine-to-five life in academia, that he'd ever been active duty, or that there was always the possibility he would have to return to an infantry unit.

Reality hit her hard as they drove through post on roads called Riva Ridge, Po Valley, and General Pike Loop. Somewhere in her memory, she recalled these names from a WWII history class she'd taken in college. They passed a twenty-four-hour gas station with coin-op laundry and a Popeye's chicken, then row after row of dingy brick barracks. The institutional architecture, soldiers in camouflage running alongside the road in formation, and dearth of landscaping depressed her. Neighborhoods named Monument Ridge, Adirondack Creek, and Rhicard Hills posed as some kind of ersatz suburbia. The Fort Drum Inn looked less like an inn and more like an elementary school. Uniformly drab townhouses lined cement sidewalks. The base stretched out across hundreds of numbingly neat acres, devoid of character. Everything looked alike. She could imagine going to the playground with Audrey and returning to the wrong house on the wrong street.

At the housing office, a disinterested and unhelpful civilian explained that it was doubtful they could get a three-bedroom, given their family size. Instead, he informed them, they were on the list for a two-bedroom. Luke groaned. They didn't have time to wait and see if the three-bedroom came available. Luke had to report to his new position next month.

As they walked to the car, Calli's temples began to throb. Fort Drum's regulated facade, cookie-cutter neighborhoods, and lack of character overwhelmed her. This is not where I'm going to live, she thought. No fucking way. If Luke was concerned, he hid it well. Too well. Was this place okay for him? How could he think that she'd be happy there? That Audrey would be happy there?

Audrey, oblivious in the back, seemed not to notice that their future looked much different from their past. There would be no more My-Gym, visits to the Smithsonian to see the dinosaurs, or first-class nursery school guaranteed to fast-track Audrey into a private school of their choice. Whatever comfort they'd had was gone. It was like Luke had put them on a rocket and flown them to the moon.

"I'm not living on post," Calli said, settling into the passenger seat.

"Let's check out Sackets Harbor," Luke suggested gently.

After their disastrous tour of Fort Drum, they headed west toward the lake.

Sackets Harbor boasted two claims to fame, they soon learned: the War of 1812, and Funny Cide, the thoroughbred who'd won the Kentucky Derby and the Preakness Stakes in 2003. Calli already knew that it wouldn't be as cozy as Nantucket, but she hoped that a small village on the water would have some redeeming qualities. But the approach to Sackets didn't bode well: more failing farms, Victorians in need of a facelift, trailer homes and double-wides, prefab Colonials in incomplete developments.

But as they drove over a one-lane bridge on Military Road, the landscape changed into neat properties and manicured lawns. They passed Battlefield State Park, where reenactors in nineteenth-century garb milled around chatting with tourists. Calli became optimistic as they got closer to the center of the village. Old Glories hung from telephone poles and porches. A makeshift sign read CONCERT IN THE PARK SUNDAY AT 5 P.M. Children fed ducks in the harbor. Life.

WELCOME TO HISTORIC SACKETS HARBOR.

These goddamn welcome signs everywhere, Calli thought. Like they have to convince me that I'm welcome.

The tiny village sat on the eastern shore of Lake Ontario about five miles north of the Tug Hill Plateau, otherwise called the Snow Belt. Maybe winter in Sackets Harbor would bear some vague resemblance to winter life in Nantucket, where everyone hunkered down and enjoyed the dwindled population. But Sackets Harbor was far from a destination for those East Coasters who wanted to hit the beaches, eat in upscale restaurants, shop in boutiques, and hobnob with the occasional celebrity. No, Sackets would never be that.

The upside was that Sackets appeared to have a personality. There was quaintness to it. Georgian Revivals and brick Federals, small Victorians and Italianate mansions dotted the main road. Scattered among the classics were a smattering of Cape Cods and Saltboxes. Maybe a small village would be just the place to call home while Luke was out in the woods training with his men. Maybe it would be easy to make friends here.

Luke and Calli relaxed as they rambled into town. The main drag, only two blocks long, was lined with towering old trees. Each lamppost boasted exuberant arrangements of colorful pelargoniums, chartreuse sweet potato vine, and a profusion of vinca cascading down from their baskets. People walked dogs. There was a wine store, a couple of restaurants, a bookstore, a bank, and a church. There was even a comedy club. Calli wished the two blocks were four, but she'd take it. If this was the best in the area, then she'd settle. She watched as people emerged from the wine store smiling. This might not be so awful, she thought.

"I'm starved," Luke said. "Let's find a place to eat."

"There's a barbeque spot at the end of the block down there," Calli said. "Wanna try that?"

They parked the car, removed Audrey from her car seat, and

entered the restaurant. Immediately, Calli smelled disinfectant that reminded her of the time in fourth grade Sheila Talbot had thrown up right next her desk. For days, the astringent smell hung in the classroom, making Calli want to vomit herself. It was the same kind of disinfectant bars used after the beer swillers, cigarette smokers, and sweet-drink spillers had left for the night. Perhaps this place was a hopping spot after dinner.

"We're supposed to meet Louise, the real-estate agent, in an hour."

"We've got time," Luke said, cracking open a plastic menu.

"This place smells like a frat house."

Luke grinned.

"Luke, I'm serious," she said trying not to laugh.

"I know you are. That's why I love you."

"Maybe next time, we'll try one of the other restaurants for dinner. It's nice to have choices. This place is cute, Luke. And so much better than Fort Drum. I think you were right—"

"What was that?" Luke cut in, one eyebrow inching up mischievously.

"Luke!"

"Come on. Say it again."

"You were right, okay? You were right."

Two days later, they put in an offer on a three-bedroom house with gray shingles and a tall oak with a swing in the backyard.

2

Years before Calli met Luke, his unit had been sent to Panama to find Noriega. A mission called Just Cause. The fighting was brutal. Twenty-three men died in the battle and over three hundred were wounded. Luke was lucky to come home alive.

Around the time Luke and Calli met, a journalist named Ned Haworth wrote an article about the battle, which ended up becoming a book. The book sold thousands of copies and attracted the interest of a big-time director, David Hess. Named after the Panamanian military camp where the Ranger Force bore the brunt of the fight, *Rio Hato* was going to be a big-budget production, and Hess, who admired Luke for his bravery, wrote him in as the hero. For months, Hess picked Luke's brain: What did it smell like? How did the air feel? What was jumping out of a plane like? What music did he and his men listen to?

Calli, a bit bewildered by the absurdity of the situation, was nonetheless impressed. In all her years of performing with orchestras, she'd never been singled out for anything. Mastering her beloved French horn and graduating from Juilliard seemed like a pale accomplishment next to Luke's courage. And Luke, of course, took the attention in stride, answering Hess's endless questions, graciously giving interviews to promote the film, heaping praise and gratitude on those men he'd fought with.

Shortly after they were married, Mr. Hess flew Calli and Luke first-class to LA the day before the movie premiered. At LAX, they spied a limousine parked at the curb right outside the baggage claim. "I bet that's for us," Luke whispered, and it was. Inside there were supple leather seats and crystal glasses and Champagne.

As the car pulled under the Four Seasons porte cochere, Calli scanned the mob coming and going in front of the building. Who was famous? Who was who? Calli was awestruck by Luke's calm. He swaggered across the driveway as though he was already a Hollywood veteran.

The next morning, Luke and Calli took a long walk over to Rodeo Drive, bemused by the glitz and glamour. Luke took Calli's picture standing under the Rodeo Drive street sign. A Juilliard friend and his wife met them for lunch. Calli didn't remember what anyone said; she was so nervous about the night ahead. Even a glass of Prosecco at the hotel bar did nothing to abate her nerves.

When they went back to the room to get dressed, Luke changed his shirt three times. So he was nervous after all. Calli, meanwhile, took two hours to apply her makeup. When she was done, the concierge called: another limo was waiting to take them to the theater.

Downstairs in the Four Seasons lobby, they met up with a couple of the men who had been in Panama with Luke. They'd been hired as military consultants on the film, and now they were waiting for their own limos with their wives. Everything felt larger than life.

Calli's heart raced as they approached the Academy of Motion Picture Arts and Sciences. She was going to walk the red carpet. It didn't matter to her that she wasn't famous; this was their fifteen minutes of fame. Stalwart and elegant, Luke smiled at her as they pulled up to the curb.

When their driver stopped, droves of people surrounded them. Everyone wanted to know who was stepping out of the line of limos. Would the paparazzi shrivel when the two of them emerged? Had the stars already arrived? Craving a cigarette, although she'd quit so long ago, Calli stared out at the crowd. Someone opened the door for them. Flashes, shouts, the red carpet and velvet ropes. They spotted Ned Haworth nearby. He motioned for Luke to make the celebratory, slow walk with him up to the front. Calli walked behind them, taking her time, aware but not unhappy that no one cared about her. By now, she was used to following Luke.

As a young woman, she never would have imagined she would be in her husband's shadow, but here she was. For so long, she'd been on a path to becoming an award-winning chamber musician. She'd always thought she'd win at the fierce competitive sport of classical music. That she'd be principal horn of the brass section at the London Philharmonic or the Metropolitan Opera orchestra with her fortissimos. But after her final senior performance of Wagner's *Siegfrieds Rheinfahrt* at Carnegie Hall, during which Calli had been noticeably off tempo, her Juilliard advisor had pulled her aside. "Calli, you need to give yourself more space to succeed and fail," he'd said. "Be yourself. Keep working hard. And *relax*."

More time and space? She'd spent every waking moment—and hundreds of sleepless nights—preparing to become the performer she knew she could be if she just worked hard enough. Between rigorous semesters at Juilliard, she'd spent four summers at the Walden School, the acclaimed music academy in Dublin, New Hampshire, where for five weeks each year she was groomed to be a top-flight performer.

She didn't have more time. It was time to get a job.

Anxiety had always accompanied Calli's performances, but instead of easing as she approached graduation, it only got worse, at times knocking her completely off kilter. Rather than growing more confident, she became increasingly insecure. During rehearsals, she'd crave reassurance, asking her peers, often to the point of irritating them, "Do I sound okay? Did you hear how I slowed on that tempo?" For days before a performance, she couldn't sleep. She'd watch the clock miserably: 2 a.m., 3 a.m., 4 a.m.. By the time the birds started chirping, she'd be crying from frustration and exhaustion.

In her senior year at Juilliard, there had been rumblings of an invitation to audition for the Met, but after her Carnegie Hall debacle, the invitation never arrived. Unable to tame the anxiety that taunted her, after graduation, Calli had no choice but to return to her parents' home and try to get some distance from her dreams.

Now Luke and she waltzed through the throng of agents, actors, wannabes, publicists, photographers, and every kind of moviemaker. People shouted at Ned and Luke. They stopped every few feet to have their picture taken together. Calli stopped, too. Watching Luke thrive under the lights gave her a slight pang of resentment for giving up on herself after Juilliard. Fear of success? When they finally made it inside to the lobby, she was already nostalgic for that intoxicating red carpet.

In a few moments, they'd be seated and the movie would begin. Hundreds of people who had never been to war would be watching what happened to Luke. Calli had not finished Ned's book; it frightened her. His depiction of the battle seemed too intimate, too vivid.

When the audience was seated, David Hess, Alexander Freese, and Charles Bangle, the producer, director, and star of *Rio Hato*, walked up in front of the screen. For a few minutes, they thanked everyone for attending the premier of a project that they felt very proud of. Then they did something Calli didn't expect. They asked Luke to stand up. They thanked him for his bravery and courage and especially for his aid in making the film as authentic as it could be. She beamed for him.

For two and half hours, Calli gripped Luke's hand as the audience relived the Panama battle. She never cried, fighting to stay composed for Luke and because she knew that they were expected to attend the afterparty. Exhausted with bitten lips, she scrambled to put on a fresh coat of lipstick before the lights came up and the chaos of congratulations began. The first person to check in with Luke was Charles Bangle, who had portrayed him.

"That was great, man. Thanks," Luke said, shaking Charles's hand.

"Really? God, I was so nervous sitting here with you. Did you like it, really?"

A flood of people surged toward him. Caught in a tidal wave of back slaps, smiles, handshakes, and questions, Luke was swept into the lobby, where the party had already started. Calli trailed the group closely. Her mission was to meet as many famous people as she could. She knew that she had this one chance. Celebrities, she told herself, were just like any cross section of people at a big party: gregarious, demure, amiable, aloof, obstreperous, and restrained. Luke was taken to a room for interviews while she was left alone in this koi pond of glitterati. She migrated toward Charles, who was pleasantly on the side of the action with his family. He introduced Calli to his sisters and parents, who had flown in from Virginia. Drinks were passed around and she gulped down a surfeit of red wine. Calli asked someone to take her picture with Charles so she would have it to show everyone at home.

Brazenly, a little drunk, she said, "Do you have a girlfriend?"

"Noooo. Why do you ask?"

"I think you'd like my sister Dinah."

"Really, what's she like?"

"Brilliant. A Princeton grad, got her MBA at Wharton. Works in New York at some investment-banking firm. Tall, gorgeous, successful. The swan of the family for sure."

"And you're the ugly duckling?"

"I'm more musically inclined, you might say. I went to Juilliard, but I'm—"

"Juilliard's no joke!"

Calli looked across the crowd for a moment. Charles was right, but what did she have to show for her years of training? A bit role in this world of great performances, for one night and one night only. She was thrilled for Luke, but it irritated her that he'd left her out here on her own. She gazed at all the stars, the sycophants, and actors with limp handshakes. Charles, at least, was a real person, but where was Luke?

Suddenly, someone far more important than Calli drifted over, took Charles's arm, and told him to come out of the shadows, that it was time to mingle with the guests.

3

Calli walked through the badly lit front hall of Veronica McLeod's home clutching a modest housewarming gift, making her way toward a gaggle of women she didn't know. It had been five weeks since they had moved to Sackets Harbor, and she was going to her first Family Readiness Group "coffee"—a social gathering of the Army wives for dinner. Veronica and her husband, Luke's Sergeant Major, lived about thirty-five minutes away from Calli. Just enough time in the car to deflate her enthusiasm and spark her nerves. Veronica and Bill were in the middle of a major renovation. The torpid decorating—a hodgepodge that didn't cohere to the whole—repelled her. Their clumsy Victorian must have been splendid at some point in the early 1900s. The millwork on the balustrades alone must have taken a carpenter months to complete.

When she stepped into the foyer, no one acknowledged her, said hello, or offered to take her coat or the small hostess gift she'd brought. She felt like she was back in high school. Lots of looks and stares, which did nothing to combat her sense of dread. It was like she'd landed on another planet where she didn't speak the language and clearly didn't fit in. Fortunately, a few moments later Veronica emerged from her kitchen.

"Calli, I am so glad you made it," Veronica chirped. "There's a bar in the kitchen. Bill's in there making margaritas." A drink. That's what she needed. She handed Veronica the candles and napkins.

"Thank you for having me," Calli said to Veronica, who was already wandering off. Veronica looked over her shoulder and smiled back at her. Calli took off her coat and dropped it in the corner of the front foyer. She made her way to the kitchen—more importantly, the bar.

"Howdy!" Bill said, giving her a hug. She'd met Bill several times in the past few weeks since they'd moved to New York, a bear-like, warm-natured man who always made her feel welcome. "What can I get for ya, Calli? Wine, beer, margarita?"

Calli studied the wine selection. Cheap white Zins. An Australian Merlot.

"A margarita sounds good. I haven't had one in years."

"Ten-four."

It always startled Calli to see soldiers out of uniform. His threadbare green Grateful Dead T-shirt, frayed on the hem, homely Wrangler jeans, and Birkenstocks were more fitting for a hippy than an Army Sergeant Major. He had a gold molar and too high-pitched voice. Under his left eye was a heart-shaped scar that may have come from chicken pox—or a battle. Calli had first met Bill on Fort Drum when she'd dropped off lunch for Luke. He insisted she call him Bill and asked her what she thought of Fort Drum. He smiled at her like they were in on a little secret together.

Before she knew it, she had a margarita in her hand and salty tortilla chips in the other. Calli took inventory of the kitchen, the counter space, cabinets, stove, and oven—all vintage eighties. As a cook—and a snoop—these things fascinated her. She wondered if Bill and Veronica actually cooked or if they subsisted on fast food. The kitchen was a jumble, the refrigerator stuffed into what may have been a closet or pantry. Across the room, five other women were gabbing. She knew she had to take those three steps and intro-duce herself. Calli imagined their conversation, telling them about Audrey, her many talents, about her own talent with the French horn. No, I don't play much anymore—mostly Christmas and Easter. Maybe she could tell them how she met Luke when she was singing in a bar.

Her receiving-line manners, groomed during years of ballroom dance classes and her parents' strict adherence to Emily Post, kicked into gear. She crossed the room and introduced herself. "Hello, I'm Calli Coleman."

Each of them, in turn, introduced themselves, first names only: "I'm Kim. Hi Calli, I'm Lisa."

She could hear her mother say, "Why don't people use their last names when they introduce themselves? It's just bad manners." Fumbling, she stood in the peculiar line with them, crunching her chips to fill up her mouth, smiling at the other wives. Them smiling back, heads bobbing up and down as if in agreement with something that someone had just said. The conversation hit a lull. Calli fidgeted. She was sweating.

One of the women, Lisa (it was Lisa, right?), was suddenly standing next to her like they were old friends. "Hi!" Calli was hyperaware of how Lisa immediately imposed herself into Calli's space, standing so close that her foot was practically on Calli's toe, forcing her to lean back. She wasn't interested in being close, literally or figuratively, to Lisa, who instantly began to prattle, "God, I only slept three hours last night and then got up to watch QVC and bought the coolest ankle bracelets and rings. Have you been to the Commissary here? The pool? I just moved..." Lisa went on and on, without slowing down to realize whether Calli had answered her.

I am in hell, Calli thought. Lisa's frenetic story had no beginning and certainly, it seemed to Calli, no end. "Nice to meet you. I'm going to get another drink. Need anything?" Calli politely excused herself. If she was profoundly uncomfortable with Lisa, Calli felt right at home pouring herself another tall margarita, standing at the sink, staring out the window into the black night. Soon a timid wife with stringy hair and clumped mascara asked her, "So what unit is your husband with, Calli?" And there it was.

Within days of moving, Calli had learned how the Army wives sized each other up by their husband's unit and rank, ultimately to determine a pecking order. Nobody cared that Calli was in a band or played French horn and guitar or loved to read novels written by women or lived with an Italian chef in Arenzano on the Italian Riviera when she was in her early twenties. Not one person she'd met so far knew that she was an exquisite cook—the only lasting thing to come out of the relationship with the Italian chef. No one asked where she went to school or what her father did for a living. Country clubs, private schools, and financial firms were irrelevant tribes here. Here she was Mrs. Master Sergeant before she was anything else. Here her role was to support her husband and the unit. To help him climb the ranks.

But before she had a chance to answer, Bill McLeod spoke up from across the kitchen, "Do you know who Calli's husband is? He's Master Sergeant Coleman, the guy from *Rio Hato*. He works up at Division Staff."

She winced.

He might as well have told everyone she was a stripper at the local titty bar. Once they knew about *Rio Hato*, they'd seize up. It had never mattered to anyone in Baltimore what Luke's rank was. He was the guy from *Rio Hato*. If she was honest with herself, Calli had thought that Luke's microcelebrity would shield them from ever having to leave Baltimore, where she had so many roots and memories. Her parents were beloved professors—her father at Johns Hopkins and her mother at St. John's. Everyone adored them, especially her mother, an English scholar with an accent to match and an air of aristocratic mystery. More women than men confessed to Calli that they had fallen in love with Lucy Wendover. "I just adore your mother," they would say. "Your father, he's a lucky man." For years, Lucy had pulled off her role with panache—she wasn't an aristocrat, just an affluent, well-cultivated woman with a judicious knowledge of English literature and a bewitching effect on her students.

Calli's sister, Dinah, had a similar charm. When Calli had

suggested, several years earlier, that Charles Bangle would take to her, she'd never expected they would actually intersect at a premiere, and she was even more surprised when they actually fell for each other. Dinah had kept her maiden name when they married.

Calli loved to call Charles a movie star in front of her younger sister, despite Dinah's protests that he was an *actor*.

It was their father, Haines Wendover, who anchored the family. Haines was old-school Baltimore through and through, and Baltimore society, with its Bachelors' Cotillion and white-tie galas and summers in Nantucket, responded in kind. Once Calli found her footing among them, she never lost it.

For all her polished social graces, Calli didn't know how to behave now. She took a deep breath, smiled, and scuttled away. The others may have thought her aloof. Maybe even rude. But what, she wondered, did she really have to say to them? She didn't have any stories to share about previous deployments or duty-stations where the best shopping was at Wal-Mart twenty miles away. She could hardly keep up with the stream of acronyms that seemed part and parcel of military life. Even this meeting—for the Family Readiness Group—had to be decrypted for her by Luke. According to him, most bases had one, organized by the wives and NCOs—another acronym she was just getting the hang of—to function as an info hub when a unit was deployed. Calli had accepted the invitation partly out of curiosity, but mostly out of obligation.

She skulked like a cat into the living room, feigning interest in the Victorian architecture of the elderly house. She gazed at the moldings, the mantle, the exotically gothic-shaped windows, the wonky floorboards, tattered curtains, artwork snatched up at the county fair. Every room had a different shade of unrestrained crepuscular purple. Purple on purple rooms everywhere.

Veronica, impossibly sweet, soon announced that dinner was served. Calli joined the others in the dining room, where they were treated to a Mexican potluck presented on a plastic tablecloth—the kind that could be wiped off with a sponge. Calli quickly served herself a vast helping of green enchiladas out of a white casserole dish, refried beans, rice, and flan. The other wives busied themselves at the buffet, gossiping about promotions and Fort This and Fort That. Calli retreated to the den, where she found a youthful, attractive wife with a thoughtful face who crossed her right leg over—and around—her left leg. Her earnest green eyes were good news. Her skin, the color of caramel, was dewy and flawless, while her long jet-black hair boasted strand after strand of exquisite miniature braids. The young woman seemed like an exotic East African princess. She couldn't remember the woman's name—or if she'd even met her yet. She reintroduced herself.

"Hey," she said, which came out more like *Haaaay*. "I'm Josie Merchant. My husband Tristan is in Charlie Company. We met in there." She pointed to the kitchen.

"Hello, Josie. I'm Calli Coleman. Do you mind if I join you?"

"No, please sit. I don't really know anyone here."

"Oh really?"

"I just moved up from South Carolina. My husband and I got married a month ago. I'm kinda new at all this Army stuff."

Still, she seemed to know much more than Calli did, using words like *brigade* and *battalion* and *lieutenant*. Envious, Calli hung on every word, hoping to learn from her.

"Ladies," Veronica called from the living room, "come on in. Take a seat. Some of you might have to sit on the floor. We'll go over the minutes from the last meeting first."

Calli looked around the room. Every one of the women—even Josie—was reaching for her purse. Taking out cash. Calli hadn't even brought her wallet.

Calli leaned over to Veronica. "I'm so sorry, I don't have any cash on me. What is it for?"

"It's okay, Calli," Veronica announced cheerfully, louder than Calli wanted. "Everyone pays five dollars to help pay for the food. Since it's your first time, don't worry about it."

Her face suddenly hot, Calli wished she could melt into the floor.

A brittle carapace fused around her as she remembered a moment in a grocery store with her grandmother who, after rooting through her wallet, admitted that she didn't have enough money on her to pay for the groceries. The checkout girl shouted out to the manager across the store, "The lady doesn't have enough money. I need a key to undo the register." Calli—even at age eleven—had been aghast that the checkout girl had wrongly assumed they were poor.

The end of the meeting couldn't arrive fast enough.

4

When Luke's orders came down to leave his teaching position at Johns Hopkins ROTC and go back to the regular army, surely he knew, Calli reasoned, that he would be stationed somewhere that would deploy him. The 10th Mountain Division, she'd learned since arriving at Fort Drum, was the most deployed unit in the world. "First Sergeants are in charge of Companies of over 150 soldiers who train—to go to war," Josie Merchant had explained the night they met. Calli wasn't sure that Luke had 150 men working for him. If he did, he hadn't mentioned it. He only told her about Division stuff, the operations center, and his thankless operations job working for the G3. Whatever that was. He never mentioned deploying, to Iraq or anywhere else. And Luke wasn't a First Sergeant. Josie must have heard Calli wrong. Luke was a Master Sergeant. Or at least, that's what she thought he'd told her.

Maybe somewhere deep inside him, he prayed that the deployment orders would be cancelled. But they weren't.

She heard about them not from Luke, but from Luke's Operations officer's wife, Tracy. At McDonalds. Calli didn't like her very much. They didn't have much to talk about. She ended sentences with "that's where we're at" and had a coffee-stained incisor that might as well have been rotten. There always seemed to be a bit of dried spit-up in her hair, and she divulged everything Calli never asked about her marriage.

When the Colemans first moved up to New York, Tracy called Calli to organize a playdate at the indoor playground on Fort Drum. They watched her four kids and Audrey bounce in the blow-up bouncy house, crash into each other in the inflatable princess castle, and climb through the bulging maze that resembled a hamster's tube. Army kids screamed and dashed around them, chasing after each other like minnows.

Afterward, in the packed McDonalds outside Fort Drum, uniformed soldiers rotated through the lines, moms and their young kids licked their greasy fingertips, and Tracy, trying in earnest to forge a friendship, ended a sentence "when they deploy soon..."

"Deploy? Wait, what are you talking about?" Calli asked.

"Oh, I'm sorry," she said. "I thought you knew."

"I didn't think Division was going."

"Oh. No. They're not. Luke volunteered. He's going with 4-31 and Second Brigade."

Calli felt the tears well up immediately as little pebbles of disgust that couldn't be dissolved formed in her blood. Not only had she moved out of her sheltered Baltimore away from all her friends to peculiar northern New York, where she knew no one and next to nothing about the Army, now this. Why hadn't Luke told her?

Tracy, embarrassed for breaking the news to her, apologized again. Calli drove home numbly, Audrey attached to a cold bag of French fries. Back at the house, she planted Audrey in front of a *Thomas the Tank Engine* video. In the privacy of their home, where no one could see the snot sopping her lip, she called Luke but got his voicemail. She called her mother, hysterical. Lucy tried to console her. Calli didn't think she knew what to say. Mother taught nineteenth-century English literature at St. John's. What did she know now about war?

By the time Luke arrived home that evening, Calli was furious.

"Why didn't you tell me? Did you think I wouldn't find out?

Why did I have to hear it from Tracy? Weird Tracy. Seriously. At McDonalds. When are you going? For how long? I cannot believe this!"

"The orders haven't been cut yet," Luke said deliberately. "Anything is possible."

"Anything is possible? You're damn right. You could be killed. I just don't understand why you didn't tell me. Do you think I'm that fragile? Don't you think I'd find out eventually?"

"Calli. Stop. You're yelling at me."

"You're going to fucking Iraq and you didn't think to tell me."

"Calli. Please."

"How long? How long!"

"Twelve months?"

"A year? Are you fucking kidding me? When? Come on, Luke. What else haven't you told me? When are you going?"

"Four weeks."

"Oh, my god."

"I really thought that the orders might be cancelled."

"No! You must think I'm some kind of idiot. All the other wives know. Of course they know. They must be laughing at me. 'Poor Calli. Her husband hasn't told her he's deploying. She doesn't have a clue.' What a joke I must look like to them. Thanks, Luke. Thanks for making me even more of a pariah. What planet are you on? Is this how you treat your men?"

"My love. Please. I'm sorry. This war keeps changing. . . "

"Fuck you, Luke. Save your bullshit," she screamed. "It rings a little hollow if you ask me."

"If the Iraqis are not willing to fight for the security of their own country, then we have to do it for them."

"Blah, blah, blah..."

"Okay, yes, I knew there was a possibility I'd deploy. But you've got to believe me—I didn't want to worry you." The refrigerator hummed behind him, and Calli wondered if Audrey could hear them arguing.

"That's an interesting way to pose it."

"Calli, listen to me. I don't think you're an idiot, but you're still new to all of this."

She laughed sardonically as she lifted herself to sit on the kitchen counter.

"Come on, Calli, please. You know what I mean. You've said it yourself a hundred times."

"You lied, Luke."

"I didn't."

"But you didn't give me all the facts. Isn't that the same thing?"

"I wish you'd understand."

"Understand? Understand what?"

"Work is—work is," he stuttered.

Calli slammed her hands down on the counter, "You can't have it both ways. You can't separate home from your work, not when your life is on the line."

"I didn't lie," he said furtively.

"Keeping the truth from me is a lie."

"Okay, you're dangerously close to pissing me off. Stop now. Stop it," Luke said with his hands clenched together, as if he didn't want to admit something. "I don't want to go, but this is my work. I'm a soldier. Soldiers go to war."

"*Soldiers go to war*," she said mimicking him. "God Luke, really?"

"What am I supposed to do?"

"Just fuck off!"

Luke's eyes closed and he cradled his head in resignation. Calli, feeling trapped in this new life she'd never asked for, jumped off the counter, opened the back door, and took large strides out of the house into their backyard, her fury now upstaged by anguish. He wouldn't explain himself, would give her nothing, and expected her to assent. She was horribly aware now how removed she'd become from him. What kind of mysterious creature had Luke become? They weren't the same people they'd been when they moved here, as if they'd packed that couple in a box that had been forgotten on the moving van.

Out in the yard, their old tree swing caught her eye. She sat on the worn wooden bench, pushing herself back and forth, moving toward a grove of birch trees and then back toward the house. The swing's pendulum motion lulled her, soothed her. Her eyes closed as she listened to the flicker of tree leaves. She breathed slowly, long, deep breaths that filled her lungs with a calm that helped disperse her anger. Calli hated fighting with Luke. Soon enough, she heard him come up behind her, standing beside her while she swayed slightly on the swing. Looking away from him, she said, "Sometimes I feel like you're a different person with me than you are at work. I remember when we met that soldier a long time ago. That guy. Remember? That soldier who crashed the premier who told me that you made him cry. *Cry!* Because you were so tough and made him run forty miles with a seventy-pound rucksack. But I don't know that side of you. I've never seen that side of you. Soldier Luke. Who is that? I can't imagine who that man is. You don't show him to me. Why are you protecting me? I can't stand listening to the news. To the radio. Everyday it seems like soldiers are killed or blown up. What will I do if something happens to you? I'm not strong like you. Don't shake your head. No, no, I'm not. I don't want to lose you. I can't lose you, Luke." Tears raced down her cheeks.

"You won't lose me. I'll come back to you. I promise."

⫸ ⫷

When she opened the back door into their mudroom, she heard the phone ringing. Skipping over Satchmo, she reached it on the fourth ring, "C! Henry here. How are you? Did Lukey leave you at home while he's out in the woods playing soldier? I'm on my way to meet with some bigwig for a job interview and thought I'd check in."

Henry Banks, Luke's best friend, called daily. Actually, he called Luke daily, and if he couldn't get Luke, he called the Colemans' house looking for Luke. Calli and Luke always joked about Henry's phone calls. He must live on his phone. If he was en route to a bar or coming home from some amazing event he'd just been to, he'd call their house, and if Calli answered, she'd spend at least an hour on the phone chatting. He regaled her with his tales of his adventurous life. He and his wife Eula lived in genteel Guilford north of Baltimore, where stately elms and oaks hemmed in multimillion-dollar properties around homes designed by some of the greatest East Coast architects of the early twentieth century. Calli had always been slightly envious of Henry and Eula—their Georgian mansion with a pool, three kids, ski trips to Vail, summers in Rumson. Luke and Calli called Henry the Man of Leisure Extraordinaire—aka, The Mole. He used to call Calli to ask her if Luke could go hunting or skiing or on some riotous escapade. One day when he's out of the Army, Luke will get to play with Henry again, she thought. She suspected they were planning a trip to South Bend next fall for the Notre Dame-Boston College football game—when Luke was back.

Henry's father had fought in Vietnam. He remembered moving frequently as a child, packing boxes, spending time at his grandmother's while his father was deployed. After the University of Virginia with Luke, they enlisted with the Army Rangers. They served in Panama in 1988 together—Henry got out a couple years after. Luke stayed in. Calli was glad Luke had such a great friend—a friend who got him.

"C. What's going on? If there's anything Eula and I can do, just let us know."

Just pray he comes home alive, she thought.

"Henry, I . . . did you know Luke is going to Iraq in four weeks?"

"Oh, darlin'. I can't imagine. I wish there was something I could do."

"So you knew."

"Luke just told me. Last night."

"Why didn't you call me?"

"I was waiting for you to call me."

"Oh."

Calli had met Henry and Luke the same night. After drifting for years, she had quit her band—aptly called Late Folly—and moved into her parents' house on Nantucket where she could stare at the dark brooding Atlantic Ocean and mull over what to do next. "Calliope, you have one year," Lucy Wendover had threatened. "You're too old not to know what you want."

By then, her few women friends were already married and had babies. Most of the time, Calli hung out with men. Not marrying-type men but more like boys trapped in men's bodies who wanted to bang on drums, shoot Patron, and wax creatively about Coltrane's tenor sax. She was tired of being the only chick in a cover band. She needed to break away. To be brave enough to go out on her own or give it up altogether.

Her parents were finishing their academic years in Maryland and the Nantucket tourists hadn't yet arrived. Early May in Nantucket was quiet, cars in the traffic circles were obliging, and parking spaces were still abundant. The daffodil festival would kick off the season. Lucy Wendover had a friend who owned a year-round restaurant in town who needed help in the kitchen. Calli felt like her life was a balancing act between food and music. One always led her to the other. A job behind the scenes gave Calli something to do during the day and still allowed her to roam at night.

There was a restaurant with a lively bar crowd called Slip 14 on the Old South Wharf where she liked to go. One day, she approached the manager and offered to play her guitar and sing for the bar crowd. The modest earnings didn't matter, just the chance to be with people who wouldn't judge her. Years of auditions and stinging criticism had crushed her desire to compete. It was better, she concluded, to be warm and comfortable in a small pond than cold and flailing in the ocean.

She'd learned everything she needed to know about working in a restaurant kitchen from a chef she'd dated in Italy. The guy, Gigi—short for Luigi—was a former drug addict (coke, heroin, who knew?) who'd turned to food as his newest addiction. And sex. He was hyper-obsessive about Calli. "I've never been with such a girl. Such a beautiful girl. My American girl. My Aphrodite. Perfect Aphrodite." His libido never ceased, and he'd want her to fuck him anywhere and everywhere, including the disgusting kitchen floor of his restaurant in Arenzano. "Let me suck your tit," he'd beg her in a simian-like trance, tracing the outline of her breast with his index finger and thumb, and with a flush of heat she did not stop him. After he lustily rolled his tongue over her nipples, nibbling the flesh like caviar, he'd undressed and entered her while the stale scent of olive oil and shrimp that lingered in the black rubber floor mat spread across her skin. He could make her orgasm stronger and longer than she imagined possible. He wanted her to be loud. It made him preen. "Scream my name. Scream Gigi. Gigi. *Si! Si! È buona! È buona!*" and when she did, he'd gloat, "I am master." Screaming *yes, yes, yes* at the top her lungs so that anyone within earshot could hear her didn't matter. Sometimes they'd be eating at a restaurant and he'd slide his hand under her skirt and stick his finger in her, making her come while they were at the table. Gigi would sit, exalted, with his index finger resting under his nose the way one does with a desirable Cuban cigar, breathing in her scent like an aphrodisiac. Her heat and musk lingered on him. He watched her in her post-orgasmic bliss like a proud Olympian who'd won the gold. No matter what they did, it never made her feel embarrassed or foolish. For some reason, she didn't care what people thought of her in Arenzano. Gigi paraded her as the American import. "This is Calli. My American girlfriend. She so beautiful." Soon she shape-shifted out of the box she'd built around herself in school and inhabited the character of the titillating sexual woman he fashioned her to be. They'd smear food all over each other and lick it off. They'd have sex four times a day. Life existed between fucking, cooking, and sleeping. To Calli, Gigi was a phase. A step in her post-Juilliard cleansing program. Impulsive and amusing, the relationship was fleeting. Gigi's hair held onto an aroma of stale grease that Calli never warmed to. She couldn't imagine spending the rest of her life with him. "One day, we have many, many children and grandchildren," he said. "And they will all look like my Aphrodite." The intensity of their relationship sharpened rather than mellowed. The longer Calli lived with Gigi, the more she realized he was addicted to her. "Men in bar look at you. They want you." As obsessed as a teenager, he'd lose his temper completely if she didn't go with him to the bar to watch Italy play Spain in soccer. "What? You don't love me?"

"No, that's not it. I just don't feel—"

"No! No! You take another lover. You ruin me. You don't love Gigi no more."

"Anymore. And that's not it. I don't have another lover. Go. Go watch the match with Marco and Dudi. I'm going to stay home and read. Please, Gigi. Believe me. Go have fun with your friends."

Gigi punched nine holes in the wall of their living room when she mentioned she might move back to the states.

His cloying personality eventually exhausted her. She craved normalcy and routine, the reliable rhythms she'd followed as a serious student of music. One Wednesday, Calli found a guitar at the weekly outdoor market. Within weeks, she'd taught herself to play, left Arenzano, and headed back to the US. Alone.

The May crowd at Slip 14 was preppy, sophisticated, salty, and slightly tipsy. One night, as she was about to finish her set and get herself another glass of wine, two tall men walked in. She noticed them immediately. It was hard not to notice the one with his high and tight haircut and deep, velvety eyes. The other's charisma immediately charmed the bar's female patrons, who sat with their designer vodka martinis or Sancerres tracking his path to the bar. To Calli, it looked as if the entire crowd stopped to watch these two men enter. She stumbled on the words to "American Pie." She felt confident that no one noticed. As they found stools around the bar, Calli noticed that the one with cropped hair and brown eyes hadn't stopped staring at her. She felt his gaze like a police helicopter searching for a bandit with a high beam.

When Calli finished playing, she purposely went to the bar

opposite the two becoming men. Almost immediately, the charismatic one left his perch and walked over to Calli.

"Hello there, darlin'. I'm Henry Banks. Who might you be?"

"Hello." Calli put out her hand to shake his. Then turned away. And to the bartender she said, "Hey Jace, may I have a Chardonnay?" Calli could feel her cheeks flush. How embarrassing. The entire crowd pretended not to be watching the exchange. She turned to Henry and said, "I'm Calli Wendover. How are you? Are you having a good time?"

"How could we not be having a good time here on Nantucket? We've stumbled upon a veritable virtuoso."

"Ah, you're too kind."

"No, no, I mean it. And now that we've found this place, I believe our time will be exponentially more enjoyable. May I buy your drink for you?"

"Oh, that's kind of you but not necessary. Fortunately, Jace here gives me my drinks for free. I sing and strum. He pours. It's a symbiotic relationship. I'm all about quid pro quo."

"I see. Well, Miss Quid Pro Quo, my friend over there . . . the goofy one with the creative coif. Well, see, he's in the Army and—"

"Stop it. Army? Really?" Calli didn't know anyone in the Army.

"Yes, he's a Ranger down at Fort Benning on his way to the Army War College in Carlisle, Pennsylvania."

"Where's Fort Benning?"

"In a lovely spot called Columbus, Georgia. About an hour or so from Atlanta."

Calli didn't want to admit it, but she didn't know what a Ranger was. She said, "It sounds lovely."

"Quite. Anyway, my friend Luke and I came for a little man getaway. Fishing. Boozing. Good meals. And we agreed that perhaps you could show us around. Maybe give us some insight into where the locals go."

"I see. I see. Well, Henry, you're in the right place to start." Henry's roguish features and crisp, pressed pink-checked shirt caught Calli's attention, but it was the earnestness of his face that made her decision. He definitely didn't look like her former band mates. "Sure. I'd love to."

Calli learned that Henry was married to a woman named Eula, who was in France with their kids, and that Luke was about to leave the Rangers to take a break from the infantry. After nine years of missions, including a combat tour in Panama in 1988, it was time to take an administrative position—a desk job at the Army War College in Carlisle. "I flew back to the US to host Luke here for a long week-end anywhere he wants. Nantucket cropped up because he'd heard there was great fishing and amazing restaurants," Henry said.

"And lovely ladies," Luke mused. Not only was he tall, six foot five, he also had delicious brown eyes, a straight nose, and a dazzling smile. His striking features matched well with his gentleness and elegance to make quite an attractive man.

Calli immediately fell into step with their inside jokes and camaraderie as if some mystical gravity pulled her into their universe. They were sensitive not to be crude around her but still teased her. "Calli, I bet it must be nice to live for free in your parents' house," or "Are you what they call a 'townie'?" They didn't insist on pseudo-intellectual rounds of who-has-the-most-musical-knowledge. Luke and Henry opened doors for her, stood up whenever she left the table, and looked her right in the eye when she spoke. Conversations concentrated on Nantucket, literature, travel, love, marriage, nothing and everything three people could manage in three days. They were gentlemen, Calli thought, not thirty-something boys who think they're going to be Mick Jagger someday. Not some recovering needle jockey who needed sex to make himself feel like a man. One afternoon, while they walked on Sconset Beach, Henry loping ahead, Luke asked her, "How long have you played guitar?"

"Ah, I've been waiting for that one."

"Why?"

"Oh, I don't know. Seems like a filler question."

He raised one eyebrow and tilted his head.

"When you don't have anything else to say but don't want that awkward silence."

"It's not a *filler question*. I'm interested. Come on, how long?" He put his hand on her arm, briefly.

The breeze blew her hair in her face while she contemplated the answer. The beach was filled with late-afternoon long shadows, while the sun darted in and out between the puffy clouds. She could feel herself getting defensive, but why, she didn't know. "It's a long story. I don't want to waste your time."

"Give me the short version," he said, winking.

"You're relentless!"

"Curious. Inquisitive. Challenging."

"Yes!"

"Go on."

"Okay, here goes." She told him everything up to her last performance at Carnegie Hall. "But the best part. Are you ready?"

He looked thrilled. "Yup."

"The truth. Well, I, uhh, I..." She looked over her shoulder, down the beach. "I gave up."

"You gave up."

"Wow, I've never said that out loud before."

"I'm honored."

Before Luke could question her more, Henry shouted at them, "Hey kids! The sun is over the yardarm. Let's go get a drink."

For three days, she showed them the island. "Hey, do you want to drive out to Great Point today?" she'd suggest. "You should definitely see the Lifesaving Museum," she'd offer. Every night, they'd meet back at Slip 14 to listen to Calli play and sing. A static charge hummed on her skin in the moments before she'd see them, but both options were unrealistic. She knew Henry was married—and happily—and Luke was in the Army. She definitely didn't want to contend with that lifestyle. She could already hear her mother: "Army? Calli, that's not the life for you. Did he go to college? Here we go again." For the three days together, laughing with Luke and

Henry, the whole universe ignited like the finale at a Fourth of July fireworks show, and Calli surrendered to the unusual events, like a monkey's wedding—rain and sun together.

Calli caught Luke staring at her more than once. She'd seen him do this every so often, but he never acted on whatever he was thinking. On their last day she took them to the far western side of the island, where they climbed over the dunes and spotted a newly beached whale.

"Look at that! Is that a whale? Oh my god, poor thing."

The blustery weather caused the waves to crash violently with a frothy foam onto the sand, and the whale rolled gently with the ebb and flow. "Come on! Let's see if it's still alive," Henry called out over the wind as he and Luke ran down the beach. "Calli, aren't you coming?"

"No way! It's too cold, and I'm not getting eaten by a killer whale. I'm perfectly fine to watch you two bozos from back here." She hung back against the dune to stay out of the wind and spray of the chilly water. Smiling as the two men jogged toward the poor whale, the smell of saltwater—a scent that rivaled almost-burnt toast, freshly mown grass, and a bouquet of fresh basil—would always remind her of this short time with Henry and Luke. Men who were themselves, able men. She didn't have to be the strong one all the time. She watched them approach the whale and reach down to touch it—not paying attention to much else but their mission. Simultaneously, the ocean launched an enormous deluge of glacial salt water over them. Startled and sopping, they cracked up, "What the heck?"

"Holy shiiiit!"

"I thought the whale was going to bite me."

She laughed so hard she felt tears stream down her cheeks as they ran back to her.

"Oh my god! Oh my god! Did you see that?" Henry screamed.

"I thought the whale was still alive, and then the water hit me; it scared the shit out of me," Luke said.

Calli, who was laughing so hard she couldn't speak, bent over and hugged herself.

"Oh, you think that's funny, do you?" Luke said, his good humor shining through. "Look at us. We're soaked. This is worse than Ranger School," he said, weeping—something he did when he laughed really hard.

"Old Man, you're getting soft," Henry said. "Let's get out of here. We need to get dried off before our flight. Buddy, we're leaving in two hours."

It was the shock of the words that made Calli stop laughing. Luke and Henry were leaving. They hadn't talked about the future. For three days, the three of them had lived in the present with anecdotal glimpses of their pasts. But the subject of tomorrow never arose. Ringing through her body was the urge to beg them to stay, but as with any grand finale that closes the show, Calli awakened in her sensibility. She'd had these three days, and now it was time for her to focus. She dropped them off at their hotel, shivering and wet.

"Okay, you knuckleheads, I guess this is goodbye. I won't belabor the point since it's obvious that you have to get into dry clothes, but if you ever decide to come back up here, give me a call. I don't know what I'm doing when the summer ends. Anyway, let's keep in touch."

Luke stared at her deeply. "Would it be okay if I call you? Later?"

"Sure. I'd like that," Calli said. And to Henry, "I can't wait to meet Eula. She must be wonderful."

"Oh, she is. You'll meet her. I'm sure." Henry pressed his lips firmly on her forehead, pulled back a little to breathe and look Calli in the eye, and kissed her forehead again.

Luke leaned down softly and planted an intimate, yet gentle kiss on Calli's lips. Stunned and discombobulated, she drew back suddenly, as if he had stolen her hope that the last three days were just an aberrant reverie. That kiss opened the door, and the two of them slipped through to that sacred place lovers go when they think no one is looking—that place where they are overrun by feeling and no one and nothing can ever separate them.

$$\ggg \quad \lll$$

Eula and Calli didn't get to be friends until a couple years later. Henry and Eula spent two years in Paris, using it as a base to teach their kids French. When they decided to return to the US, Henry secured a (short-lived) job in Baltimore working for one of the shipping companies. Between his and Eula's fortunes, he didn't really have to work, and after a while they settled back into the rhythms of their more than comfortable life. It wasn't until Eula and Henry offered to host an engagement party for Calli and Luke that Calli finally met the woman she'd heard so much about. A Southern elite from Oxford, Mississippi, who reinvented herself as a Baltimorean after she married Henry, Eulalia Firestone Banks was out of Calli's league. Henry had once mentioned that Eula was an avid disciple of Albert Hadley. Calli had to Google Mr. Hadley, understanding only then how their house was a tribute to the designer. To Calli, Eula was a beguiling debutante transposed into the glamorous Baltimore socialite world.

Before the engagement party, Eula went out of her way to make sure the event would suit Calli's tastes. "Now Calli honey, tell me your family's hobbies. Does your daddy drink bourbon or is he a wine man? Isn't your mama an English professor? I just know I'm goin' to love her. I can't wait to ask her about who her favorites are," Eula squealed over the phone. "And you know, I don't cook much besides Opal Anne's famous fried chicken so I'm hiring a top chef to cater—you know, Christopher?" Opal Anne was Eula's childhood maid back in Oxford, and Calli had no idea who Christopher the famous chef was.

"Yes, honey, Christopher. From C-Squared. Downtown. He makes the most divine buttermilk-brined chicken and waffles and these little wild mushroom tarts with caramelized onions. Trust me. You're going to just die. A foodie like you. You'll be begging Luke to take you there every Saturday."

"Eula, you don't—"

"Hush now. I looove to throw parties. Show these Baltimore gals what a real Southerner can pull off up here. Sometimes I just get so sick of being Yankee-Doodle-Dandied. They think I'm Scarlett fucking O'Hara. Some ostentatious belle from down south. No ma'am." Eula giggled.

Cultivated bouquets of peonies, roses, and lilies in angular crystal vases were scattered throughout their well-edited home. Perfectly aged Barbarescos and Brut Champagne flowed while Eula skirted among her guests, purring her Southern drawl, introducing Calli as her long-lost friend—even though they'd only met a few times. Her impeccable collection of Warhols and Mirós infused the rooms with whimsy. A Stanton Macdonald-Wright was hung in the dining room and Helen Frankenthaler's *Mountains and Sea* was on the landing. But on the wall of their great gallery was Eula's pride and joy, Olitski's *Green Goes Around*. The painting epitomized Eula's sensuous life, the ambiguous mist reverting to the edges of the canvas.

Emerging artists were given space, too. "We all have to start somewhere," she would say. Eula was gracious and sophisticated, as witty a conversationalist as Dorothy Parker. Unpretentious but not unproud. She loved wine—and she made Calli laugh with her self-deprecating jokes and commentary on the Baltimore social scene. "You know how that small-minded Alice got into garden club?"

"*The* garden club. No, do tell."

"Well, instead of being nominated like the rest of us, she had her mother-in-law call in some hifalutin' favors claiming that Alice had some incredible garden outside of Wilmington that had been designed by Christopher Lloyd."

"You know I have no idea who Christopher Lloyd is, right?"

"Calli," Eula said earnestly, "I just hate it when people social climb so clumsily. You and I would never do something like that. Well, we don't need to." Calli didn't belong to garden club, but Eula's protectiveness amused her. It seemed as if Eula had predicted their friendship far before Calli did. Calli fell in love with her.

Eula became Calli's Yellow Pages, drinking partner, and confidant. Most nights after languid cocktails and dinner with Henry and Eula, they'd be sitting talking—she could be holding a full glass of Chardonnay in one hand, chatting about kids—and then, like the Dormouse, she'd fall fast asleep, only to wake up twenty minutes later to continue on with her story as if her narcoleptic episode had never happened.

Eula confided in her. Calli knew about Eula's starter marriage to a NASCAR driver named Rusty Wallace, an obscure fact in Guilford and a secret from her children. A gossamer marriage, doomed, that ended amicably after two years sans children. She exposed to Calli the solitary tryst she had had with Henry's older brother, Duke, six months before her wedding. Duke had seduced her. Eula had succumbed, wildly mad at Henry for taking his Porsche on a tour of the US to compete in the Free Flow tour, a skateboarding competition. She blamed it on the wine, wedding angst, and an ethereal Palm Beach night on the Bankses' Little Harbor 75. She never pretended to be perfect. She only spoke of it once—Henry at her side.

Eula and Calli talked about books they'd read—she was an English major, at Barnard—and tiny haunts in the East Village crammed with four-tops that served dirty martinis in rocks glasses. Art may have been the only thing Eula loved more than wine. Her privileged background had permitted her to live in Florence for several years studying architecture and the Masters. But her passion was American artists. "I am a damn American!" she'd pronounce with moxie, usually after a few sips of wine. "I can't draw or paint, but I admire them all!" Calli didn't always understand the art on their walls, but she recognized Eula's devotion. Art cast a spell on her.

Calli's admiration for Eula grew the more she called Calli. Included her. Together with Henry and Eula, Luke and Calli were at their best.

She had been so busy mining Eula's glamorous life for values that she could appropriate, like heirlooms, that she'd forgotten she and Luke were at the mercy of the Army. The Colemans had to work. Luke committed himself to his men and the military, even if it meant his image didn't match the income. Being in the Army was sacred work. But it wasn't for everyone.

>>>>> <<<<<

When they moved to Sackets Harbor, Calli curtailed all communication with anyone from Baltimore, too ashamed of her new life. Everything about their new residence depressed her. The culture in northern New York seemed beyond provincial. Her inability to tell Eula how poor Jefferson County was, how contrary the inhabitants to the Bankses, made Calli ashamed that they lived in such struggling community.

Calli didn't know where she fit in. Calli wasn't a true-blue socialite, but she wasn't Army, either. The majority of the Army came from an utterly different background than she did. Modest towns in flyover states. Girls who got pregnant before high school graduation with their man-boy-soldier-husbands waiting to whisk them off to Fort Someplacebetterthanhere. Young men saddled with a wife and baby. Some soldiers were criminals. For many of these young soldiers, the Army was the last stop for young men and women with few other options. Officers emerged fresh out of ROTC or military academies, twenty-one-year-olds in charge of eighteen-year-olds. Education was measured by deployments and time in service. At the end of the day, it didn't really matter where you went to school. The most important lessons were out there, in theater.

Calli's education, on the other hand, had been top drawer. It'd never been more obvious to her how charmed her life had been. For most of her childhood and adolescence, her parents had received the Social Register. Those orange letters on the black-bound directory of breeding and preferred social contacts. The Wendovers weren't social climbers. They only happened to be from the right standing, which permitted them to mix and mingle with prominent American families. How incredibly lucky to have gone to private schools and country clubs. Debutante balls and dancing class. And how strange that none of those things mattered now. Calli's life before Sackets Harbor was starting to feel very far away.

Even as Henry continued to keep in touch with Luke, Eula's calls and emails faded. What would she think of Sackets Harbor? Calli wondered. The reenactors and quaint restaurants might amuse her. But what about the derelict houses and Old MacDonald's farm with the hand-painted sign offering hayrides? Calli imagined that life in Baltimore kept getting better for Eula, while life in Sackets Harbor idled in low gear. For several months, she rarely answered when she saw Eula's rare number on her caller ID. She missed Eula dangerously, but she didn't feel up to being the Calli that Eula knew.

5

Luke would deploy in a month.

She still had a hangover from their contentious fight. The first couple of days afterward, she avoided speaking to him as much as she could. He seemed genuinely sorry in his way, putting his socks in the hamper versus leaving them on the bathroom floor and wiping his toast crumbs off the counter after he made breakfast. Yet her questions went unanswered, and as deployment day loomed closer, Calli didn't know how to escape the trap she'd found herself in.

I can't love him right now, she thought.

When they reconciled enough to make love, Calli went through the motions of passion. She didn't want it. She didn't want to be that intimate. Lying with him naked, she thought over and over, what if he doesn't come back? The thought consumed her as he glided himself in and out. He was there, she was not.

It was unusual for Calli to be this removed. She had a healthy passion for making love with Luke. It was never the hammering sex that she'd had with Gigi, but a tender and mutual enjoyment of two people in love. When they first moved up to Sackets, just over a month ago, they'd spent an afternoon at Remington Beach, lying in the summer sunshine, Audrey home with a sitter. Lake Ontario's temperatures were moderate, cooling Calli and Luke, and they floated on a blow-up raft Calli had purchased on post at the PX. They floated. Away from the beach. Away from people. Giggling with each other about nothing as they stretched out on their backs, holding hands.

"Do you have a hard-on?" Calli said.

"Yes, I'm so horny right now. You're so beautiful."

"Do you wanna . . . should we try it out here?"

"Really? What about the people?"

"What people?" Calli said as she slipped her hand down Luke's trunks to grab his erection. She was able to wriggle his wet suit off and observe him fully naked, lying on the plastic float with his phallus pointing to his face. Calli smiled as she felt the butterflies between her legs flutter and warm her. Seeing Luke like this, she felt slick inside and desperate to feel him inside her. Luke untied her bikini top and rolled one of her nipples between his fingers.

"I love how your tits get erect," he said. "I love to suck on them." He bent his head and gently nibbled on her nipple. Calli's eyes closed as she moaned, "Oh, Luke, that feels so good."

Soon his finger was inside her, slowly entering and drawing back. She felt his knuckles curl into her perfectly. He licked her breast then suckled on the other nipple, gently biting her. Calli had his erection in one of hands and stroked him. "Too bad we don't have any support out here. I'd love to get on top of you," Calli said.

"Well, there's always later, my pretty lady."

Calli climaxed first. Then she helped Luke to bring him to orgasm holding his penis. Moving him until he was spent. Both of them broken open with ecstasy.

But now, with the deployment in the bed with them, nothing could wake her out of this somnolence. She pretended. She felt disgusted with herself, as if spiders were crawling under her skin. She hated that she had locked herself away from him. So she pretended. If she didn't, Luke would keep touching her, rubbing her, kissing her. And she didn't want him to touch her. She hated that she faked, but she also wanted it over.

Calli's sleep habits became erratic. Many nights she fought insomnia. During the day, cooking shows seemed to soothe her.

Calli hadn't told Audrey what was going to happen. She wasn't sure how or when she would tell her. She wasn't sure how much Audrey would understand. *Your father is going to war. For a year. He may never come back.* How would a child make sense of that?

The day before, Calli and Luke had gone to the JAG office to prepare their wills. A free service for all military and dependents. A small tremor vibrated in her left hand as she sat opposite the officer's foreboding desk. As with many of the military offices, the JAG officer's space had no character. The officer never looked them in the eye and spoke as if reading a script she knew, but she was not confident enough to speak without looking down. "In the unlikely event that something should happen to Master Sergeant Coleman," the JAG officer began in a monotone. Calli wanted to strangle her. The stupid woman behind the desk in her ugly soldier's uniform. Raven hair pulled back in a severe bun, the JAG officer rarely looked Calli in the eye, even when she wasn't reading the scripted form. Calli wondered if this woman could imagine sitting on the other side of her desk with her most beloved husband worried sick about the prospect of his wife going to war. Was she married? Did she have kids, parents, friends? People whose lives would be forever changed in "the unlikely event."

In the car on the way home, Calli said, "I didn't like that JAG woman at all."

"She was a little mannish," Luke giggled.

"Why do they have to wear the same uniforms as the men? What? Does everyone have to look the same? It's so communist. There's nothing feminine or sexy about women soldiers."

"That's completely the point, Cal."

"Ugh. I could never have been in the Army."

"You got that right, Miss Band. Miss Guitar."

"What's that supposed to mean?"

"Calli. I was joking with you. Relax. Come on. I love that you were in a band. What's wrong?"

"What's wrong? Seriously? We just spent an hour with the JAG officer going over our *wills*. I feel sick to my stomach. I don't think I can do it, Luke. I'm going to ruin Audrey. Goddammit. Poor Audrey will be stuck with me."

"Calli, stop. Just stop it. You're a wonderful mother. Audrey adores you."

"She adores *you*! What am I going to tell her? Jesus. I didn't sign up for this."

Calli decided not to speak the rest of the ride home. Luke offered, "Would you like me to pick Audrey up at preschool so you can rest?" After he dropped her off, Calli lay on their bed quivering. Something had to change. Her body taut with the acridity of the deployment. Since when was she so skittish? Luke would be leaving soon. Too soon. She felt weighted down by desolation—the deep, entangled fear that wasn't foreign to her anymore. When Luke and Audrey returned, Calli apologized.

"I think I need to do something for me," she said. "I can't just sit around here watching the Food Channel then go foraging for ingredients while Auds is at school. I'll turn into a huge pig."

"Whatever you need, my love. I'm here for you."

"I'm going to start a supper club. You know, one of those monthly—or even quarterly—nights where everyone hosts a dinner? Do you think anyone would want to do it with me? Maybe that cute girl Josie I've talked to on the phone a few times. You know, Tristan Merchant's wife? I don't know. And maybe some of the women I've met here in Sackets. That woman Kelly. Kelly Mumford, who works at the bakery and makes those amazing cakes? Maybe she knows some other women. I need friends. I need someone else to talk to besides you."

"That's a great idea. I love it. You love food. You love to cook."

"I've never been in a supper club before. I don't even know how to start one."

"I'm sure you'll figure it out. You're pretty smart."

"You think I'm smart?"

"You married me, didn't you?"

The next day, Calli printed off flyers and stuck about a dozen in her purse to hand out to the women in Sackets:

WINE & DINE
INTERESTED IN A GIRLS' NIGHT OUT?
POTLUCK TUESDAYS?
WANT TO MEET NEW FRIENDS AND CHOW DOWN?
LOOKING FOR 8–12 WOMEN. CALL CALLI IF INTERESTED.

Then she called Josie Merchant.

"Josie, it's Calli Coleman. How are you?"

"I'm good," Josie said, not convincing Calli.

"Have you been to the JAG office yet?"

"We're going today. I'm not looking forward to it."

"We just went. It's a reality check, that's for sure."

"I can't wait."

"Listen, I'm thinking about starting a supper club. You know, something to do when the guys deploy. I invited some women here in Sackets. Kelly Mumford, she's this really neat woman who works at the coffee shop here in Sackets, well, she's in. And this other woman I know out here. Maybe you know some people. Even if we start small. I've never done this before, so I don't really know . . ."

"Yes! Yes I'd love to," Josie said. "Maybe Daphne Hollis would be interested. Her husband, Huey, is Tristan's First Sergeant."

"I think I've met Daphne."

"You met her at Veronica McLeod's. Remember?"

"Yes, yes, I remember now. Big blond hair?"

"Exactly. She's wonderful."

"I'm thinking about next Tuesday night. I'll make dinner for everyone."

"Calli, thank you! I think this is just what I needed."

When Calli hung up, the world didn't seem as gray. Or bleak. Or heavy.

>>> <<<

Daphne, a tall, zaftig woman, had a bighearted personality. Confident and well-spoken, she was a nurse who traveled often to work with laboratory pigs. Calli hadn't warmed to her at Veronica McLeod's, and Calli had only seen her once with her husband Huey since then, at a party. She remembered Daphne looked relaxed, sitting on the counter with arms animated while telling a joke or story, laughing along with the other soldiers and their wives—and hospitable, even though it wasn't her house.

Calli finally called Daphne. "I admit. I'm really nervous about the deployment."

"Everyone is. They're not going to a great area. We'll just have to drink a lot of wine while they're away."

"I don't believe what Luke is telling me is the truth. About how he wouldn't ever go out of the wire. What does Huey say?" Daphne had been through a deployment before so Calli considered her a worthy resource.

"Oh, Huey tells me everything. Even stuff he's not supposed to," she chortled.

"Does Huey know Luke?"

"Of course he does. Everyone knows Luke." Calli bit her lip. Once again, she felt like she was dangling from a chin-up bar trying to do one more pull-up to keep up with everyone else.

"Hey, changing subjects for minute, would you be interested in meeting me for lunch?" Perhaps she needs some support, too, Calli thought.

Daphne was already waiting at the table at Poppins, the restaurant in Sackets Harbor where they'd decided to meet. She couldn't guess Daphne's age, but she thought Daphne must be in her late thirties, buxom, bleached blond, with a foxy face and smile that announced, "Here I am. Take me or leave me." She wore tight clothes that amplified her silhouette and unapologetic sexiness, and she pulled it off. She was the kind of woman who ought to have owned a classic Harley Davidson. Calli imagined her in her garage restoring a 1960 cherry- and-cream Aermacchi Chimera 250.

Although she was disarmingly statuesque, her gentle voice and reassurances that Luke wouldn't be fighting all of the time eased Calli's nerves. "I know it's really scary, but they'll be okay. Look. I brought you this." It was a teddy bear Beanie Baby with a camouflage pattern. "Huey's taken this on deployment before. And he made it back."

"Oh, Daphne, thank you."

"It's good luck. You keep it."

At lunch, Calli learned that Daphne was thirty-eight and had an eighteen-year-old son from an earlier, misguided marriage. "Yeah, you know how it is when you're twenty. That invincible thing. Who needs condoms? Get married on a mountaintop in bare feet. Then the relationship flames out as soon as it started. But I was left with a little package." She laughed, shook her head.

Calli prodded her, "So you kept the baby?"

"Yes. Of course. Daniel lives with his grandparents now. In Tempe." The words hung heavily in the air. "It's easier this way. He can go to college. Not move around with Huey and me. It works." Daphne went back to eating her lunch and then said, "I was married a second time, too." And here, she waved her hand in front of her face, breaking out into laughter that made Calli laugh, too. "Yes, it's true. Third time's a charm."

While she spoke, Calli thought about the first few times she'd met Daphne; she was wrong not to endear herself to Daphne then. She was lovely, guileless, and amusing. The key to Daphne was her sense of humor. Daphne would probably fit in anywhere because of her upbringing as a Canadian Army brat. She was born in Germany, raised in Toronto, and had a nursing degree from Arizona State. "I just love food," Daphne twittered, more at herself than at the comment. "Last night I ate a bucket of KFC crispy chicken and a bag of corn chips. I was starving."

Calli loosened up, soaking in the laughter like an animal in the desert that finds water. The revealing conversation was unbelievably refreshing. Daphne was alive. Calli was surprised at how easily they got along, and as the conversation drifted back to youthful mistakes, she felt at ease enough to share her quirky relationship with Gigi—even the abundant sex. "Once we did it in a telephone booth at lunchtime," Calli admitted. She had never shared Gigi with anyone. Not because she was ashamed, but because it was a faraway love—a fantasy that lived and died in Italy.

"I've done that!" Daphne chimed in.

"You had an Italian chef boyfriend?"

"No, no. The phone booth sex." The two women were practically in tears, lunch long forgotten.

Months ago, she wouldn't have given this woman the time of day because she wasn't Eula. Before, Calli had been threatened by Daphne's large personality and confidence. Calli was still wading into the shallow end of the military pool, the high-school wallflower at her first dance. Now she wanted to sit and talk to her all afternoon.

"Hey, would you like to join my super-exclusive supper club?" Calli asked.

"I love the idea of a supper club. I need to make some friends. I don't know if I can make every meeting because of work, but I'll definitely be there when I'm in town. Ooo, fun. Thanks!"

Calli was shocked. Friends? She couldn't believe that Daphne didn't have a phalanx of friends at her disposal. Calli's ride in the backseat had finally ended—she was able to step forward and offer something of substance to Daphne: a reason to get out of the house once a month and eat copious amounts of appetizers and decadent desserts and drink lots of wine.

On the way home from lunch, Calli considered the first tentative sounds of this unusual symphony of women, Daphne's enviable bravery and wit like the double bass and Josie's charming naiveté like the treble clef on a harp. Together, she hoped, they could form a tonic balance in spite of the binds of war and phrases like "in the unlikely event."

6

Walking with Satchmo by herself in the grassy field at the end of Mill Creek Lane—their lane in Sackets Harbor—Calli tried to shut out the news: *Four soldiers were killed in Iraq today.* As Luke's training went on, it was harder to let headlines like this bounce off her. Back in Baltimore, war had felt distant, distinct from their lives. Now, in Sackets Harbor, war was encroaching in a way she'd never experienced before. Too many men from the 10th Mountain Division had been killed in Iraq and Afghanistan. Many had been badly burned or wounded, some abducted. Luke had been in the Army for close to eighteen years, in combat twice, but this was Calli's first deployment. No matter what she did, at moments she was immobilized by fear. If she leaned into her worry, she might melt.

Calli tried to explain the deployment to Audrey, simplifying the scenario into phrases like "Daddy's going away to fight Bad Guys" and "Let me tell you a story"—curious Audrey would sit on the tree swing while Calli pushed her. "Auds, do you know about Bad Guys?"

"Yes, mama. Like the Big Bad Wolf? Mrs. Gardner read that to me in school."

"Yup, just like the Big Bad Wolf. Well, remember the pigs and how they were the good guys in the story?"

"Yeah," Audrey responded.

"Well, Dad's kind of like one of those pigs. The pig in the brick house. He's got to go away for..." And here Calli never knew what to say. A long time? A week? A year? Did Audrey understand a year?

"Is the Bad Guys going to boil up like the Wolf?"

"*Are* the Bad Guys."

"*Are* the Bad Guys? That's a story, mama."

"Really," Calli said. "How's that?"

"*Because*, mama, everybody knows that pigs don't talk like people."

"Oh Audrey, I love you." Calli felt grateful that huge ideas with Audrey could be simplified. It certainly wasn't that way with Lucy. Or Luke.

Luke and she never used to fight.

"I'd like you to consider becoming the FRG Leader when we deploy."

"Are you fucking kidding me, Luke? Those women don't even like me."

"Calli, listen. Tracy Applebee is a nincompoop. Besides, she's probably moving home with her mother in Kansas. All the other wives are, what? Twenty-two at most?"

"NO."

"Fine. I think you're being a little childish."

"Shut up."

"Shut up? That's nice."

"Luke, goddammit. You're asking me to be okay with the idea that you're going away for twelve months. Okay with the fact that you're going to fight terrorists in Iraq. Okay that we won't see you except for your two-week leave—and that's nine and half months into the deployment. Okay that I'll be here raising Audrey alone. Okay that we—"

"Calli, okay. I get it."

"No, no you don't. You don't have a fucking clue. I hate this. All of this. I don't have that many friends up here. My family is four hundred miles away. Fine. I'll be the goddamn FRG leader if that's what you want. I'll host coffees and pretend I know what the wives are saying when they speak in military lingo. Sure. No problem. That's just perfect. I can see them all laughing now. Calli, the FRG Leader. She thinks she knows it all."

"Yes, it is what I want."

"Of course it is."

Luke walked over to her and wrapped his long arms around her and then leaned in to bite her neck. Squeeze her boob.

⫸ ⫷

"I'm considering hosting a bon voyage party. Before you deploy," Calli told Luke. It wasn't protocol to host a party. "I'd like the opportunity to meet some of the other wives and soldiers."

"I think we can make that happen," Luke said.

"I do have one request, though. Do you think you and the men can smoke your Cohibas outside?"

"If we must," Luke mocked.

Dwight at North Country Liquors on Military Road smiled when Calli walked in because the last two times she'd been in his shop she'd walked out with a case of Sangiovese in her arms while he carried out a case of Knob Creek to her car. He'd surprised her when he told her about an authentic Italian deli—Bucatini's—in the nearby village of Clayton next to the opera house. The deli owner, Mischa, offered to order hard to find pastas, sun-dried tomatoes, and espresso from New York if he didn't carry them. Calli prepared a culinary Valentine: antipasti—an artful composition of salami, spicy capicolo, prosciutto di Parma, mortadella, and bresaola; pinzimonio and extra virgin olive oil; tuna pate; dark-purple calamata olives; roasted red pepper salad; and handsome hunks of Parmigiano-Reggiano served next to pots of honey kissed with truffle oil—all on huge white platters. Baskets overflowed with focaccia, bread sticks, and crackers. She never skimped on food or drink, borrowing the sumptuous Italian tradition of pulling people out of the knots and tangles of their lives with a gathering.

Daphne and Josie came to the party. Huey and Tris, their respective husbands, weren't in Division with Luke but were part of the same brigade that was slated to deploy to Iraq in two weeks. Calli's desire to keep Daphne and Josie close to her had never been stronger. Their particular friendship was forged out of a common bond. That's how it worked with Army wives. The transient lifestyle didn't give much time to weigh the pros and cons of someone's character. Snap decisions had to be made, to fend off loneliness and isolation.

And Eula and Henry were there. "We wouldn't miss it, darlin," Henry beamed. "And it'll give us a chance to see this dreadful place you've been complaining about."

"It's not that bad. I've found the cool spots. But I do have to warn you, it's not swanky."

"We don't need swank, darlin. We just want to see Lukey and you." They drove four hundred miles up from Baltimore to say good-bye to Luke. They always did things like that. Eula and Henry embraced Luke's long military career, the nobility of it. She admired their eagerness—Henry's especially—to stay in their lives when it would have been so easy for them to just let the Colemans fall away. They were all vibrant that night in spite of the reason for the party, cautiously tiptoeing away from the subject of deployment, which sat with them like an unwelcome guest.

"Calli, your friends are just wonderful," Eula purred, taking a seat next to Calli. "Seems like you've settled in. I just adore that tree swing out back. I bet Audrey loves it."

"You're so sweet to come all this way," Calli replied. "And thank you for the adorable outfit for Audrey. You're too good to me."

"It's not nearly as awful as you made it out to be. But you were right about the wine selection at the liquor store."

"What, you couldn't find your favorite Champagne?" she said, a bit too sharply.

Slightly hurt, Eula said, "No, I just meant their selection is limited—not bad."

"I'm sorry. That came out the wrong way. This place is great. I'm really getting used to it. Maybe tomorrow we can take a walk and I can show you the old movie theater. It's got a ton of potential. Who knows? I've been thinking about telling Dinah and Charles. Maybe they'd be interested in fixing it up." Calli said, trying to convince herself as much as Eula.

The party was festive as the women roosted in the living room dancing and drinking. A couple of the younger Alpha Company wives had loosened up after Calli refilled their wine glasses a few times. The piquant whiff of cigar smoke danced along with them while they sang Jimmy Buffett's "Why Don't We Get Drunk and Screw," which Calli played on her guitar. Out on their deck—the men stood around with their cigars and Knob Creek, bravado, and chest beating; and on the other side of the house, the women laughed and hooted, one swaying like wild Clematis while the others danced on chairs.

Three more soldiers had been killed in Afghanistan the day before. Two soldiers had been abducted in Iraq the week before and found—in pieces—today. Yusufiyah, the sector where Luke would be during his deployment, was about twenty-five kilometers southwest of Baghdad. It wasn't in the Green Zone. The predominantly Sunni farming population was punctuated by romantic adolescent terrorists who gained entry into Baghdad from a highway that ran straight through Yusufiyah, and they brought with them IEDs.

The dreaded IED. The clandestine warrior; the paramour of the Taliban and Al Qaeda, the true enemy of the American soldier. When he deployed, Luke would have to dodge roadside bombs, dead dogs stuffed with explosives, zealot fundamentalists with their trigger-finger cell phones. Sometimes Calli wondered what would happen if Luke was blown up. Would he be disfigured, burned, an amputee? Would she still be able to love him? These toxic thoughts about Luke slithered around her mind, made her feel hideous.

She'd be the sole caregiver: Audrey, Satchmo, and Charlemagne, their fat cat, needed her.

"I'm not a good military wife," she told people. Their marriage was an egalitarian union, but it was lorded over by the Department of Defense. She despised that they had to go where the Army wanted them to go. Do what the Army wanted them to do. She wanted what she always wanted: normalcy—a normal, healthy family. But a good soldier had two families—the one at home, and his men. Luke's commitment to both was one hundred percent. She liked the idea of eating dinner together every night, spending the weekends fixing up a house that was foolhardy to buy because, although it had "good bones," it needed more work than they had time or money for. She imagined Luke coming home late from work on a Friday night because he was stuck in traffic, not because one of his new soldiers disobeyed an order, went AWOL, or decided to go salmon fishing in a rough current, leaving Luke with the burden of telling the family he'd drowned.

But this was the job Luke had chosen and the one he'd had when she decided to become his wife. Not many people knew both sides of Luke—Soldier Luke and Family Luke. Soldier Luke felt foreign to Calli sometimes—authoritative, emotionless, pragmatic.

But Luke was also brave and strong in ways that made him sexy. What she loved most about Luke was his fierce loyalty to her. He always loved her. He knew she was his "it" instantly. He never wavered or deviated from that love. He never would.

>>> <<<

Josie and Tristan stopped by the Colemans' early the night before the deployment. Tristan was a young lieutenant—part of the diaspora of young college men who had graduated ROTC as Second Lieutenants and who had recently been stationed at Fort Drum. All lined up to go to war. Luke called him "sir," even though Luke was forty and Tristan was twenty-five. In the military, a non-commissioned officer like Luke always addressed an officer like Tristan as "sir." There were times, under certain circumstances, when this rule was broken, but it was the officer's move to say, "Please call me X." Even then, when the two soldiers were in a military setting, both had to use the formal "sir."

Josie and Tristan had moved to Fort Drum about the same time as the Colemans. Both Josie and Tristan were from South Carolina, so being in northern New York pressed against their southern sensibilities. Conspicuously attractive, Josie had svelte, lanky legs and tawny skin that reminded Calli of Brazil nuts. She would snicker Waffy-Taffy-candy jokes in her southern drawl. A skilled baker, she claimed to be a chocoholic and addicted to desserts.

Josie and Tristan had been married for less than one year. Their foray into married life had been consumed by war: training for the war, preparing to go to war. No marriage should start this way, Calli thought. They giggled with each other when they thought no one was looking and always held hands. They will make it, Josie is strong, Calli thought. She won't seek comfort in another man while Tristan was away. This restraint is good. We need it. We will have plenty of time during the deployment to cloud our minds with other furies—sending our husbands into the hornets' nest knowing their marriages are secure will keep them safer.

The night before Luke's deployment, they were dressed as if going to a cocktail party, Josie in a pastel linen shift and Tristan with pressed khakis and bow tie that made him look like a little boy going to Sunday school. Tristan announced, "A friend of mine from ROTC who is stationed up here and deploying with Second Brigade up and announced that he was getting married—tonight. Shotgun wedding, anyone?"

Then Josie asked, "Would y'all like to meet us down in the village after the weddin' to take a walk around the battlefield and watch the sunset together?"

"Yes, yes, we'd like that," Luke chimed in.

"We'd have to bring Audrey," Calli said.

"Well, I was hoping so," Josie said. "Ya know, I love Miss Audrey.

Especially when she's dressed up in one of her princess costumes. She's so cute! Maybe we can even buy her an ice cream."

Tristan wasn't leaving until Tuesday. They still had three nights together; Calli had only one with Luke. When they met up in the village, none of them spoke of the deployment. None of them wanted to slog back to the countless conversations they forced themselves to have about "the official notification process" or "hazardous duty pay." They laughed with Audrey, who was costumed in her Snow White outfit. Live jazz dawdled in the air from the large white gazebo in the village.

As the sun started to set over the water, plunging slowly, inevitably out of sight, Calli's mind avoided the unpleasant ticking of the clock. Nothing could halt tomorrow. She slipped into autopilot for Luke and Audrey. For Josie and Tristan. Yet inside, she was wailing. A Canadian breeze put goose bumps on her skin. It was time to head home.

They walked off the Sackets Harbor Battlefield together toward the village. As they approached Poppins, the restaurant where Josie and Tristan planned to eat dinner, Calli realized that they had to say good-bye to Tristan now. On the sidewalk, they hugged. Tristan picked up Audrey, "Good-bye, little lady. I'll see you soon. Can I get a kiss on the cheek?" Audrey, not fully understanding, started to laugh.

"Of course you can have a kiss." She giggled and blew a zerbert while she made the *zrbtt* sound against his face.

Tristan chuckled and put Audrey back on down on the sidewalk. He brandished a toothy smile that tried to hide his concern and sadness. Josie said to Calli, "I'll call ya tomorrow night, okay?"

Calli said, "Don't be worried if I don't answer."

"I'll call ya anyway. No matter what."

>>> <<<

That night at dinner Audrey was her usual curious self. "Why is our nose attached to our brain?" And just last week she'd asked Calli, "Why do we have skin on our legs?" Both good questions.

Calli had to be strong for Audrey, explain the world to her. She was just now beginning to dance, and told Calli, "Mom, I'm just getting my wiggles out." She was the most beautiful creature on the planet. She was everything that was benign and hopeful and good.

Will I be enough for her while Luke is away? Calli wondered. She'll be different when he returns, all her babyness sloughed off. With heartbreaking urgency, she wanted Audrey to understand that Luke was leaving. There'd be no more dates at Dunkin' Donuts. It wasn't fair for Calli to expect that of her, and her mind wandered. How often would she ask Calli, "Is Daddy at work? When is Daddy coming home? Can I do this when Daddy comes home?"

7

Deployment Day.

It wasn't like Christmas or a scheduled dentist's appointment. They headed to church in the morning like they always did on Sundays. Calli did chores the rest of the day—last-minute details, gardening, and laundry. Why plan something elaborate when all she craved was normalcy, she thought. They had spoken so often about how much they loved each other and Audrey. So often they prayed for Luke's safe return, and they'd gone over "in the unlikely situation" until they didn't have much more to say.

At five o'clock, they left for Fort Drum under bright blue skies, that thrilling August sunshine. Audrey was with them.

"We're going to Daddy's office, Auds," Calli told her.

"We're off to Fort Drum," Luke chimed in.

"Fort Drum. Fort Drum. It rhymes with bum, and some, and rum!"

"I could use some rum," Calli mumbled. Luke took one of his hands off the steering wheel and clasped it over Calli's.

"Remember when I threw up in Daddy's office and he had to clean it up?" Audrey said, chuckling.

Calli remembered many Saturday mornings when Luke would take Audrey—have a date with her, they called it. They would stop at Dunkin' Donuts, gorging themselves on sweets and hot coffee.

Today was a sham.

In slow motion, they drove on post to Luke's office, got out, and solemnly walked past other families; the faces reflecting the same surreal and vast emotions she was feeling. In his office, Calli sat next to Luke's enormous rucksack that was packed with seventy pounds of equipment and clothes for his year in Iraq. The 1970s wood-frame couch was covered with fetid orange wool upholstery that chafed the back of her thighs. The entire contents of his desk—pictures of Audrey and Calli in frames or pinned on his bulletin board, his paperwork and binders, his knickknacks and Magz sculpture—had been removed and packed in a cardboard box stowed somewhere in their garage. Audrey wandered around chatting with some of the other soldiers. Some of the men were waiting to fly tonight while others were there to say goodbye, their turn not up yet. Calli wanted to say something. She didn't have any words. She kept thinking, Is this the last time I will see the man I love?

There were others—families, mothers and fathers, wives and children—all milling around pretending to be at ease, but the atmosphere was undeniably somber. Some were outside in the twilight with their soldiers; others mingled inside. Smooth skin, adolescent beards, no wrinkles or gray hair, the weight of their job not yet felt.

Some would never come home—but who?

"Calli. I've thought about this, and I think it's best if you leave before the bus arrives to take the soldiers to the airfield. It will be easier that way. For all of us," Luke said heavily.

"Okay, fine," she said. "If you think so."

To distract himself, he stuffed his running shoes into his bulging bag. He checked the locks on his gear. He and Audrey walked off to the weapons room to draw his assault rifle. It was illogical to let her go with him to get his Colt M4, but Calli was unable to say, "Stop! She's only three!" When they returned, Luke placed the dormant rifle on his barren metal desk.

After a few hours of shiftless conversation and many reassurances that Luke would call or email Calli as soon as he could, the time came for Audrey and Calli to leave.

As they readied to go, Dylan, her brother, appeared to her. The last time Calli saw him, Lucy Wendover was holding him in her arms at the Baltimore-Washington Airport in August 1977. Dinah and Calli were boarding a plane to Miami to stay with their grandmother while Dylan had surgery to correct his neural tube defect. The tube had never closed completely during their mother's pregnancy. By two, Dylan had already had three surgeries.

Calli was ten years old then and she knew. She waved to him. He waved at the girls from their mother's hip. "Wave bye-bye to Calli and Dinah. Wave bye-bye. Blow them kisses," Lucy had prodded, holding Dylan tightly, staring down into his angelic face. The girls boarded the plane. Calli didn't look back. She had to hold Dinah's hand and watch out for her; she was only six years old.

Dylan's death haunted Calli as she clung to Luke. A part of her tried to remember that last day with Dylan, to recognize similar symptoms. She already knew how much it ached to lose someone you loved more than yourself. The emptiness left behind never diminished; though she'd learned to live with that damage. She didn't want to have another empty place in her soul with only memories and pictures to remind her of his presence. Would the Universe do that to her? How do I let go and remember how Luke feels holding my hand? Calli wondered. She could touch him right then, and she wouldn't touch him again for such a long time—months and months. She wouldn't see his eyes or smell his skin.

Somehow she managed to untangle herself from him and climb into the driver's seat of the car. Luke helped Audrey into her seat and buckled her in. Calli turned and looked at him as she had so many times. Sooner or later, she knew she would have to look away, but right at that moment, she gazed at him for every nanosecond she could. In his digital green camouflage uniform with his gentle mahogany eyes tearing, he looked at her. She looked at him. She reached across the back seat and grabbed his hand. She wanted to grab him and tear off his hand to keep with her. She never wanted to let go. Calli squeezed and squeezed, praying all the while that she would hold him again.

Luke held onto her hand. Both of them crying. "I will return," he told her. "I love you! I will."

He closed the door. Stared into Calli through the window. She didn't hesitate to turn on the car. Audrey waved her little American flag out the window at him as they drove away. The newest chapter of her life had started. She drove off and didn't look back. She couldn't.

>>> <<<

Someone advised them to buy a Dictaphone so Luke could record bedtime stories for Audrey. They'd purchased two recorders and, as it turned out, in addition to the two hours of stories that Luke had recorded for Audrey, they both had been recording their thoughts about each other for the coming year. When they did finally kiss good-bye, it made Calli feel a little better to know that she'd have his recorded voice to comfort them. As they drove off post, Calli switched on the tape to hear Luke's voice speaking to them as they drove home: "Calli and Audrey, my dearest loves. Know that I will miss you every second of every day that I am away. In nine and half months we will see each other again—how wonderful that day will be. May is not that far off and I know you can do it. I can't wait to hold you in my arms and kiss your skin. I can't wait for the three of us to make a cheese sandwich, with Audrey as the cheese in the middle of us hugging each other tightly. I promise I will be safe. I love you, Calli. I love you, Audrey. Give Satchmo and Charlemagne a huge squeeze from me. I love you both . . . all the way up to the moon and back!"

Calli realized that these recordings would be the only way she could hear Luke's voice while he was away. She played the tape again. It was time to move ahead. A strangely phlegmatic calm rose up in her.

Once home, she quickly jotted out an email to their families. She knew they'd want to know how the good-bye went. Then she checked her inbox and saw that she had an email from Luke. He must have written while waiting in his office to leave to go to the airfield.

My Dearest,

All I want to say, my dearest heart of hearts, is that I love you with all my morsels. We can make this work, Trust in the Lord, be strong and be courageous, for I am with you. All things are possible for those who believe. I am counting the days till I see you in person, though I will see you every minute of every day in my heart. You are my soul and salvation. Even through the mushiness, I can still smile. I LOVE YOU!!!! To be continued.

Luke

>>> <<<

Luke is somewhere between here and Kuwait this morning—Calli's first thought as she woke up alone in their bed. It seemed so big—the thought and the bed. He might be in Germany or Ireland refueling, or possibly already en route to Kuwait. She was grateful for her Clonazepam—without it, she would have been up all night thinking about the year ahead. Although she'd never been in AA, she supposed the same mantra applied—"day by day." Today I have three hundred sixty-four days to go. She slugged downstairs for coffee.

Audrey called Calli from her bedroom, "Mama. Mama. MAMA!" Calli would be alone with her for next twelve months. Luke wouldn't be walking through the door to give her a break. He wouldn't be there to let her have some time off on a Saturday morning while he took Audrey to Dunkin' Donuts for their date. Every night, Calli would give her her bath, read her a bedtime story. Calli would comfort her, console her, hug her, love her, chase away her nightmares, and assure her that her Daddy was coming home. There's no getting around it, Calli thought, I am a single parent—for now. Duty calls. She had to go to Audrey and welcome her day with a smile. Even if smiling was the last thing she felt like doing.

>>> <<<

After Calli took Audrey to preschool, she drove to Verizon to have Luke's mobile phone disconnected. The parking lot at the Salmon Run Mall in Watertown was half empty. Overhead, the drone of a plane—a plane swollen like a bloated tick—vibrated and headed out of Fort Drum. An anxiety she hadn't experienced since her last days at Juilliard hit her hard. She opened her car door and retched on the black asphalt parking lot. The stench of bile and vomit flew back in her face.

The plane was probably overflowing with soldiers just like Luke, heading to the cradle of civilization for a year; some forever. A numb dreariness covered her like a cold sheet and she wanted to curl up with it, lie down in her bed with it, and close her eyes to block out the world.

Only three hundred sixty-four more days until that plane flies back to Fort Drum to deliver Luke to me, Calli thought, standing in front of her car door staring at the sky.

>>> <<<

Her list was different. No sandwich meat. No potato chips or pretzels. Only one bag of coffee. Calli didn't notice how short the list was until she was in the market and the cart didn't seem as filled as it should have been. She wouldn't need to buy Luke food until he came home for his leave in May. For the past few months, once or twice a week she drove the twenty-five miles to Fort Drum to take Luke his lunch. It was an excuse to see him as much as it was a way to make sure he ate lunch rather than starving, only to come home and eat pretzels and cheese like a vulture before dinner. Now that he was deployed, she didn't want to go Fort Drum. She didn't have anyone to deliver lunch to.

Calli had lived alone before Luke and knew how to cook for one person. A chicken breast, a pork chop, a frozen turkey burger. Audrey didn't like everything and didn't eat very much anyway. Calli picked at Audrey's leftovers, scraps of grilled cheese, mouthfuls of spaghetti, a few chips here and there, not wanting anything to go to waste—the seagull diet.

Tuesday night supper club became the highlight of her meal planning. All the women in her supper club made such comfort food: pastas with warm, gooey sauce; creamy soups; salads chock full of dried cranberries, roasted sunflower seeds, velvety goat cheese; fresh-baked rolls and desserts like fudge brownies and chocolate lava cakes; bountiful appetizers of cheeses, breads, chips, dips; and nothing that included the words "lite" or "sugar-free" or "low-fat." This week was her turn to host, and she decided on a sausage, red pepper, and onion frittata.

Calli looked forward to Tuesday nights. She was surprised how much she looked forward to them and recognized that the lens through which she had initially viewed Daphne and Josie was a flimsy one. She had reduced them to stereotypes, overlaid her expectations on them, predicted that that would act out the one thin role she prescribed for them. These women were far from having one aspect—no they had numerous sides—and now their stories, like vines, intertwined and took root with Calli's.

Calli thought, I don't envy us, the offerings we make, like the Inca in their *capacocha*, but instead of children, we give up our husbands.

After dinner, Calli put Audrey to bed and then Josie, Daphne, and Calli watched a movie. "Did you hear that?" Josie asked a few minutes in.

"What?" Calli said.

"It sounded like mens' voices," Daphne said.

Calli walked over to her window and looked down to her neighbor's, "Oh no. There's an ambulance at Diane's house. I hope everything is okay. She has cancer, and her mother, Eunice, is quite old. She lives with them."

They met the day after the Colemans moved in, when Calli was walking Satchmo. "Your wild flowers are beautiful. I love how they border your walkway," Calli said. The woman stood up from her bright pink Adirondack chair to greet her. She was bald under the headscarf and wore an overwhelming scent of blossomy perfume as if she was trying to mask another smell. She had no eyelashes or brows.

"Thank you. It's my outlet. I love flowers."

"Me, too. I'm Calli Coleman. We just moved in down the street. My husband, Luke, and I have a daughter, Audrey, and, of course, this beast—he's Satchmo."

"Welcome, Calli. I'm Diane. It's just me and my husband here with my mother, Eunice."

Now the three women were at the window, examining the situation.

"Should we go down there?" Josie said.

"Daphne, you're the nurse, is it good that the ambulance has been there so long? Shouldn't they have left by now?" Josie said with concern.

"Either someone's dead..." Both Calli and Josie stared at Daphne in disbelief.

"Dead?" Calli exclaimed.

"Or it's not incredibly serious."

A little later, the ambulance pulled away from Diane's house. "What's that gold sedan behind it?" Calli asked Daphne.

"Probably a volunteer medic." Just as the ambulance and sedan drove past her house, another medic in an SUV pulled up. The ambulance paused, the driver of the SUV hopped out, and jumped into the ambulance. Clearly in a rush, the SUV driver had parked in front of Gus Pepys's driveway, blocking it.

"Gus isn't going to like that," Calli said. "He just got back from his third deployment, twice to Afghanistan, once to Iraq. He's a little on edge these days."

Calli had met Gus and his wife, Goldie, a few times. They had three sons who were older than Audrey. They didn't come out too much.

Sure enough, within minutes of the ambulance's departure, as the women watched, Gus emerged from the house and cantered toward the medic's car—with a sledgehammer in his hand. He slammed it down on the hood of the SUV, then smashed the windshield. *Slam!*

Calli was so startled she jumped. "Oh my god!"

"Whoa!" Daphne said.

"Jesus. What's he doing? What's wrong with him?" Josie said.

Without thinking, Calli ran to open her front door and yelled out to him, "That's a paramedic's car!"

Before she could finish, Gus said, "They ALWAYS park in my driveway!" His stunned wife stood in the garage, motionless and mute. And just as quickly as he started, he stopped and walked back into the garage.

Confused and scared, Calli retreated into her house, thankful that Audrey hadn't seen anything. "Should I call the police?"

"Calli, you have to call the police—or someone. Call the fire station. I figure the paramedic is one of theirs," Josie said.

Calli called. Of course, no answer. Rattled, she thought to call Louise, the local know-it-all.

"Calli, you need to call Jacob. He's the chief of police in Sackets." Calli overheard Louise relay her saga to someone else. It sounded like Louise was in her car. "Hold on. Janella Thomas just pulled up next to me. She said definitely call Jacob. Look, hon, I gotta go."

Calli dialed 411 and asked for the Sackets Harbor Police Department. "Hello, may I please speak to the chief of police?"

"Um, he's not here, sweetie. What's this about?" A woman with a gravelly voice asked.

Calli hesitated, then said, "Well, I know this sounds strange, but there's a man across the street who just took a sledgehammer to a paramedic's car."

"Where are you, sweetie?"

"On Mill Creek Lane."

"Listen, sweetie, is the guy still out there?"

"No. No he's gone back in his house, but I'm here with my little girl and my husband is in Iraq—"

"Gotcha, sweetie. Don't be afraid. Can you get to your car and come down here to make a statement? I don't have anyone right now who can come to you."

Don't have enough people? Calli thought. What if I was burgled? Would the woman who called her sweetie find someone then?

Calli left Audrey, asleep, home with Josie and Daphne and drove down to the police station. The Sackets Harbor Police Department consisted of a small office in the same building as the fire department. The biggest crime these people had to deal with might be dog poop someone left in the park.

Calli told her story, signed her statement, and left.

Josie and Daphne met Calli at home. "How'd it go?"

"Fine, I guess. They didn't really ask me very many questions. The whole thing is fishy. It's weird. Typical northern New York small-town police. Do you wanna stay and finish the movie with me? Wanna wait? Keep an eye out for the police? I wonder if Pepys has PTSD? I wonder if he'll try something on the police?"

While outside crickets sang and a moderate breeze whispered, the women watched the movie. Waited. Occasionally, they peered out the window. Calli felt safer with them in the house with her. Her sweet stench of body odor caught her off guard when she lifted her arm to fetch her glass of wine off the coffee table. She had never felt nervous in Sackets before, but with a soldier across the street who appeared to have lost his mind, Calli's anxiety spiked.

Sackets Harbor was a small village of thirteen hundred, and she lived less than a mile away from the center, where the police were stationed. What was taking so long? Daphne decided to drive home and get her toothbrush. "I'm coming back. If it were me, I'd want you to spend the night, so don't even try to tell me no."

"Hey, here're the keys to my house. Will you grab my toothbrush, too?" Josie said.

Calli didn't argue with them. She didn't know that much about PTSD, but it didn't take much to figure out that something was terribly wrong with Gus Pepys. His deployments had to have taken a toll on him. On his family. Calli always told people how fortunate Luke and she had been. Luke's deployment to Iraq would most likely be his last one since he planned on retiring when he got home. "Twenty years and not a minute more," he'd said many times. But for many soldiers, it was not uncommon to deploy multiple times. Some of the younger soldiers had spent more time overseas than they had on US soil during their early careers. Of course the war would break down their coping skills. How much war could one person witness before the nightmares and noises overpowered them?

Josie and Calli closed the wooden slatted blinds at the front of the house, turned out the lights, and peered out, waiting like two amateur private investigators. Josie giggled.

Now camped on her tiny patio in a big down jacket, Louise called. "Anything?"

Louise lived next to the Pepyses, and after Calli's frantic call to her two hours earlier, she was waiting like Josie and Calli.

"Not yet. When do you think the police will come?"

"Oh, they'll come. Just wait."

Calli motioned to Josie to come upstairs with her, to watch from Calli's bedroom, where she thought they'd have a better view. In the bedroom closet, Calli kept binoculars. She took them out to share. They commando crawled across the floor, closed the blinds, and then peered out between the slats.

Louise called again. "Can you see anything happening?"

"No. Nothing is happening. What is taking so long?"

By eleven, the police still hadn't come and Daphne had returned. Bored with playing sleuth, Daphne and Josie decided to watch more television. Calli called Louise. "Hey, I'm finished being Nancy Drew for the night. I'll see you tomorrow, ok?"

Calli ran downstairs to lock all the windows and doors. They had moved to Sackets for its safety and charm. Back in the bedroom, Calli pulled out one of the shotguns Luke had inherited from his uncle. She laid it on the bed next to her, remembering her angst at seeing Luke's gun in his office the day he deployed.

Calli didn't tell Josie and Daphne that she had retrieved the gun. She didn't want them to be more concerned about her than they already were. She went downstairs to join them.

"What do ya'll think is going to happen to him?" Josie said.

"Hopefully, he'll be arrested," Calli said.

"His career is ruined," Daphne said, "and he will probably lose his pension. One thing's for sure: That dude definitely is not deploying again. He's got a serious anger problem. You said he was a colonel, right? Can you imagine him in command? I wonder if he was like that over there? I mean, Huey has anger problems, but I can handle him. He's just a yeller. I can't imagine Huey being aggressive." Daphne laughed. "One of Huey's men is on his third deployment in five years. His wife is twenty-five. That's tough on any couple. Huey told me he has a dozen or so soldiers who are on their second, third, and fourth deployments. Young men, young wives," Daphne said.

"That was really scary. I've never seen anyone attack a car before. Much less with a sledgehammer. It was like a bad country song. Ya'll know, those songs where the scorned woman attacks her cheating lover's car?" Josie said.

Calli said, "I feel really badly for Goldie. God. How awful. I wonder if he's hit her. Or their kids? I mean, if I saw Luke do something like that, I'd be terrified of what he might do to me...or Auds. That guy needs serious help."

"Yeah, but the Army won't help him. Well, they'll help him, but he won't think it's help. These guys are programmed to believe admitting they're having problems tarnishes their report cards, so a lot of them don't tell anyone. They can't be on antidepressants, or seek mental health treatment, or else they're considered unstable," said Daphne.

"Unstable? That guy *is* unstable," Calli said.

"That's so fucked, Daphne," Josie said.

"The Army is fucked up. We're just a means to an end. Do you think they really care if our husbands are depressed? If we're depressed? Hell, no. Just scribble out a prescription and send us on our merry way," Daphne said.

"I know. For some reason, a few of the younger wives keep calling me. Even ones who've been through this before. They say, 'Calli, it's hard. And it may never get easier.' So, on that uplifting note, I'm going to bed," Calli said. "The guest room is all ready for you two lovelies."

Upstairs, aware she'd be unable to get any rest otherwise, Calli took a sleeping pill, pushed the shotgun to the floor, and went to bed.

The next morning, convinced that Gus Pepys had been arrested while she was in her coma, she got ready to take Audrey and Satchmo for a walk. Daphne and Josie slept in. But out the window, she saw Gus Pepys being escorted into a Military Police car. Whispering to Audrey, "Let's play the silent game. You go first and I'll count how many seconds you go without speaking. Okay? Good!"

"Okay, Mama. Then your turn and I'll count."

"Yes, perfect. But you go first. I'm sure you'll win."

Calli crept out the door, trying not to bring attention to herself. She held Satchmo on his leash and put Audrey into the jogging stroller. Out of the corner of her eye, she caught Gus Pepys staring at her from inside the MP car as he was driven away from his house. His wife. His family.

For an hour, Calli speculated while she walked around town, Will he come and break into my house while I sleep? Will he bring his sledgehammer? Would he kill Audrey, too? Satchmo and Charlemagne? Would Luke have to be called home from Iraq?

When she returned, she saw Louise and two other neighbors outside of Louise's house, chatting. Louise kept saying, "I should have told you to call the State Police . . . that guy would be locked up by now."

"The MPs took him away about an hour ago. That's pretty serious," Calli said.

"I always thought that guy was creepy. He never spoke to any of us neighbors. Just walked around like he was better than us. Once Goldie was outside watering her zinnias and I said hello to her. She barely acknowledged me."

"Maybe he beat her. Maybe she was afraid to speak. I don't know," Calli said.

"Don't worry, honey. You'll be okay. He's gone now."

8

Calli kept herself busy with the house. She painted their front door cardinal red. She didn't spill any, but there were dry marks. She smoothed it out over and over again, but it still looked shoddy. Once the door was finished, it was time to attack the overgrown weeds invading the plant beds. Horsetail weeds were a nightmare to abolish because of their tremendous root systems. Down on her knees, Calli dug her gloveless hands in the loamy ground, digging hopefully for the enthusiastic root system that snaked its way almost two feet down. Fresh earth sheathed her hands and arms while a worm wiggled away from her trespassing fingers. Calli's hands scratched tenderly, blindly, for each thread of horsetail. Beneath the top layer of dirt lay the fresh allure of life, an echo of new beginnings and longstanding legacies. Horsetail was prehistoric. It survived when the dinosaurs hadn't. If she broke the root system, two more would grow in its place.

An hour passed quickly yet only a small patch of weeds had been eradicated. With her aching back begging her to stop, Calli committed herself to one hour of battle. And then she'd stop—for today. Finally she sat up and settled on her haunches, breathing deeply like a yoga teacher had encouraged her to do. Stick out your tongue and roar like a lion! she'd suggest at some point during a class. Her dirty hands and black nails looked alien. She wasn't a gardener. Surveying the rest of the yard, Calli caught sight of the newly planted landscaping at the empty house next door. Most of the ground cover and shrubs lay dying or dead from lack of attention. Leaving the horsetail to counterattack, she got up and walked over to the empty house. Sad, sagging plants hung low and smelled lethargic. In a humble attempt to keep some of them alive, she yanked out her hose and watered. The effort felt futile. Everything was going to die anyway.

>>>> <<<<

It was 117 degrees in Kuwait, according to the Weather Channel.

Although it wasn't cold yet, Calli invested in some DVDs for the long haul. Movies that would probably help distract them, *The Sound of Music, The Wizard of Oz, Toy Story, Annie*. She thought about picking up the phone and calling Eula when her dark moods were lurking, but she never did. Eula wouldn't understand. Josie and Daphne understood, but why saddle them with her gloomy vibration when they had the same darkness resting in their bones.

Even Mother feels sad, she thought. Calling her mother only made her feel more despondent. And there was no good reason to call Madelon, Luke's mother. Worry her. Calli needed to talk to someone. She needed to fill the little niches that pockmarked her days.

Calli abandoned the idea of calling anyone. Instead she decided to make some bread to send to Luke in his first care package while Audrey was at school. Her bare cupboards didn't have all the ingredients, so she got into her SUV to go to the market.

Suddenly feeling garrulous, she said to the checkout woman at Price Chopper, "I'm making bread for my husband."

The chubby woman said, "That's nice, sweetie."

"He really loves this rosemary bread. It's great right out of the oven with butter and buckwheat honey. Have you ever tried buckwheat honey? It's completely different than most honey. I found it at a farmer's market and now I'm addicted."

"Does it come in one of those little bears?"

"Um, I don't think so. But regular honey would work, too."

"I love that honey out of those cute little bears. Have you ever tried it on bananas?" Out of the corner of her eye, she noticed a newspaper headline on the periodical rack. For months, she'd been reluctant to read, listen to, or watch the news, but the cover of the paper had a picture of President Bush with a huge quote: "Everywhere that freedom stirs, let tyrants fear."

"I really wonder about this," Calli said, nodding toward the paper.

Checkout Lady rolled her eyes. "I hate Bush. I am sorry, but I do. We shouldn't be there. Don't you agree?"

Calli said, "My husband is in Kuwait on his way into Iraq. And unless something horrible happens, he won't be home for another twelve months. The only thing that matters to me is that he comes home alive."

Conflicting emotions festered in her like a pustule as she left the market. It wasn't in her to hate the president. But perhaps she did. Yelling at Audrey, kicking Charlemagne once when he was climbing on her ficus, and saying fuckin' this and fuckin' that—she was definitely angry.

Calli had screamed at Audrey a few times lately. She spanked her hard yesterday bellowing, "Stop it. Stop it. STOP!" Now she couldn't even remember what Audrey had done.

A vein bulged in her arm.

Audrey hasn't done anything wrong except have me for her mother, Calli thought. I can't do this to her. She needs me to be strong and supportive; not a coward who verbally abuses her—who spanks her?

What would she do when she went home to Baltimore next? Calli didn't want to deal with anyone right then who might scratch at her vulnerabilities. Lucy Wendover often seemed to have difficulty in analyzing her own daughter's behavior, making sense of it, under-standing her. Even though Thanksgiving was still weeks away, Calli needed to find a way to gracefully excuse herself, to do something radical and different. Kelly and Roger Mumford—friends of Calli's in Sackets—had asked to her join them for Thanksgiving with their family. They'd asked Josie and Daphne, too. The Mumfords were thoughtful, gentle people who would let Calli be present—herself—during Thanksgiving.

Calli was lucky. There were many kind people in Sackets Harbor whom she considered friends; they had supported her and Audrey—opened their homes to them for dinners. Calli embraced nights when she didn't have to cook and clean up. Having civilian friends up here made life easier. Somehow they knew not to poke at the sore—per-haps they'd seen this before. Another version of Calli—an Army wife doppelgänger —had been there when the war broke out. No one asked her about the war at those dinners; they talked instead about good literature, Italian cooking, travel, dogs, anything—anything but the war. Anything but Luke. The vacant space in her heart grew in diameter with each passing day. It was a reprieve to come up for air occasionally and just be. Somehow Kelly and Roger let her guide the conversation toward or away from Luke, never probing her or voicing their opinions about the president. They didn't have to. She knew how they felt and they were compassionate enough to let Calli come with Audrey to their house for dinners. To relax and be.

She had decided she was going to tell them yes. She would join them for Thanksgiving.

Dear Calli,

I knew the upcoming election would produce reactions and spin that ranged from the sublime to the ridiculous, and I see from the debates that it has already started. My favor-ite line, one that comes from almost every candidate, is: "I'm against the war, but FOR the soldiers!" What kind of malarkey is that? This is not the draft, so the soldiers there believe in what they are doing—for the most part. So, how can you be against something but support the very people who are committed to it? That's like saying, "Let's cut down the forest, but I want to preserve the trees!" I really hope someone takes the issue further and forces the candidates to explain exactly what it is they mean by that comment. So far, everyone has just left it at that. Unfortunately, the liberal media has done an excellent job of wearing people down and Americans are buying into all the headlines.

And you are right about not feeling the impact of war. I always like to ask people what they would suggest. Okay, we're out of Iraq tomorrow—lock, stock, and barrel. Then what? How would THEY have handled the aftermath of 9/11? Nobody really has an answer. It's all about Peace and Love and all those romantic and completely unrealistic notions that need the cooperation of—guess who—THE TERRORISTS in order to work! Of course, we all want tranquility in our lives. Of course, it's easy to downgrade the importance of Iraq when it's so far away. But there is a price to pay for burying our heads in the sand.

Mother and I always support you. We love you so much. Please call your mother; she'd love to hear from you more often. And, of course, I always enjoy hearing that lovely voice of yours, too. Will you be joining us for Thanksgiving?
Love,
Dad

After reading her father's elegant letter, she considered how he always weighed politics and reached a set of judgments in harmony with his own needs. An extension of her needs in this case. That he could make a personal statement into a strong political solution revealed the depth of his talent and his love for Calli. A nuanced ideology emerged to Haines Wendover even when support for the war had begun to pall. His words provided a safe space for intellectual debate in Calli's life where few existed. Haines's intelligence soothed her. Would Audrey someday admire her in this way?

When Calli dropped her off in her designated classroom on Tuesday, Audrey barely noticed when she left.

"Bye Auds, I love you."

"Bye bye, Mama."

"I'll see you after school. I love you."

Audrey tottered off. The puzzle in the corner of the classroom drew her toward it. Calli read somewhere that the children will "follow" their mother. Any ounce of positive energy Calli had she used around Audrey in the hopes that she wouldn't get down, too.

The two of them had a ritual every night.

"Auds, give Mama a kiss. Yes, right here on my lips."

"Okay, Mama."

"Should we pray for Daddy's safety?"

"Okay, Mama, yes...okay, let's." Their hands held each other tightly while they bowed their heads.

"Dear Lord, please keep Daddy safe from the Bad Guys. Keep all of his men safe, and all the military safe. Please watch over them. Please watch over all the loved ones at home and keep them safe and in your loving arms. Watch over Audrey as she sleeps and give her good dreams of ice cream and oceans. Amen. Do you want to say anything, Auds?"

"God watch over Daddy and his men. Amen."

"That was beautiful. I love it. I love you."

"I love you, Mama."

Many times a day Calli said, "You know Auds, Daddy loves you all the way up to the moon and back!" Audrey had asked Calli last night to "explain" the Bad Guys to her. At first, Calli thought maybe she was scared, but then she realized it was a stall tactic. After Calli explained, Audrey then asked her to explain how Babar lands his plane.

Calli came up with a little story that Audrey liked. "Okay. A while back the Bad Guys did something, well, bad. They hurt a lot of people. So the President of the United States, whose name is...?"

And Audrey said, "George Bush."

"Decided that we needed to teach the Bad Guys how to become good guys. In order to do that, he needed all the soldiers to help him. Who is a soldier in our family?"

"DADDY."

"Right! So Daddy and all the other soldiers are over in Iraq teaching the Bad Guys how to be good guys. He tells the Bad Guys…"

"You Bad Guys, you be good guys, and don't you come hurt my Audrey and my Calli."

>>>> —<<<<

Before Calli got into bed that night, she read an email from Luke: *These little Kuwaitis can make some omelets! I try and have at least three starches with meals and I am eating four times a day. I actually have lost weight in just a week.*

She hung onto the tenuous threads that kept her buoyed each day. The conditions in Kuwait sounded deplorable: they lived in a tent city, all thirty-five hundred of them. The tents held seventy people on cots. At least they had air conditioning.

Sweet Luke, he claimed that the best thing about the place was the food. They had meals four times a day, including at midnight. Did he dream of cool Sackets Harbor? One of his jobs was to schedule time for the boys to be outside in all their gear each day, to condition themselves. *They have worked their way up to ninety minutes each day and then,* he wrote, *they usually have to return to the tents, drink a couple of liters of water, and sleep for an hour or so, because the sun takes it right out of them.*

Calli wished Audrey was old enough to speak with her about Luke. To share with Audrey about the heat in the Middle East, the Kuwaitis and their omelets, how long Luke would be deployed. But Audrey was too young. Calli knew that the best thing she could do was to keep Audrey happy with as little information as her three-year-old brain could understand.

>>>> <<<<

One day, Tracy Applebee called Calli. "Hey, Calli. Do you and Audrey want to come over?"

The last thing Calli wanted to do was spend more time with Tracy, but begrudgingly she decided that it was good for Audrey to get out of the house and away from the television.

On the way to Tracy's house for the playdate, Audrey announced from her car seat, "Mama, my tummy hurts."

"Oh Auds, really? I'm sure you're fine." Calli didn't believe her. She kept driving, determined to have some adult conversation. She'd had all the *Toy Story* she could take.

"Mama! My tummy! Oh no!" About fifteen minutes into the drive, Audrey gagged then threw up all over herself and the back seat of the car.

Grossed out by the sour smell and the irritation of having to stop, Calli pulled into a Rite Aid parking lot and tried to console her. Oatmeal puke stuck in her curls and on the sides of her car seat cover. Rain pelted Calli as she leaned into the car to inspect the damage. Gagging, she held her breath, trying to smile at the poor creature. "It's okay. You're okay. Oh, you poor girl. Mama's here. Don't worry. We'll get you cleaned up. We just have to drive home."

Thankfully, Calli had programmed Tracy's number into her phone. She called to tell Tracy that she couldn't make it.

"Oh, I'm so sorry. How is Audrey now?"

"Well, she's vomiting all over the place so I really need to get her home."

"Yes, well, I just wanted to tell you that I'm going back to Kansas for the deployment. My family is there. I can't deal with this place. I guess I'll see you when the guys get back."

"Oh, okay. Um, well, good luck. I really have to go now, Tracy. But thanks."

After calming Audrey down, she retreated back to the driver's seat and drove home. Calli pounded the steering wheel with her fists at the first stoplight. *Tracy* couldn't deal with this place? Calli didn't know why she felt angry with a woman she didn't care for to begin with. Nothing made sense to her. Maybe she was jealous. Tracy could make a home elsewhere for a while, but Calli felt as if her home was on Mill Creek Lane, where she lived with Luke. Where Luke's things were. Where he could imagine her cooking bacon and eggs or baking cookies with Audrey. She was determined to make her home in Sackets Harbor, New York.

When she finally had Audrey settled in on the bathroom floor, trying to teach her to vomit into the toilet, the tears came. Luke was not going to walk through the door of this home, not today, not tomorrow. What kind of a home was that?

9

Calli read Fannie Flagg's *Can't Wait to Get to Heaven*. A sense of courage and natural graciousness characterized Flagg's words: *Life was a gift; not something to figure out. Life was something to enjoy.* In the long twilight of this war, she wondered what the outcome would be. Would they truly be safer? Would she have spent this year in vain? She wanted to enjoy her gift.

Women whose husbands had just returned said, "Oh, don't worry, the year goes by quickly."

Calli bit her lip. "Easy for you to say." Their loneliness was over. And while Calli was happy for them, she was jealous.

His Bay Rum aftershave, razor, deodorant, toothbrush and toothpaste were prominently placed in the bathroom cabinet. A crystal decanter half-full of bourbon sat front and center on the bar. His ratty old slippers with a hole at the top where his right toe peeped out rested under his side of the bed. Their house needed to bear the unmistakable signature and spirit of Luke. Nothing of his was moved. She missed his southern Virginia drawl gently mocking her and how his laughter shone through the house. She missed how he snored and how she'd kick him to roll over. That was real. And while, yes, she did sleep somewhat better thanks to sleeping pills, without him, she was alone in the bed. Kicking Luke to roll over was part of their marriage, part of their friendship, part of their lives that she would be missing for a long time. Did the other wives get used to these deployments?

Daphne had been dealing with Huey's deployments for years; in Calli's eyes, she was a pro. The day Huey left, Daphne drove to Calli's house after she dropped him off, her fingernails gnawed to stubs and a vacant look in her eyes. Calli said, "You're going to be ok. You know everything will be fine." Calli then joked, "Look at me. I'm covered in flour thinking I can bake bread. Things could be worse. You could look like me."

The night Tristan left, Calli had gone to Josie's. Daphne, too. Josie's usually meticulous braids sprouted small tendrils where she hadn't cared for them, and her eyes were swollen like a boxer's. The three of them settled into the overstuffed furniture in her living room, staring at each other.

Josie cried, "I never thought this day would come. I didn't want it to come. I'm so empty."

"You've got me," Daphne hiccupped, having had a few glasses of wine. "And Calli."

"I'm so lucky," Josie cried again.

Calli wished she could play some music or light some candles that would make them feel better. Empowered. Optimistic. But they were empty and drunk. "It's a weeknight and we're together." That was about the most optimistic thing Calli could offer up.

Then Daphne said, "We should call ourselves the Diva War Widows."

Calli grimaced. The idea of being widow, even if it was just a nickname—bad omen.

Calli said, "How about the Diva War Brides?"

"I'll take it," Josie said.

>>> <<<

Calli opened her email and found a message from Luke. He asked her to forward it to the other wives.

Camp Buhering, Kuwait

Dear friends and families of the Alpha Company,
On behalf of the Commander, CPT Eric Case, I would like to send a quick update from the far side of the world. Please excuse the informality and please do understand that I will be purposely vague on some points contained below.

First of all, we are all SAFE and SOUND. Though several of us are spread out in a couple of different locations north of here, all are well and in good shape. Morale is high as we prepare for the next leg of the adventure. I must explain the picture above before we go any further. Our battalion mascot is the Polar Bear, aptly named Big George. I found this picture on my computer and thought I'd send it as a heading until we get our FRG newsletter cooking. Obviously the Polar Bear here is LTC Calvi, our battalion commander. For those of you that do not know him, he is the senior officer and we are blessed to have him at the front leading us. In my "just shy of 19 years" of active duty, I can say without reservation that we have the most solid and cohesive command team in the Army. Please have faith in our command.

A quick recap for you on the last two weeks: As you know, we left Fort Drum in a cloud of dust and have been moving forward ever since. The plane ride was almost fifteen hours, and given the change in time zones, it was almost twenty-four hours later that we arrived in Kuwait. The post where we are staging is smack in the middle of nowhere, in the desert! The temperatures have hovered between 115 and 130 daily with lows around 100 at night. Needless to write, look for some thinner Polar Bears when we return. The dining facility here is outstanding, and the Kuwaitis can feed thousands in relatively no time at all. No one is hungry here as there are four meals a day. All the water is trucked in daily, both bottled water and bathing water. Each unit has trailers set up with sinks and showers in them. Just outside are gigantic water containers, which are filled from 18-wheelers. The only problem is that the water cooks in the sun all day to about a thousand degrees! I force the men to drink water throughout the day. I would guess on an average we drink about 10–12 liters of water daily. In this heat, it is an absolute must! We also spend at least an hour or so outside in the heat of the day in our full kit: helmet, gloves, body armor, kneepads, and weapons. I think we are getting acclimatized, slowly but surely.

We have been able to do some training before we head north. We left one morning around 0200 and drove about 1.5 hours away to a rifle range to make sure our weapons were all zeroed and ready. We have done some driving drills in order to get all our drivers accustomed to the new, heavy, armored Humvees that we will use. We are able to do PT every day, which helps relieve the stress and keep our minds healthy. And, of course, we are getting plenty of rest. Given the somewhat less-than-rigid daily plan, the men have done very well. We live on cots in very close proximity to each other in air-conditioned tents, so courtesy is a must. I have been very impressed with your sons and husbands and promise to look out for each and every one of them.

Some of your husbands are north at the moment. We are expecting to join them soon. We all certainly rely on each other, regardless of rank, for everything. That's the only way we will be able to win and endure the year of separation from you. I hope that you all will freely and willingly help each other out as well. I know that at the moment communications from your sons and husbands are somewhat slow. Please know that there is almost a division's worth of soldiers here, and the facilities just aren't capable of handling all the email and phone usage that we would like. I suspect that once we get settled at our FOB (Forward

Operating Base) and get into our routine we will be able to communicate somewhat easier, so please, please HANG ON! I have encouraged all the men to write letters and send postcards. The mail is free. I would also add, having spent a few days deployed over the years, that letters and care packages are HUGE morale boosters for us. One last point on the communications from us: There will undoubtedly be a vacuum of news when we leave Kuwait—do not be alarmed. The transfer and change out with the unit we replace will be a little time consuming and the communications assets will not be readily available. As soon as I can get to a computer, I will send a quick update.

In closing, dear friends, please know that we are all well and in good health. It is my pleasure and most of all my honor to serve your husbands and sons and especially you. Be safe, be strong, and be courageous. My very best to each and every one of you.
Luke Coleman
Master Sergeant
The Immortals

Calli reread the email, her thoughts spinning. It was impossible to imagine such heat. A vacuum of news? Why was Luke writing email to all the wives? The *Immortals*? She hoped, even if the other soldiers couldn't reach their families, that Luke would tell her when he was moving north to Iraq. It would be any day now.

And then the real fight would begin.

⟫⟫ 10 ⟪⟪

Veronica McLeod asked Calli to lead an FRG meeting, to talk to the other wives about the deployment. Calli could never have imagined that she would have an Army family, but her family back in Baltimore didn't understand what she was going through, as much as they tried. The other wives and military families may not have been the "kind" of people Calli thought she'd need, but in the past few months, the course of her life had changed. The path she'd thought she was on had sprouted a huge detour sign, and suddenly the people around her weren't Army wives so much as women taking the same route through marriage and parenthood that she was, at least for these twelve months. Perhaps leading the FRG meeting was the right thing to do.

At any rate, Veronica seemed to think that Calli was the perfect candidate.

"Calli, Luke is very admired."

"He signed his message *The Immortals*. Do you have any clue what that means?"

"It's their company nickname. Their Company Commander came up with it."

"There's a Company Commander, too? Veronica, I can barely even remember the difference between a battalion and a brigade. How many people did you call before you called me?"

"You were the first person on the list. Listen, I know you haven't had the easiest time. Army wives can be bitches sometimes. But not everyone is that way."

"Yeah, I know. I've made friends with some of the other wives. Finally."

"I know. It was Daphne Hollis who recommended you to lead our meetings. She mentioned that you're getting some email from Luke that might be helpful to the younger wives."

"Daphne? Really?"

"Yes, and she said you'd say yes."

"Oh, really. Well. Um. Can I think about it?"

"Of course you can, sweetie."

Calli's jaw clenched as she remembered the time she almost fell through the ice at her grandparents' farm. The kind of ice that looks like water but is only strong enough to hold a goose or a heron, but probably not a full-grown woman. Calli wondered, Is the Universe throwing all this at me because I need to learn something?

She didn't know why she was struggling with this. When the war started, people asked her, "Is Luke safe? Will he have to go to war?" She told them, "Oh no. He's safe working at Hopkins. He's non-deployable." None of their friends were in the military. Except for Henry, but he'd been out for over a decade. Most of their close friends worked in executive positions at law firms, financial institutions, or large companies. Eula and Henry didn't need to work. Few of her women friends worked outside the home; most of them were raising their children, hosting play-dates and comparing notes on motherhood and child rearing. Calli remembered that these women's biggest concerns were how they would pay for private school and where they would go away over the summer—Nantucket or Bethany Beach, Jackson Hole or the Outer Banks.

She didn't want to be an FRG Leader. Captain Applebee's wife, Tracy, should have been the FRG Leader, but she'd fled home to her parents' in Kansas claiming that she couldn't deal with another deployment. She'd been so blithe about this deployment a few months ago, but where was she now?

If Calli became an FRG Leader, would it help Luke? Will his men be happier if the wives are happier? If they have more information? Calli wondered. Her mind wrestled about what to share with the wives. Every email? Perhaps she should just send a weekly update to their friends. She thought, This is just the type of situation that Luke and I would discuss in the evening when he came home from work. Inevitably, he'd give me his sage advice on how to handle the situation.

Pretty soon, the wives were calling her: "I'm scared, Calli. What do you know? Anything?" Fear was spreading like an octopus's tentacles. Many of the men had moved into Baghdad, and with the move, everyone's anxiety levels spiked. Up until then, there'd been a sense of denial even after the men left because they were in Kuwait: Kuwaiting Around. There they'd been safe from IEDs, terrorists, tenuous infrastructure.

Another wife called. And another. She wasn't sure why these women were beginning to turn to her. She suspected that it was because she was older than most. But that reason was not realistic. It had to be the email from Luke. One of the young wives asked Calli if it was going to be more violent where the men were going. More violent than where? Calli wondered. There's a war going on.

Did Calli know the APO address, did she know this, know that, a young woman wanted to know. Luke was better at writing Calli email than the others. She tried to tell the wife to keep busy, to have faith, but she knew it was hard on her, on all of them when they had only had one contact with their husbands thus far. Most were young. Undereducated. Underprepared.

She really didn't want the responsibility or the added stress of being FRG leader. Wouldn't it be nice to hide out for the year like Tracy Applebee? Calli didn't think she had the courage to share bad news with the wives if she needed to. She hadn't been brave since she was a girl when she rode her pony pretending to be an Indian. Together they'd soar over four-foot fences, jump into deep, cool streams, and gallop full speed across the pasture with dirt on her face. As a girl, she'd challenged River Brewer to a swimming race even though he was a year older than she, taller, stronger, and she'd won. She'd been brave at fourteen when she body-surfed the huge waves at the beach after a storm when the black flag was raised. Now, Calli felt like a coward. She thought, If I can help make it easier for the others, then perhaps it will make life easier for Luke. I'm good at being a cheerleader for other people. Now she'd have to spend hours a day fielding questions and dispelling rumors about the soldiers. She'd already been recruiting different groups to help send the men care packages filled with items from home. Josie sent her a list of items—procured from her sister, whose husband had already deployed once before—that were helpful when the soldiers were in the Middle East. She never thought she'd be soliciting help from their friends and family to send baby wipes, Q-tips, and beef jerky, but she was.

One night after Audrey had been bathed and read to, Calli called her sister Dinah.

"Is Charles home?" Calli whispered.

"No, he's out with some producer. What's up? Are you alright?"

"They want me to be an FRG leader."

"What's that?"

"It's the person who's the conduit between the wives and the front lines. It means I have to work with the Army. It means I have to go to meetings on Fort Drum and call people when something bad happens.

I can't stop thinking about how the wives and mothers in Iraq must feel. Is that strange? Their husbands risk their lives every time they leave the house. They must be afraid, too—really afraid—that their children will be left fatherless. It's not impossible to me that there is a woman in Iraq who feels exactly like I do."

Dinah responded, "Cal, you've got such a huge heart, and you might be the only person I know who is wondering about the Iraqi women. Maybe this is God's plan for you."

"I don't like this plan," she snorted.

"Seriously Calli, listen. You can be reluctant, but it's pretty clear to me. You're so strong. You don't know it, but you are. You're in survival mode. But so are the other wives. Galvanize them. Who knows? You might even find that you like some of them."

"Ha! Maybe some of them might like me."

And with that notion of sorority, she decided that becoming the FRG Leader was the right decision.

Dear Immortal Wives and Mothers,
I understand that not everyone has heard from their men.
I have received a few emails from Luke, mostly complain-
ing about the heat. I am hopeful that these notes that I am
forwarding are helpful to those of you who aren't receiving
as much communication as you'd like. I have not spoken
to Luke on the phone since I understand that the phone is
far away and there is a long line of soldiers trying to call
home.

Veronica McLeod and I are working on a plan to get us
all together on a regular basis. But please, if you need any-
thing in the meantime, anything at all, contact one of us.
It's easy to feel alone and scared—we need each other and
our supportive friends. Don't be shy. Call or write if you
need a sympathetic ear.
Enjoy the day.
Calli

My most beloved Calli,
The flight from Kuwait to Baghdad was pure misery. We
sat on the tarmac in full combat gear for about forty min-
utes with no air flowing in about 115-degree heat. And when
the plane finally took off, it took another twenty minutes
or so for the cooling system to kick in. I drank three liters
of water and was completely covered from head to toe in

sweat by the time I landed. It's been a while since I've been that miserable.

Saw my first Bedouin today—he had a herd of camels and was walking along in 116-degree heat. Crazy as loons these people are. I miss you terribly and am just so thankful that the Universe has brought us together. The future's bright, baby, hold on for the ride! I have to run for now, beautiful. I love you and look at your star every night. Have a great day and I will write more soon.
Love,
Luke

A few days later, Calli took Audrey apple picking at an orchard two hours away. They had hundreds of acres of trees and thirty varieties of apples. The perfect escape from Sackets Harbor, Fort Drum, and everything else.

Luke and she used to go on drives on days when they had nothing better to do. They'd get into the car and pick a destination that wasn't more than a day's trip away. Take all the back roads to get there. They'd seek out a pub where they'd have a beer and a burger. Then head home again via a different route, commenting on the landscape as they went. Could they ever live there? What would their house would look like? Where did the people work who lived in that community?

She remembered reading excerpts from *Remembrance of Things Past* by Marcel Proust, who wrote, "The voyage of discovery is not in seeking new landscapes but in having new eyes."

Thirty varieties of apples.

Setting out due south, then west, she and Audrey sang every word to every song from Annie—three times they sang "It's a Hard Knock Life." When they arrived at the orchard, the parking lot was packed. Droves of people seemed to be heading into the main building, where a large sign with peeling paint on petrified wood said HOT APPLE CIDER DONUTS. Toothsome fried food always drew people away from their task. The orchard lured them in with their wide variety of jams and jellies, winter squash, Palatine cheese, locally produced honey and maple syrup. Gourds, straw, corn stalks, and pumpkins.

Opting out of eating fresh, hot apple cider donuts and fifteen-year-old cheddar cheese, they trotted up the hill to fetch their basket. She was suddenly aware that a grown woman and a little girl weren't going to be eating bushels of apples. She didn't have anyone to give applesauce to. She had just driven two hours.

Audrey, ever the curious one, started in on her inquisition: How many apples are there on the trees? Why are some apples red and some are yellow? How do you make applesauce?

She was adorable in her pink down vest and rain boots, her wavy blond hair framing her head like a young lion's mane. Calli felt so in love with her—scared for her. She was doing her best to be a good mother but was terrified that she was failing. She didn't know how to answer all her questions all the time, stalling when Audrey would ask her when Luke was going to be home.

Calli found the smallest basket she could—a thick slatted wicker apparatus with a nylon handle. They hiked down into the enormous orchard surrounded by Criterion, Candy Crisps, Ida Reds, and Pink Ladies all in straight rows like soldiers practicing their marching drills. She helped Audrey pull one apple from one tree at a time as avid applesaucers passed them with wheelbarrows full of the red, round gems. She imagined the scene in the *Wizard of Oz* where the personified trees, angry that they've been picked for their low-hanging fruit, slap Dorothy. When they had picked about two dozen, they headed to the scales. There they encountered a grim-looking sexagenarian reading a paperback on a tattered lawn chair, his white beard down to his belly button, his coveralls muddy in the knees and crusted around the cuffs. His hooded Carhartt looked two sizes too big. He didn't look at them immediately, intent to read his pages—even though there was no else around.

Audrey said, "Can I get up there?" pointing to the large scale sitting on the counter of the ramshackle outbuilding with a National cash register straight out of *Paper Moon*.

"Of course, let me help you," the man said as he gently picked her up, placing her on the scales where the apples were supposed to go.

"My dad is in Iraq. He's teaching the Bad Guys how to be Good Guys."

Calli couldn't believe it. This was the first time she had spoken about Luke to anyone other than her that Calli knew of. The man paused. "You weigh thirty-eight pounds. And you are very tall. I'm sure you must miss your dad."

To Calli he said, "I was in Vietnam."

"Thank you for your service. You must enjoy working here in the orchard." Audrey, no longer interested, seemed content to sit in the scale while Calli fumbled for words, aware that the pause was evident enough. "Okay, Auds, let's get down so we can weigh our apples."

"Is that all the apples you picked?"

"Yes, well, we don't really need that much..."

"The apples are on me. Thank you and your husband for the good job he's doing. I hope he makes it home soon."

Touched, Calli reached out her arms and hugged him. Held him. "Thank you."

⫸⫸ **11** ⫷⫷

Dear Calli,

How are you, my darling daughter? Please feel free to keep me in the loop. I enjoy reading your emails and learning of Luke's goings-on. This is the closest I have ever come to knowing someone directly in the front lines, even during Vietnam. Besides Luke, my colleague Isabelle's son, Andy, is now in his fourth week of Marine Corp boot camp. My old law partner is a former Navy Seal Captain, another of my friends is a Submarine Commander and will be retiring next month. Father Bill's son just finished USMC boot camp several months ago and has just received his deployment orders to Iraq. War is serious business.

I have a collection of letters given to me by Mother's father spanning from 1942 until 1949. The letters cover his enlistment, boot camp, enrollment in officer training/cancellation thereof, training in upstate New York, and deployment to southern France. He joined Patton's 3rd Army and went through Bastogne (Battle of the Bulge), the Ardennes, Rhineland, and eventually Germany. He returned to the states in 1946 after almost two years in Europe, enrolled in college, and eventually landed a job in Buffalo, along with a wife and family.

Sometimes it is difficult for us to place ourselves within the vastness of history and figure out exactly where we fit in. Somehow we do, and your journaling and your letters to Luke are the best way to collect the present for the benefit of those to come. Oftentimes the most cherished items of our time here will be the memories and thoughts put down on paper. Nothing else can approximate the feelings conveyed. Encourage Luke to do the same. Make him write every day about his feelings and experiences, even if it's just on his personal log. Eventually, and perhaps not in our lifetime, they will become invaluable.

Mother and I love you so much and are very proud of you. We'd really love for you to consider moving back home. We'd really like to buy you a house here. Your mother needs you home. And how is that beautiful granddaughter of mine? Don't be a stranger. Mother would love it if you called more. So would I.

I love you, Calli.

Love,

Dad

Calli closed the letter. Mother and Dad are on their "move home" campaign again, Calli thought. Right after Luke deployed, they tried to persuade her to move back to Baltimore to be closer to them. Many wives did just that; they moved back home with their parents to help out during the deployment. Captain Applebee's wife did it—ran her ass straight home to Kansas.

But Calli needed to be exactly where she was—the women, the other wives, got it.

Lucy and Haines loved her. She knew this, and yet she didn't want to be away from here. This was her house—her house with Luke. Their house. This was where they'd last been together. She wanted to sleep in their bed. She needed to be around their things, the things that reminded her of their life together. Moving to Baltimore would mean abandoning those memories and feelings, even if only temporarily.

They'd taken a different tactic this time. Now it was "we need you home." They needed her home to help them get through the deployment. Calli thought, Mother is really delusional if she thinks my being home with help her. I can't take care of her. I can barely take care of myself.

Haines's offer to buy her a house echoed in her mind all day. Oh, how easy it all sounded. A firm believer in subtle, paternal coercion, Haines was practiced in making his daughters offers they couldn't refuse.

Daphne told Calli, "You need to learn how to prioritize and let go of things. The most important thing is to take care of Audrey. Everything else must wait or be omitted."

"Okay, I'm going to tell my parents that I've decided not to go anywhere at Thanksgiving," Calli said. "I'm too tired. And I don't want to travel over the holiday, only to come home and be on the road again three weeks later for Christmas. I know I will be letting everyone down, but I have to do this for me—for Audrey. I actually feel really good about this," Calli said. "I'm hopeful that when Luke gets home, I will have worked through a lot of this."

She wanted to call her father and tell him about Gus Pepys. About her fears about losing Luke. But she didn't want him to worry and insist that she move back to Baltimore. They didn't get it. Their rarified life in Baltimore never changed, war or no war. A letter to Lucy and Haines would be more efficient than a phone call. If she called, they'd never let her finish.

Dear Mother and Dad,
I have been giving much consideration to your offer. While
I still haven't come to a conclusion, I thought I would share
with you some of my thoughts: At this moment, I cannot

imagine not being here in Sackets. I completely understand your concerns and am overwhelmed by your love and offer to help with a move to Baltimore. I know that no one will consider me a failure if I leave—however, there is a tremendous responsibility that I have agreed to take on as the FRG Leader. At the risk of sounding like I am patting myself on the back, no one else can do the job as well as I am doing it. As you both are experiencing the anxiety and stress of the deployment, so are all the other wives and parents with whom I'm in contact on an almost daily basis. Many, many wives and parents of the Alpha Company soldiers have been so thankful that FINALLY the FRG is communicating with them about what is going on with their husbands and sons. Many of the wives are like zombies, barely making it through each day. My communication and accessibility is one of their only lifelines. Is this good for me? Probably not. Does it drain me? Yes. But, the bottom line is, helping the families back here makes me feel closer to Luke. If I can help them work through their anxieties, then they won't necessarily burden their husbands who need to focus on being soldiers and on their mission. Thus, they are in a better position to help Luke and protect him from the Bad Guys.

When I've talked on the phone with Eula or other Baltimore friends, I've felt so awkward. Not because I don't think people love me and want to be friends with me, but because I am the only one whose husband is deployed to the front lines of the war. It is a very lonely feeling, and no matter how much people try and sympathize, they cannot fully comprehend what I am going through. Mother, I am sure it must be the same feelings you had when Dylan died. People who love and care about you want to help and listen, but unless it's your family member, they cannot understand. If I moved back to Baltimore, I would only have our family to lean on. While this is a great comfort to me, I would miss being here where there are many, many people going through the same thing I am. I would especially miss Daphne and Josie.

I have written to Luke about this. His bottom line answer is, "I want you to be happy." We have always thought it would be wonderful to "retire" in Baltimore and start the next chapter of our lives there. We would love to be close to you, and I'm so honored that you want to help, and another part of me is too proud to take such an enormous offer to help financially, etc. I didn't want Luke to feel awkward about accepting such a generous offer, but he has assured me that he won't. Does any of this make sense? Going back to my original statement, I haven't made a definitive answer, but I wanted to assure you that I do think about it often. Thank you so much and I love you both very much. I am blessed to have family that loves me because I have met many people in the Army who don't have such blessings.
Love,
Calli

🠶🠶 12 ⧏⧏

Luke and the men had been in Baghdad for a few weeks and she still hadn't gotten a single phone call from Luke. He did write her every day. Sometimes it was just a brief I love you, but she wanted so much more. They'd agreed that he would write as much as possible, even if it was one sentence to let her know he was safe. She consoled herself, knowing that he was alive and well. At least she thought he was well.

She wondered how many Americans really felt the war like she did. It was hard for her not to think about WWII: the food rations, victory gardens, the increased taxes for all Americans to support the war effort, particularly the wealthy. Back then, there was a sense of unity, a common fight. She thought, We're not together in this war. "Support the Troops." People say those words, but don't act on them. She heard, "Of course I support the troops ..." An obsequious phrase with no concrete meaning to her. She hated it—it demeaned. War was heinous. It was not her responsibility to make the war easier for her family and friends; to give them a different, insightful perspective. Calli rarely spoke about the war. The divisive politics flooded the news, the papers, cocktail parties, casual conversation, schools, everywhere. Sometimes Calli couldn't tell who was against the war and who was for it.

Henry told her once, "War is a tough business that must operate under flexible conditions."

Calli said to him, "I think that all Americans have a stake in the war no matter how many people don't like it." Some wives, like Daphne, were better able to articulate their feelings about the war.

"The war, like the deployment, is black and white. It's good news or bad. We are right. They are wrong. There's no in between," she'd rant to Calli and Josie. Calli's apolitical stance seemed to frustrate Daphne.

>>> <<<

One day, her guitar—a 1968 Gibson Les Paul "Black Beauty," a present she'd bought herself years earlier—called her for the first time in months, like a ringing phone. Why had she neglected it for so long? Calli opened the Gibson's case. "How are you, old friend?" she said, as her fingers stroked the ebony fret board and Black Beauty's distinguished slim tapered neck. It felt great to hold the guitar again, both comfortable and exotic. Without thinking, she put her capo on the third fret and her fingers started the picking pattern: C G/B Am G/B—"Landslide" by Stevie Nicks. I've never felt the guitar reverberate through my arm and into my body like this, she thought.

Her passion swelled as she strummed. Calli began to sing the bittersweet words to the song, reflecting on her own marriage. Playing again thrilled her. The heavy wood made the tone rich and full. Made her feel alive. She thought of her father's words. Of Henry's words. Of all the angular words the wives had said to her. Now—now she was finally willing to give herself room to clean up the rough spots in her life. Creativity had always nurtured her. For an hour, she played with aching fingers, reminiscent of those nights in Nantucket when she lost herself in the palette of melody and harmony. Her creative side had brought her together with Luke. That was the Calli she had to return to, even if she stumbled to get there. That person Luke had fallen in love with. Calli felt an awakening.

She stopped playing Stevie Nicks and let her own embryonic chords materialize.

She called Daphne. "I'm playing! I'm playing my guitar! I'm going to write a song. I've never written a song. I know I can do it. Why didn't I write before? Yes, yes, this is what I'm supposed to do."

>>> <<<

She was at the zoo with Audrey when she got the call from Veronica McLeod.

"Hi, Calli. It's Veronica. How are you?"

"I'm fine," she responded, only half-listening. Audrey grabbed at her legs: "Mama, the bats are scaring me!" Children scampered through the dark hall. "May I call you back?" she asked. "I'm sort of tied up right now."

There was a pause on the other end of the line.

"There was an incident…"

4-31 Soldier wounded in action
Bravo Co
Injuries considered not serious
Soldier has been returned to duty
Name: PFC Turner
Bravo Company was on patrol when struck by a roadside bomb. PFC Turner had minor shrapnel to his elbow. No one else was injured. He was treated and released.

Calli found a bench outside the bat cave where she could write down the incident information. Her mobile phone with her wasn't something she usually remembered to throw into her purse when she left the house. No longer a luxury item, it would be an append-age. As she scribbled down details, acronyms, names, she thought, I am supposed to be a domestic goddess sitting on various volun-teer committees, being June Cleaver, raising money for some cause I believe in. I am supposed to be making delicious dinners for my handsome husband who's had a long day at the office and be there when he gets home to pamper him. I am supposed to be worrying about the disobedient puppy chewing on furniture, the cat that pees on the rug, and how I am going to shuttle Audrey from ballet to soccer practice. Didn't Alexander Pope write, "There is majesty in simplicity"?

Calli sat stunned on the zoo bench. Five years ago, their lives changed forever. Calli remembered 9/11 and made a long list in her head about much she had changed. Here she was at the zoo receiving a call about the soldier who'd been hurt. This wasn't Hollywood. This was real life. This wasn't some movie or book that she could stop or put down. It was happening—life after the blockbuster. Now. The bullets had started to fly. And close to Luke. If she was receiving a call, then Luke must have been nearby. Now she was expected to call the other wives and share with them this news. Read the incident report to them exactly as Veronica had read it to her. The FRG system was in place. She had to call the Key Callers, the other three women who then disseminated the information down the line. Trembling, she repeated the call three times. Her voice quivered a little more each time she read the incident report. She had to hide her feelings from Audrey. Audrey couldn't know. Couldn't see Calli unravel.

It had begun. The war was on her front step now.

⇶ **13** ⇷

INCIDENT

2 soldiers wounded in action

Charlie Co 4-31

Injuries considered not serious

Soldiers have been returned to duty

Names: SSG Wycoff; PFC Parra

Charlie Company was on patrol when struck by an RPG. Vehicle caught fire. SSG Wycoff sustained burns on his right arm. PFC Parra sustained burns on his right leg. No one else was injured. They were treated and released. Please do a call-out.

INCIDENT

Soldier wounded in action

Alpha Co 4-31

Injuries considered very serious

Soldier has been sent to Baghdad

Names: 1st LT Richard Strong

Bravo Company was on patrol with LT Strong when he was struck by an IED. He sustained serious injuries to his right arm and right leg. He will be sent to Walter Reed Army Medical Center once he is stabilized. Please do a call-out.

> *INCIDENT*
> *There was an incident in 4-31 fighting forward in Iraq*
> *Soldier Killed in Action*
> *Alpha Company*
> *All affected family members have been notified*
> *Name: SPECIALIST Taylor*
> *Soldier was killed in a small arms firefight. Alpha Company was on patrol when they came under attack. An incident briefing will be held today at 1:30 p.m. Please do a call-out.*

At the incident briefing about Specialist Taylor, the tension popped, and everyone in the room seemed to be thinking the same thing: Thank god it wasn't my husband. Even though they were six thousand miles away from Iraq, war was in their backyards, on their decks, in their kitchens, and sitting in their living rooms. Specialist Taylor had been on security duty for one of the Majors when a sniper shot him.

When there was an incident, the Army put a blackout on all communication from Iraq until every person in the unit had been notified back in the US. That meant no calls or email for sometimes up to a week with no warning. The silence was awful. No emails from Luke. Calli hadn't been able to sit down and focus on anything since the incidents began.

The Rear Detachment team urged the wives to get passports if they didn't already have them. They'd need a passport to fly to Landstuhl—the largest military hospital outside the US, in Germany. The Army would pay their airfare. If they were flown to Germany, it would be for one reason: to say good-bye to someone too injured to make it to Walter Reed or Brooke Army Medical Center. The Rear D reviewed the official notification process with them again. If their soldier is KIA, they would be told in person. Passports not needed.

Today it was an RPG. IED, RPG, IED, RPG, IED, RPG—it would make a nice little ditty. They'd only been away for five weeks, and already the casualties had begun. Before the incident briefing, she'd stood in their kitchen staring. She stared and stared, waiting for something to happen to shake her out of this stupor. Calli couldn't believe this was happening. She thought of other people who'd gone through wars, other war brides.

A week earlier Lucy Wendover had sent her *Letters and Verses*, by Clara Boardman Peck, her great-grandmother.

Calliope, please take care of this book, the inserted letter had read. *In 1951, your great-grandfather, Laurence F. Peck, took your great-grandmother's letters and poems and had them sent to Dodd, Mead, and Company in New York City to be made into a book for their children, Prudence Peck Waldroup and Girvan Waldroup. Prudence was my mother, as you know. It was never publicly published, but it was printed by Vail-Ballou Press and bound in a unique black leather book with gold inlay. It's a glimpse into history—what was going on in your great-grandmother's life. She was a wife and mother during two wars. It's evident she dedicated herself to her children and her family.*
Love,
Mother

Ironic that her mother had ended the letter in such a way. What did Lucy know of war? And Calli hardly considered her dedicated. But Calli was curious about this book. Perhaps it would give her some advice or insight into how to better deal with these casualties.

In the end of *Letters and Verses*, her great-grandfather wrote, *This is the last of CPB's letters to be found. Its few words are indicative of her joy and happiness in her family to the end.* She died, very suddenly, on April 23, 1950. What a love story. In the early part of her memoir, Clara was blithely living her life in 1914; traveling in Europe with her best friend before they debuted to New York City society. In the early part of 1914, the thought of a world conflagration seemed to most people incredible, and no reason to forego a trip abroad. The impact of the war on Clara, when she was caught with other Americans at the edge of the maelstrom, the exhilaration of glorious adventure rather than horror at the nightmare, was interesting to Calli to read. Their stories—journeys—ninety years apart. On July 17, 1914, from her room at the Grand Hotel Metropole in Bad Nauheim, Germany, Clara wrote to her mother:

> *I did look up and there was a Zeppelin airship directly over my head. It's hard to call back that first fine rapture, there've been so many since. Now, if I hear a rush and a buzzing and an increasingly near rushing sound, I rush to my room and hide my head under a pillow. The airships here are like the yodelers in Switzerland. But that morning, Ah! It was thrilling...*

A few weeks later on August 7, 1914, from the Hotel Royal in Rome, she wrote again to her mother:

> *Dear Mama,*
> *We are here with a ravening horde of other Americans yapping round the Embassy. Nobody dreams of deviating from one set form of salutation and the interest in the answer is never failing. The greeting is: "Say, how much money have you got?"*
> *But I will go back a few days. Day before yesterday Charlotte and I went up to Milan from Menaggio in another despairing attempt to get passage home on some Italian ship. We failed but in driving from the hotel suddenly ran bang into Mrs. Touzlain, our dear friend and hostess who was keeping watch over our trunks in Germany! Our encounter, I think, interested Milan! We decided that since money could not be obtained in Milan—the thing to do was to come on down to Rome. So I, feeling at last definitely busy, rushed down again to Menaggio for the bags and*

to settle the bill. The very kind—oh, more kind than you in America realize—manager there gave me all the money left to me on my letter of credit; please remember that manager as a family friend.

Tween you and me, toward three o'clock yesterday afternoon after two days of the crowd and the heat and the fleas and the cinders I—I sorta lost my taste for the war. But not really. No. There be thrilling times, and if they can't get money through and we are stuck here for some time, why, you remember that it's Rome, wonderful Rome, I'm in and having the time of my life.

Mrs. T's experiences are really worthwhile. She left Nauheim at an hour's notice. Six miles from the border the train was stopped, everyone ordered out and told they'd have to walk. This was the middle of the night. She shouldered her bag and did. In Switzerland on the frontier everything was in turmoil. All the men were in arms on the borders to protect their poor little country. 400,000 Swiss mobilized in those two days and all the fleeing Americans' tales are the same. On the passes, guides tramping down out of the snow to shoulder arms. In the towns, old men and women the only ones left. Well, she finally got over one of the passes more dead than alive with fatigue. When she apologized to me for losing my trunks with hers on the border, I frankly cried. She's so little to have all alone had to go through that.

Of course, I personally am dreadfully envious! Why the deuce couldn't I have been the one to march over the frontier, I ask you. Tisn't square. No, it isn't. Just bad luck that we left a few days early. Mrs. T's letter of credit has so far been locked up, and I of course have divided my remains with her.

Bless you,

CB

One evening back in the United States in the spring of 1915, when dining with friends, Clara's brother-in-law, Laurence Peck, mentioned the Hôpital d'Alliance, at Yvetôt, France, a joint American-British hospital recently established in Normandy, for which he had taken over the task of supplying trained and volunteer nurses and requisite equipment from the United States. Clara wanted to help the war effort by serving in such a capacity, and a few days later she went for an interview. Her passage from the US back to France was later arranged in company with a small group of volunteers who were to leave in early May.

> *Yvetôt. May 25, 1915*
> *Dear Mr. Peck,*
> *This is the most attractive hospital I have ever seen, with the nicest lot of doctors and nurses in the world. They are awfully kind to us, too, which makes it complete.*
>
> *At the moment, the nurses are crowing in while the convalescent patients are being hurried out, so we have plenty of extra time to trail about and see things . . . so far it has mostly been play. You see, the hospital is full of men recovering, and I have not yet had any really hard work or seen any horrible things. To me, the most heartbreaking thing one sees are the cheering English Tommies on their way to the front. They frankly make me cry.*
>
> *The soldiers all tell us in vivid detail just how and where they got their wounds, and the ones that did have a piece of shell removed keep it wrapped in a handkerchief. They are awfully grateful for everything one does, and it gives one a warm, pleasant feeling to have them all wave when you come in the room. It has all worked out even better than we had hoped, you see, and I am awfully grateful to you for letting me have the chance.*
> *I hope you are having a good time, too.*
> *Most sincerely,*
> *Clara Boardman*

Calli discovered another letter, to a Ms. Weir, Clara's closest friend back in New York City.

Hôpital d'Alliance, Yvetôt, France
June 1, 1915
My darling Caro,
That's my address for you but I, at the moment, am having my two hours off and sitting in the completely adorable French garden in the back of the Nurse's Home. It's utterly right in every way, with plenty of open grass and simple banks of shrubbery and flowers, and my open windows are right above it. You would love everything about it, and Yvetôt itself is quite wholly French. Really and truly, the instant you see the little winding cobbled streets and small rickety houses with old women in white caps sitting knitting at the doors, you at once say, "Ay, this'll be France."

And my dear, it is. They all speak it, too, old and young. Also they all speak to me, being infirmière de l'hôpital, and every soldier and officer touches his cap to the uniform. The first few times I happily saluted back; then one of the Englishmen here, with a sudden trouble with his breathing, said that it was awfully jolly of me but well, really, it was not—er—done. It must have given quite a good many people pleasure.

I may say I'm practically never out, as we go on duty at 7:30 A.M. and get off at 8 P.M. with 2 hours off in there somewhere. Then we ramble round the country, still in uniform as it's so much safer. Every man respects it and often stops to chat and ask about the pauvres malades. In fact, every Frenchman one sees is nice. Very grave now, but infinitely kind and anxious to help the sick soldiers in every possible way.

The soldiers themselves are magnificent. During the most painful dressing of their wounds you never hear one groan, and almost always they keep a little smile on throughout.

One doesn't do it dry-eyed but oh, oh I'm glad I came. They are so grateful for a little amusement. The littlest thing pleases them, and when I come in with cards or cigarettes, they are so happy. It's an inspiring crowd to be with. I'm not going to write you details of the soldiers I'm taking care of now. It's not pretty. In fact, it's about as near hell for them as any little skit Dante ever wrote, only they don't writhe about under it. They smile. And after I've fixed them each time, I run in the other room and cry.

It's the most illuminating thing as to humans I have ever done, certainly, and the fact of being a little nearer this thing, and helping even my tiny bit the wrecks that crawl out of it, is a warm and constant glow within.

Paris was dreadful—nine tenths of the women in crêpe, darkened streets at night, and a dreadful air of gloom all over. The cheeriness and nerve of the English is harder to bear. To see a trainload of English Tommies on their way to the front, each one of them by now of course knowing just the hell he was in for, but each man cheering and singing and waving as he went by, is too heartbreaking to bear calmly. The French are complete corkers but, well, their troops don't sing.

An Englishwoman nurse in our hospital was expecting her husband from the front on leave last week. A telegram came and she opened it when on duty. It simply said, "Husband killed in action." She fell down in a dead faint, but when she came to she jumped up, smiled, and went on with her work. Then she went home to his mother in England for a week, but returned yesterday, and today is in the ward with smiling face, blue checked uniform and long green jade earrings.

Don't you think these things are pretty well worth seeing. Best love to you. Do write. Warmly,

C

Calli's great-grandmother's words inspired her. Calli searched her journal, finding poems she'd penned, phrases from articles that resonated with her. She had no idea where her old music journals were; perhaps lost in her many moves. With Black Beauty on her lap, she strolled through some chords she thought might fit her poetry. It'd been over a decade since she'd even thought about composing. She kept playing, just to see what would happen.

She quietly spent some time listening to Neko Case, Amy Allison, and Antigone Rising. She listened for something that haunted her, something that caught her interest, something that spoke to her. She knew if she could capture those things, channel that feeling, she might be able to write and sing something, put her fingerprint down permanently. For years, she'd born witness to everyone else. Now she wanted to make a contribution to the world—as a woman, for other women. Her opus needed to be for them.

14

Nothing in Calli's life was expected, even though her daily routine was the same. Every day she woke up. She listened for the phone to ring. The bad news. The wives kept calling and emailing her. They wanted information as much as she did. News. Insight. Guidance. They must have thought she knew more than she did. Every time the phone rang, she jumped. Calli imagined getting an awful call, or worse, going out someplace only to come home and see the Trifecta—the chaplain, the casualty assistance officer, and the rear detachment officer—sitting in her driveway. Information was a double-edged sword; she still had so many questions. Why was Specialist Taylor shot? How was he shot? What were they doing that caused him to be shot? Was Luke there? This poor soldier had a wife and two small sons. He was only twenty-two years old.

Just prior to the deployment, Calli made a meal for the Taylors, after his wife had had their second child. She wasn't sure what to expect since she had never met Penny Taylor. In an effort to be *a good Army wife*, Calli pulled together a decent beef stew, salad, and loaf of Italian bread to take. The Taylors' on-post housing, a Spartan, unremarkable beige apartment on the second floor, boasted an enormous television, beige wall-to-wall carpeting, a mattress with exposed ticking—the sheets bunched up in the corner—on the floor, and an overstuffed cream sofa in the living room. Dr. Phil was proselytizing on the TV. The older son, wearing only a diaper, tottered around the room with a blue permanent ink pen. The walls, unadorned, glowed from the bouncing TV shadow. Penny Taylor said, "Hey, this is my mother-in-law Sylvia and my sister-in-law Jasmine."

The women grunted greetings at Calli, silently watching *Dr. Phil*. Expecting to be there only a few minutes, she never took off her coat. "You wanna hold Khalil?" Penny ambitiously handed the baby bundle to Calli before she could answer.

Still in her coat, now sitting on the cream sofa cradling the baby uneasily, watching *Dr. Phil* with them, she had nothing to say. No thoughts came forward in her brain. No words for these women who seemed to be in a trance. "You can stay awhile, right? Hold the baby." Sylvia, her mother-in-law, asked Calli, "Do you know if we can use WIC to buy baby formula?"

And before Calli answered, Penny Taylor impatiently said to her mother-in-law but looking at Calli, "Oh, we won't need that."

Now, only months later, Penny's husband was dead. She'd returned home from the post office to the Trifecta. When they arrived at a soldier's house, the primary dependent was immediately awarded a death benefit of one hundred thousand dollars. They asked what else was needed from the Army. They wanted to accommodate the family during this time. Some wives asked for a memorial service on post, some asked for support from their FRG. Penny Taylor asked that all the meat in her freezer be shipped with her back to South Carolina. She wanted the Army to pack her up, move her small children and her. And the meat in her freezer.

Calli never asked Penny what the significance of the meat was. She was beginning to understand the financial burden these families faced. Lower-ranking enlisted soldiers made less than minimum wage, but their housing and insurance were covered, making the service a good option. Perhaps the Taylors had shopped for the meat before the deployment. He had wanted to make sure she had enough food when he was in Iraq. Would Penny Taylor look back on these days and even remember that she asked the Army to ship her hamburger and pork chops to South Carolina? She could have asked for the moon and the Army would have considered it. Calli thought, Maybe I'd ask for my steaks to be packed in dry ice, too. Grief is fierce.

At Specialist Taylor's memorial, "Amazing Grace" was plunked out on the Army's chapel organ. Women held hands. Crying, they sang. Many sat shoulder to shoulder. The lights were dim in the chapel. Specialist Taylor's body didn't return to Fort Drum. He had been returned to South Carolina. A team of Rear Detachment soldiers escorted the remains wherever they needed to go. The wives of the battalion and other Rear Detachment soldiers attended the service. His bio was printed on the program—the stock military photo in his uniform looking gallant—not smiling. His freckled face sunburned from training outside. Calli didn't know him.

Sitting on the wooden pew in the chapel, she felt like a maple with her sap drained out of her.

There would be many more calls to make in the coming months. Calls to the wives, the Immortals' wives. Many of them, new to deployment like she was, would think she was calling them to tell them that it was their husband so she'd have to quickly say to them, "It's not your husband!"

After the memorial service, Calli had to deal with another incident. Lieutenant Richard Strong had been airlifted to Walter Reed the previous night. They had had to cut off his right arm and right leg after he stepped on a roadside bomb.

His girlfriend was there to greet him when he landed. More than just the families were impacted by the incidents.

In Iraq, the American soldiers had memorial services for the KIAs. They were given a little time to grieve, but they were also so focused on their mission that they usually quickly got back to their tasks. The soldiers patrolled with their guns, sweating in the 125-degree heat, donning a full uniform, flack jacket, and helmet.

Two retired Army veterans had spoken to Calli about how difficult it was for those back on the home front, and that, more often than not, the toughest fight in the war was for those back home, who had a million questions and heard only partial truths. Calli didn't get much information, and what she did receive made her feel like a cryptologist at the NSA.

Josie stopped by Calli's later that day. Dark circles under her eyes gave away Josie's fragility. "Calli, I can't bear this." Her doe-like eyes held Calli in a vise grip. "Early this morning, I heard car doors closin' outside my house. I thought it was the Trifecta." And here she paused, her right hand clenching her left wrist to steady herself. "I got up and got dressed. I stood, waiting in the living room...ready to receive them at the door. I waited for them to knock. I waited for the knock."

False alarm.

>>>> <<<<

Calli did the best that she could to protect Audrey. Shielding her took a lot of Calli's energy. Audrey was her constant. Audrey would never know until she was an adult how Calli struggled to keep herself together. Audrey, her cherubic girl with big, blond curls. Calli would prepare her lunchbox every morning with ritualistic care, as if sending her off to school with a cheese sandwich and an oatmeal cookie could work as a talisman against all of the pain from the war. Calli was thankful that she had a gorgeous, intelligent, loving daughter who needed her to be strong for her and protect her. She made Calli laugh and smile and was a reminder of the innocence and beauty that can exist in this world. She was doing much better than Calli was. Routine was a good thing for her.

Calli had been cooking with Audrey, teaching her safety around the stove and oven. Daphne bought her a child-sized apron that said *Diva in Training*. Sometimes Audrey would walk downstairs naked with only the apron hanging around her neck, untied. Audrey was not partial to clothes. She had very specific ideas about herself— being naked was far better than being clothed. For a month now, she'd called herself Wonder Woman.

With her apron on—and nothing else—she said, "I am ready to cook, Mama." Laughter rose from a deep point in Calli's belly and hurried out of her mouth before she could suppress it. She sighed to settle down and held herself with a smile, breathing in Audrey's innocence like a bouquet of freshly cut gardenias and jasmine. Calli pulled her footstool to the stove and let her stir rice or pasta as it cooked. "My Wonder Woman," Calli said.

After the cooking lesson, Calli observed Audrey lying on the floor with Satchmo, watching a cartoon on television. He was her pillow as her head rested on his black belly. He, too, a companion. Always at Calli's side, in a haze of nostalgia, Satchmo reminded her of Luke's commitment to and love for her. He slept on the floor next to Calli's side of the bed. Reclined at her feet when she sat on the sofa. Minded her when she pushed Audrey on the swing. He lay on the kitchen floor while she cooked, watching her. Even when she took a shower, ultimately the door to the bathroom would bang open as he sauntered in to lie down on the bath mat. Unfailingly protecting her.

>>> ‹‹‹

Emails to Luke had to be upbeat and supportive so he wouldn't worry about her.

> *Hi, My Love! How are you today? What are you doing? We are doing fine here. I'm teaching Auds to cook. She wears her apron every day—and not much else. I could do a cooking show called "the nude girl and her mama teach you to cook." I'm sure it'd be a hit. Pasta seems to be top of the list. Maybe someday she'll go to Cordon Bleu. Lucy and Haines send their love. Dinah and Charles, too. They're all FINE. Did you get the care package I sent yet? It's getting*

colder. I hope it gets colder for you soon. 120 degrees seems deplorable.
I miss you and love you.
Love,
C

In her messages to her husband, Calli never confided the morass canting her to one side, opting instead for banal weather reports and words of love. Her tears welled up just below the surface, waiting to overflow like the levees in New Orleans. She was thankful every time she got an email or letter from Luke and another day was over for him in Iraq. It was all she could do not to go insane. She prayed that when the phone rang it wasn't another incident call. She prayed that there was no knock on her door. Many mornings, she'd wake up with a sick feeling in her stomach. It was not nausea, but rather the feeling she got before an audition or when she'd watch a movie and one of the protagonists died suddenly or was maimed out of the blue. But in real life, the protagonist was Luke. When these moments punctured her peace, her first inclination was to go into their guest room and look out the window where she had the best view of their driveway. Her fleeting relief that the brown sedan with the Trifecta wasn't sitting there, waiting for her to wake up so they could knock on her door, pacified her for an hour or two. But she couldn't seem to shake the feeling that something awful might have happened.

Whenever Calli would take Audrey to preschool, on the forty-minute ride there and back, she'd pray that the brown sedan wasn't waiting for her when she arrived home. As she turned right onto Mill Creek Lane, in the final ten seconds of her drive, she'd imagine what would happen if the brown sedan was parked in her driveway. She'd actually never seen the brown sedan, but she'd know it. She'd know it anywhere.

15

Calli was elated after the call.

She took a chance. Called Richard Strong at Walter Reed. She wanted to face her fear head on. Perhaps Richard could teach her how to be braver. She wasn't sure what to expect. Words couldn't begin to describe how impressed she was with his attitude and how much his sense of duty to the Army came through.

He was candid, and in very good spirits. "Do you have a phone number for Luke so I can call him?" he asked. "I'd really like to talk to him." Richard's painkillers blotted out his Army acumen. Of course there was no number to call Luke.

"No, I'm sorry I don't. But I can email him for you if you want me to."

Richard chattered on about Luke, how inspiring he was, what a good leader he was, how all the units wished they had someone like him. The more Richard spoke, the more Calli was drawn into his words. Luke's phrases echoed in Richard's comments to her. He asked, "Did I act honorably when I was wounded? I hope so. That's what Luke always instilled in us."

"According to Luke, the first words out of your mouth were, 'I hope I'm the only one who was injured. Is everyone else okay?'"

"Has anyone else in Alpha Company been WIA or KIA since me?"

"Do you know about Specialist Taylor?" Here there was a bit of a pause before Richard responded.

Sheepishly he asked, "Do you think I'm going to ruin my relationship with Luke if I go into detail about my injuries?" Calli wondered if the drugs made him ask such a strange question. Richard had just had his right arm and leg amputated and was more concerned about ruining his relationship with Luke.

"No, Rich, I think you're okay. You don't have to tell me if you don't want to, but I'm happy to listen to anything you have to say. Luke is really proud of you. You acted very courageously."

They discussed Luke's definition of character. Richard said, "It doesn't matter what you did yesterday or the medals you've won before, or the mistakes that you made in your past; your character is based on what you are and do today." Calli started to cry. That was pure Luke. Luke had made him believe that.

Richard's positive attitude and his acceptance of what had happened to him took her by surprise. It seemed as if he had known all along that this was his destiny. He looked at the soldiers around him at Walter Reed Army Medical Center and knew that comparatively, he was lucky. He knew that the people at Walter Reed were going to take care of him. He told Calli he wanted to be an advocate for his platoon to ensure they got the items that they needed. He'd asked his girlfriend to marry him. She'd said yes.

"Oh Richard, that's wonderful news."

"Danielle, as luck would have it, is an occupational therapist in the Army, stationed at Fort Benning. She's trying to get a compassionate transfer to Walter Reed or Bethesda. I plan on running again within a year."

"Running? That's incredible."

"Yes, the nurse told me that it's not impossible. She's seen it before."

"I have no doubt that you will be running. In no time. I can't wait to talk to Luke and tell him the great news."

"Yes, oh yes, please tell him. Please tell him I'm sorry."

"Richard, you focus on healing and getting better. Luke will email you ASAP, I promise."

When she had to put Audrey down for a nap, she told Richard she'd call again tomorrow. "And listen, I want to come down for a visit in a few weeks."

As soon as she said it, she knew she had to go.

She'd told him she would come.

Dear Immortal Wives and Mothers,

I never thought I would freeze when the phone rings.

The last three weeks have been the most excruciating and unpredictable for all of us. It is hard to fathom that in such a short time we've had so many incidents. What will the next ten months bring? How will we maintain our composure, be strong for our children, and not allow the war to pulverize the fragile normalcy we are all aching for? For those of us back here at Fort Drum, we are blessed to have one another to lean on. For those of you living elsewhere, you are blessed to have your family or friends to lean on. And, if you have a strong faith, you have the Universe, God, Buddha, or whomever you lean on. We must all remain strong for our men and feel proud of their service. We don't have traditional marriages, we're all on an adventure, and it's often difficult to describe to our civilian friends and family. We must try and remember what matters most: our love for our husbands and our families, our admiration for their brothers in arms, and the importance of the part they are playing in defending our great nation.

First Lieutenant Richard Strong is recovering at Walter Reed Army Medical Center. As a double amputee, he has a long row to hoe and will be in intense physical therapy. After speaking with him last night, I feel confident that Richard and his family will be well taken care of. Once I have Richard's address at Walter Reed, I will send it out in the event that you would like to send him flowers or cards. Josie Merchant, Daphne Hollis, and I are headed to Walter Reed Army Medical Center at the end of the month to visit Richard as well. If you would like me to personally carry anything to him, just let me know.

I pray that we are not in this situation again this year. As Luke wrote to me, there is never anything good to say in a time like this. These men are loved and part of something so much bigger than any of us can ever imagine. When we shut our eyes, we should remember them as heroes and thank the Universe for the time we've spent with them.

As I have written so many times before: If you are having a tough moment, or if you're feeling alone, confused, angry, or sad, please call someone you trust. To ask for help or support is not a sign of weakness, it is a sign of maturity and wisdom that we cannot go at this alone.
Fondly,
Calli

Patrol Base Yusufiyah
Dear friends and families of the Alpha Company Immortals,
The bulk of the company is now with the commander and me at Yusufiyah. It is a small compound that used to be a potato factory. The last unit here left us with some "projects" to complete, namely building new housing! We are settled in and making do with what we have. Some are in tents and others live in what was probably the big potato storage bin! All the electricity is 220 so we have roasted our fair share of electrical appliances! It's not funny, but then again, in the grand scheme of things, watching my laser jet printer sizzle was kind of amusing. Sorry about that, taxpayers! We all live in pretty close proximity to the Iraqi soldiers. It is not out of the ordinary to see our Immortals

kicking a soccer ball around with the "jundis," the Iraqi Privates. I guess that they are as curious about us as we are about them. I know this must sound like some human aquarium where we only look at each other through a tank. We actually interact with the Iraqis throughout the day. It is impossible to imagine what Iraq was like under Saddam. Life in this theater is all relative, though.

While we are getting accustomed to our living conditions in Yusufiyah, an occasional trip to Baghdad reminds us of many of those creature comforts from home that we all miss! Long showers and porcelain toilets, for example. As usual, the ingenuity of the American soldier is amazing and such fun to watch. It is amazing how quickly we can find that one soldier in the whole crew who just happens to know how to repair air conditioners or rewire lights. If we could only find someone to fix the phones here, we would be in great shape. I promise you all I am trying each day to find a phone that works. Please be patient and understand that some soldiers travel between other FOBs that have phones, and, obviously, your husband's best friend in the same unit might very easily have access to the phone when your son or husband does not. One of these days it will get fixed. Till then, we have to rely on the Internet and letters.

That brings me to another point—the mail! Thank you all for taking care of us with cards, letters, and care packages. There is probably no greater event in our days than when the mail truck arrives. Seriously, I love it when I have to get a 10-15-man detail to bring all the boxes back to the boys. I feel like Santa! I know it can be tough trying to send letters and packages each week, we know you all have your daily routines. But even just a postcard will make your soldier's day. I am working to compile some pictures on a disc, which we will send home. We just have to connect the dots on the technology side of things, and we'll be good to go.

We're eating well and starting to get into a routine where we can lift weights and try and stay fit. The cooks are taking great care of us. Most of all, we are taking care of each other. I tell you that your husbands and sons are taking care of the commander and me. These brave men, YOUR brave men.

I will try and get a note out more often; please know it is not for lack of desire. We miss you all and cannot wait to finish this job. I know you all support us, and that's what counts the most. We actually begin our midtour leave next week, so you will start seeing our smiling faces back home.

In closing, dear friends, please know that we are all well and in good health. It is my pleasure and most of all my honor to serve your husbands and sons and especially you. Be safe, be strong, and be courageous. My very best to each and every one of you.
Luke Coleman
Master Sergeant
The Immortals

INCIDENT
There was an incident in 4-31 fighting forward in Iraq
Soldier killed in action
Alpha Co
All affected family members have been notified
Name: PFC Wood
Soldier was killed in a small arms firefight. Alpha Company was on patrol when they came under attack. An incident briefing will be held today at 1:30 p.m. Please do a call-out.

After a hot shower, Calli walked out of the bathroom, grabbed the phone off the bureau, and lay down on the floor near the foot of the chaise longue in the bedroom. Sharp light from the bathroom cascaded out of the door across the dim room. Dripping water spread beneath her back and legs, soaking into the carpet. Staring at the ceiling, she felt set adrift from the phone call, couldn't remember what she thought immediately after she answered it in those moments just before the shower.

She needed to hear Luke's voice.

A thick fog dropped in and she couldn't see through it. She wondered how she would get through the rest of these months? Soon she'd have to be in a straitjacket if incidents continued at this rate. Earlier that day Josie had lamented, "There are more and more Americans in the hospitals in Baghdad. The bad guys are getting braver. They just drive up to convoys on the highways and blow themselves up or throw IEDs."

Calli's stomach churned, roiling noxious waves. Every time Luke left his FOB, an image imprinted in her head of swarthy-looking men driving little ramshackle Toyota pickup trucks from the 1970s, racing up to the side of Luke's vehicle, trying to get close enough to annihilate him. She imagined the scenes from *Rio Hato*.

Josie, Daphne, and Calli went to the incident briefings together. They'd sit, stunned, and listen to the Rear D explain to them how another soldier had been blown up. The bad guys *were* getting bolder. The mere thought of things getting better in Iraq had vaporized. She never could have imagined that it would be this horrendous.

Solace came in fits and starts. Every morning after she'd dropped off Audrey at school, Calli plucked away on her guitar, jumpstarting her muscle memory as her fingers at first were stiff and tender. After practicing, she'd stare out into nothingness, sitting with herself quietly, not sure where her mind wandered, waiting patiently for the notes and chords to take shape—a song? You can do this, she'd say to herself. Her new mantra: You can do this. Just believe and open your heart, she'd think, anchoring her mind firmly in the faith that she wouldn't judge herself.

➤➤ 16 ⫷⫷

Plans were confirmed to go to Walter Reed to see Richard and the other wounded soldiers. She thought, this preposterous rabbit hole I've slid into must have an end. I'm going to go be with the soldiers who have fought. I need to be with them—even if I don't know them.

The soldiers at Walter Reed were soldiers like Luke. Men and women who felt the Mesopotamian sand on their skin, breathed the same air as the Bedouins, walked on the roads riddled with IEDs. All things that Luke had done. She needed to be with these soldiers. She didn't care what their wounds were or looked like. They were her connection, redemption. Emancipation.

Calli had invited Josie and Daphne to join her. Madelon, Luke's mother, agreed to drive up and take care of Audrey. Calli's parents had agreed to let them stay with them in Baltimore. It would be interesting to introduce Lucy and Haines to Josie and Daphne. Josie, who still looked like she was eighteen, and Daphne, who was on her third marriage... Calli didn't care anymore. So what if they hadn't gone to the right schools. At least they'd gone to school. And college.

But on her way to Baltimore, Calli planned to meet up with Eula in Manhattan. She and the Divas would meet at her parents' house.

"Calli, have fun in New York. I mean it," Daphne told her.

"Yeah, Calli," Josie chimed in. "You go check out all those New Yorkers and see what they're wearin' and tell me so I don't look too much like I just fell off a turnip truck."

"I wish you could come with me," Calli said.

"No, you need to spend some time with Eula. She'll make you laugh again."

"You make me laugh."

"Yeah, yeah. Whatever. I don't like the Big Apple anyway," Daphne lamented.

Two weeks earlier, Eula had left a pleading message for Calli to drive down to Manhattan to spend some time with Henry and her. "Henry's got us tickets to *The Fantasticks*. We can shop and spend some time together. Please, Calli. Call me back and let me make arrangements. I miss you."

When Calli called Eula back, she suggested, "There's a photographer, Suzanne Opton, who's been doing amazing work. I'd really like to see her exhibit, *Soldier.* " Calli was more interested in analyzing the haunting faces in the photos than seeing a musical.

⟫⟫ ⟪⟪

As she approached Manhattan, traffic increased apace with the number of luxury vehicles. As she saw skyscrapers in the distance, Calli couldn't help but feel like she was entering another country, one that wasn't at war. In northern New York, the symbols of the American way were yellow ribbons on trees, Old Glorys outside homes and businesses, blue star banners and magnets on cars, thank-you posters aimed at the soldiers in the windows of restaurants, and small but visible signs in stores that read 10% MILITARY DISCOUNT.

Somehow New York retained its charm and ambiance for her, even though it was so outrageously over-the-top. In another lifetime, she fantasized, when we have gobs and gobs of disposable income, we'll have a pied-à-terre where we can go for a long weekend to take in a show, shop, and gawk at all the other millionaires.

Visiting New York City was like watching Audrey put on her dress-up princess outfits, all her faux jewelry and her pink plastic Barbie shoes. It was make-believe. Handing out twenty-dollar bills like pencils, one to the taxi driver, one for a modest lunch, a tip for the concierge, another tip for the man who parked her car in the garage. It was endless.

Visiting New York as an adult felt much different than living there as a twenty-something college student. A New Yorker would be appalled that most days she walked around in her exercise clothes with a baseball cap on or her pajamas because she didn't take the time to take a shower until she went to bed at night. Her hair was limp and greasy; her teeth had a film covering them. For this trip, though, she'd actually gotten up early to wash and blow-dry her hair, put on an outfit that was fashionable but comfortable to drive in for five hours. She even put on mascara and blush.

As she drove down the Henry Hudson Parkway, drivers around her talked into the air. Since the law passed that drivers had to use an earpiece when driving and talking on their mobile phone—the scene of people who seemed to be talking to themselves as they drove far too fast, in narrow lanes, filled with taxis, limos, and passenger cars, was comical. Conveniently, her earpiece was in Luke's car, which was parked in their garage at home, but she really didn't give it another thought as she dialed Dinah for a long-overdue return call. She figured in a city of over eleven million, her chances of being picked out of the traffic were nil.

"Hey lady, how are you?" Dinah greeted Calli breezily, as if she had no cares in the world.

"Hey, Didi. How's Hollywood?"

"It's fine. Where are you? On the road?"

"I'm on the Henry Hudson heading into the city. I could *not* do this everyday. Do you think everyone here is on Xanax?"

"Feeling a little anxious yourself? Maybe you need a Xanax."

"I'm already taking Clonazepam! Ha!"

She suddenly noticed one of New York City's finest right behind her. "Oh shit," she said to Dinah. "I think I am going to get pulled over in this horrific traffic jam because I don't have an earpiece." Calli quickly hung up. Where had that cop been hiding? She dragged the phone away from her ear, down the curve of her chin, across her chest and lap, into the center console of the car. She shook her hair. Started to fiddle with it as if she was combing it with her fingers. Maybe the cop would think she was primping for a date or just killing time in traffic by twirling her hair. Perhaps his eyesight wasn't that good.

Then, suddenly, "Pull over to the side!"

Where the Hell was the side of the Henry Hudson Parkway? The river?

"Please! Pull over to the side!" the cop's PA blared.

Frantically realizing that her feeble attempts to assimilate into traffic were foiled, Calli inched off to the right as best as she could maneuver the car. In front of her were about a dozen bright orange pylons lined up, closing off the exit to 95th Street.

"Pull forward!"

She couldn't pull forward. The orange pylons were in the way. Where the Hell was she supposed to go?

"PLEASE. PULL FORWARD."

People honked their horns, rambling by her, as she started to sweat even though it was only forty-five degrees out. If she pulled any more forward, she was going to drive over the pylon, and all she could think was that then he would ticket her not only for driving and talking on her mobile phone, but also for destruction of city property.

"PULL FORWARD, NOW!"

Complying, she moved her car forward. Mowed over the orange pylon. Down it went, dragging underneath her. On went her hazard lights, as she placed her hands on the top of the steering wheel and panicked while she waited for him to approach her. Perhaps he would be gentle since she had a yellow ribbon magnet and a blue star banner magnet on the back of her car. Maybe he had been in the service and decided to join the NYPD after a tour in Iraq. Maybe if she pleaded with him that she was the wife of a deployed soldier, he would let her drive on.

"Ma'am, may I have your driver's license and registration?"

Her hands shook with a tremor. She couldn't find the registration. Shaking as if she had seen a poltergeist, she took five minutes to finally locate it smashed down behind receipts from auto repair bills. Meanwhile, the stern cop badgered her: "Is the car registered, ma'am? Are you sure it is registered? Is the car registered?" Fortunately, somewhere inside her brain she remembered the phrase "a closed mouth grows no feet," so she didn't blurt out and yell at him, "Of course the fucking car is registered, you asshole! Back off and let me find it without your beady little eyes scrutinizing my every move in this damn car!"

Instead she said, "Yes, sir, I am sure the car is registered because otherwise I wouldn't be able to get onto Fort Drum. You see, my husband is deployed and I am just visiting the city to get away for a while."

She hiccuped and burst into tears.

"Officer, my husband is Iraq. I was distracted by all the traffic. I'm a really good driver. Really, I haven't gotten a ticket since I was twenty. The war is really bothering me, and I was thinking about the news and how horrible it is. I'm so worried about my husband. Please, you must know that I, I...I was talking to my sister. She was making me laugh and I was feeling a little better." Pathetic. She had broken the law. Still, she wished Luke was there with her. Of course, he would have known exactly where the registration was, he would have been calm and courteous, he would have smiled and not been such a hideous cliché. Being pulled over was yet another reminder that Luke was so far away and she would have to handle this situation alone. She wasn't a New Yorker anymore, she wasn't just casually driving to an appointment, she wasn't a spoiled housewife who shopped all day, letting her nanny raise her children; she lived thirty miles south of Canada in a village of twelve hundred people, twenty miles away from Fort Drum, home of the 10th Mountain Division. After what seemed like an hour, the officer returned from his vehicle and stared down at her. "Ma'am. I've never done this but I'm giving you a warning," the cop said.

"Really?"

"It is very, very dangerous to talk on the phone and drive here. Please. Do. Not. Talk. On. Your. Phone." He walked away and drove stridently back into the sea of New Yorkers, leaving her there to find her own way out into the fast-flowing stream of black Lincoln Town Cars, BMWs, dilapidated Hondas, motorcycles, and yellow taxi cabs. She inched her car back into traffic, that damn bright orange pylon dragging and scraping the asphalt. The last thing she needed was to damage her car.

Several hundred feet down the parkway was the next exit. Aiming the car once again onto the "side" of the road, she pulled over and stopped. As she did, the parkway opened back up to three lanes and cars started to speed by. She jumped out of the car, praying that some angry New Yorker didn't lop off the car door. In her pseudo-chic jeans and fitted black cashmere sweater, she crouched down to the ground. Sure enough, the bright orange pylon was lodged exactly in the center of the car's undercarriage. It would have been funny had it not been so hazardous. There she was, lying on the ground, halfway underneath her car, pulling the pylon out. She pulled and pulled, and meanwhile, right next to her she saw tires flying by—a kaleidoscope of colors, engines droning, horns honking—and smelled burning rubber from the damaged pylon. It's not Luke who is going to get killed, she thought. It's going to be me—run over right here on the Henry Hudson Parkway.

Eventually Calli made her way to the Mark Hotel on the Upper East Side where Eula and Henry always stayed.

"Do *not* park on the street. I'll cover your parking so let the valet take your car," Henry said insistently. The black-and-white-striped marble floor in the entranceway of the Mark reminded Calli of a piano, and the art deco décor wasn't quite her style. All the staff had

Eastern European accents and smiled at Calli as if they'd never had a bad day in their lives. Eula and Henry loved the Mark because it was close to Central Park, where they could jog around the reservoir and stalk people like Nora Ephron or Tom Brokaw, as if the hotel's 24-hour access to Bergdorf Goodman wasn't enough to get them through the door.

Soon enough, Henry headed off on foot to the NQR line to head south to SOHO to meet a friend for Bloody Marys. He preferred the subway, claiming it *the more authentic transportation* of New York. But Eula had them into a cab and off to Saks for shopping. "Sale, Calli! Sale," said Eula loudly as if Calli had a platinum Amex tucked away somewhere for just such a spree. "Let's check out the shoes first," Eula said, pulling Calli into the express elevator to the eighth floor. "There's an amazing black pair of Christian Louboutin peep-toe pumps with crystals I've been dying to try on. The last time I was here I dropped a grand on a pair of python Nicholas Kirkwoods that I've been wearing almost everywhere I can. Henry would just die if he knew how much they were," Eula squealed, oblivious to Calli's gloomy mood. Calli didn't know—or care—about Nicholas Kirkwood's thousand-dollar shoes. As they exited the elevator, Calli lost her breath for a moment when she saw the throng of women picking at the rows and rows of shoes like turkey vultures attacking roadkill, amid dismembered shoe boxes and lost tissue paper, while harried salesmen in Italian-cut suits balancing six to seven boxes in their arms cooed, "Oh, dahling, you look just divine in those Roger Viviers. I have a pair of Jimmy Choos *to die for* that you must try, too." It seemed to Calli that these women knew how to achieve an orgasm at lunchtime without having to take off their clothes. But her curiosity was piqued as she found a pair of black leather boots that might look good with her jeans—the new pair that she had purchased for eleven dollars at the T.J. Maxx in Watertown. When she flipped them over to see the price, Calli almost threw them out of her hands. "Five thousand dollars! Whoa. Eula, these are five thousand dollars!" Simultaneously she thought, Do you know how many water purification systems and handheld GPS systems I could buy and send to Luke's men with five thousand dollars?

"Why don't you look over at the sales rack, Cal. See if you can find a cute pair of Chanel ballets slippers. Don't get too rattled."

"What? Why did you say that?"

"It's just. Well. You're kind of bringing me down. You haven't smiled since you got here. I want you to have fun. I wanted to splurge and give you something to look forward to."

"Whoa. Do you think I'm some kind of charity case? Goddamit. These fucking boots are five thousand dollars. The women in here are fighting over stupid shoes. Shoes! It doesn't seem like anyone in here, or this whole city for that matter, knows we're at war."

"Oh, Calli—

"All these people care about is how many pairs of Jimmy Choos they can gobble up. And, and...you're just like them."

"That is not fair, Calli. Really, you are unbelievable. Don't you think I know we're at war? Don't you think I worry about Luke, too? But just because we're at war doesn't mean you have to torture yourself—or me. Why can't you relax? Come on, let me buy you a new pair of shoes. Please?"

"No thanks. I'll wait for you at the Starbucks around the corner."

"Come on, Cal, don't be like that. Do you want me to cancel our lunch at La Goulue too? I've been craving their cold duck fois gras on that brioche toast."

"No. Don't cancel the reservation. I want to eat. Seriously, it's okay. You wanted to come here and I agreed. You're right. I'm a downer so I'm just going to get a cup of coffee and people watch. Please. Don't leave because of me. Get your five-inch heels and then we'll go to do something else. Really. It's okay. I mean it," and she did.

>>> <<<

After her disastrous time in New York, Calli drove south to Baltimore to her parents' house in the Mt. Vernon section of the city. Josie and Daphne would arrive only hours after she did, but she still had to deal with her parents' interrogation and their pleas for her to move home until the Divas saved her. Fortunately, Lucy and Haines were still at work when she arrived. Calli spent some time staring at her parents' things: antique Victorian shoe buckles in shadow boxes and artwork from their travels; porcelain dishes from China, France, and England; all manner of hand sculptures (one of Lucy Wendover's stranger collections); vintage tub chairs; an apothecary cabinet; and flea-market finds created their perfectly jet-set–styled setting. An Anglo-Raj cotton quilt hung on one of the parlor walls. A sensible combination of antique furniture posed together with vintage and contemporary pieces in every room. What did all this mean? she thought. These are just things. Disposable.

Her phone rang. It was Dinah.

"Hey lady, are you there? Why'd you hang up on me the other day?" Dinah said.

"Yup. All alone at the moment. What are you up to, Didi? Oh, some police officer tried to give me a ticket for talking on the phone while driving. I got out of it."

"Ugh, Petula is sick with some kind of ear infection. I've got her a doctor's appointment later. How long you staying?"

"Just tonight and tomorrow. Although I might stay for the weekend. The Maryland Club Halloween party is Friday night, and Eula is desperate for me to go."

"How is Eula?"

"Oh you know, she's Eula. I was just with Henry and her in New York. But my friends Josie and Daphne are coming soon."

"Oh yeah, Mother mentioned that you had some friends coming with you. Are their husbands with Luke?"

"Yes, they're all together somewhere in some FOB. That's Forward Operating Base to you and me."

"Did you say FOB?"

"Yes, Dinah. A FOB. So, how's Santa Monica? Warm? Sunny? How's Charles?"

"Everyone is fine. But I want to hear about Walter Reed. So, you're going tomorrow? You're visiting one of Luke's guys?"

"Yup. I'm a little nervous, Didi. I mean, I just don't know what to expect."

"Calli, if anyone can handle Walter Reed, it's you. You can do it. You'll be great. I wish I could go with you. Charles and I have been talking about how we want to help the troops. He's working on setting up a not-for-profit to get donations so we can buy some things for Luke and his men. I just cannot believe they don't have water purification or GPS for all the guys. What the Hell is the government doing with the billions we read about in the paper?"

"I don't know. I don't read the paper anymore. No news. I can't. I turned on CNN the other day. Arwa Damon was reporting from Iraq. She was interviewing soldiers from Luke's unit in the Triangle of Death. The Triangle of Death, Dinah. Luke's not on a business trip."

"We all feel so helpless. You guys are the only ones we know who are directly involved in the war. We are really lucky to have everything we do. And Charles always says he wouldn't be where he is if it wasn't for Luke..."

"Well, Charles wouldn't be where he is if he wasn't a talented actor."

"Calli, he worships Luke. He's his biggest fan. We want to help. We *can* help. I've got Luke's email. I'll write him and see what he needs."

"Thanks, Didi. So listen, I'm going to go. My friends will be here soon. I'll let you know how tomorrow goes. Wish me luck."

"Good luck. You don't need it. But good luck anyway. Love ya!"

"Love ya, too. Say hi to the gang for me."

"I will. Give Auds a huge squeeze from her Auntie Didi."

Dear Didi,

Today I went to Walter Reed. I was really scared about what we would see there. Gnarled amputations. Bloody teeth. I know that there's a chance I could be visiting Luke here, and seeing these wounded soldiers is a screaming reminder.

My two new friends, Daphne Hollis and Josie Merchant, came with me. Josie's grandfather was with the 10th Mountain Division on Riva Ridge during WWII, so she has an affinity for these men.

I asked Luke for his advice on this trip. He wrote, "Just be yourself"—just as you said, too. But I don't know who I am, Dinah. When we walked through the parking garage, we talked about everything but what we were thinking. In the main lobby at Walter Reed, we started to see them. Some on crutches. Some in wheelchairs. Out of uniform, from places like Sadr City, Basra, Tora Bora, Kabul. Still proud. Still fighting for "active duty" status. It was hard not to stare at the soldiers with amputations. Seeing a pants leg tied in a knot where a leg used to be. I wanted to talk to them. Thank them. Ask them about what happened. What had brought them here? An IED? What had they seen? What did they remember? Richard Strong didn't remember his accident. I wondered what Richard must look like compared to the last time I'd seen him at Fort Drum. Back then he'd been at our bon voyage party dancing, smoking cigars. He barely acknowledged me because he was focused on being with the men. The last time I'd seen him he'd been standing—on his own—a young officer, twenty-six years old, training his men for war.

Richard's on Ward 57, the ward where amputees recover. From the nurses' station, two halls stretched out like arms from the desk where names of soldiers were written on dry-erase boards. Their room numbers. Stats. A permanent column where a nurse could place a dot if a young man was in surgery.

When I saw Richard, he was sitting up in bed, a Dilaudid

drip in his arm. He looked so little—thin, sallow, and feeble—nothing like the Richard I'd seen only a few months before. His right arm and leg had been sawed off when he arrived. Now he had stumps, swollen with bandages.

Richard turned toward me and smiled. Instantly, my doubts vanished.

I wanted to be with him, sit with him, soak in everything about him, regardless of his injuries. I sat down on the side of his bed. No longer afraid. I'd done it—crossed over and faced the fear that nagged at me for months. I placed my hand on his right thigh—above the amputation—and looked straight into his eyes.

It's no small feat to realize when you've shed one skin for a fresh one. Far braver than I was, Richard opened his soul to me and allowed me to gaze into what I had so feared—a severely demolished body. But his sturdy mind and clear heart embraced me. I knew exactly at that moment that no matter what happened to Luke—or me—I would be ok.

One of his nurses noticed that I had put my hand on his thigh. "You need to wash your hands before you leave his room," she'd said to me. "There's something in the soil in Iraq that causes an infection if it gets into your blood."

I didn't care, though. I wanted to be with him. I loved him. I cannot explain why, but I had this overwhelming sense of love for him; the way I love Audrey. I had to look away from him—at the wall—to prevent myself from crying. But the tears weren't sad. He had a dry-erase calendar on the wall, next to his bed. It started in October.

Richard arrived at Walter Reed on October 6, but on October 2 someone had written, "Alive Day."

Not "accident day" or "amputation day." "ALIVE DAY."

Richard cared only about his men back in Iraq. Even after stepping on the land mine, he refused to accept medical assistance until he knew that his radio man, Sergeant

Jackson, had been attended to. Just as I was leaving, I said to Richard, "I thought that I was coming down here to help you, but I can see now that the reason I'm here is because you can help me."

Later in our visit, an older couple in their seventies walked in to visit with Richard. The man and his wife had traveled down from Pennsylvania, where the parishioners in their church baked brownies and cookies to give to the patients. I was impressed that this older couple had traveled so far to see these soldiers. To bring them homemade baked goods and good wishes. The husband explained that he was a Korean War vet. To Richard he said, "You know, amputees all have alive days; they are better than birthdays because if you get that close to a bomb or an IED or grenade and live, that's a miracle."

Before he left, the man turned to Josie, Daphne, and me. Before he said good-bye, he lifted up both his pants legs. He was a double amputee.

17

Lucy and Haines convinced Calli to stay for the weekend. Lucy said, "You should stay and see your friends." Then she said, "Josie and Daphne, I admire you ladies. Haines and I want you to know that you have a place here with us anytime. We'd be honored if you stay for the weekend," which caught Calli off guard, but Calli appreciated her mother for trying.

Calli asked, "Can you stay? I'd love it if you could."

"No," Daphne began, "I have to get back to Jellybean." Jellybean was Daphne's ferret. "I imagine she's taking advantage of the petsitter—fearlessly swan-diving off my bookshelf into her hair."

"Yeah, and I have to get back to my important life in Watertown: raking leaves, organizing my knife drawer, and cleaning my underwear." Josie mused.

Calli called Eula to tell her she was staying longer. Eula responded to the news, "This is perfect. Just perfect. I'm thrilled! I am so glad you aren't leaving quite yet. Henry just bought me a case of Montrachet—"

Calli interrupted, "Eula, I have no idea what a Montrachet is..."

"Oh darling, don't worry. I know you'll like it. It's Chardonnay. And we all know you love Chardonnays. I cannot believe Henry got it for me. We'll break open a bottle later to make sure it isn't poisonous," she said giggling. "Unfortunately, I cannot go to the Maryland Club Halloween party," she said sheepishly.

"Oh? The girls will be sad."

"I have an Italian literature class."

"Italian literature?" Calli said with a snarky tone.

"Yes, yes. I'm working on my Italian, so I thought it might be helpful to read *The Prince* and *Purgatorio*."

"Eula, you slay me."

"Italian is hard! So, huge favor?"

"How can I say no."

"Would you be a darling and take the kids to the Halloween party? Henry and you? You know how Henry is. He'll go to the bar and let the girls loose and who knows what will happen if they—"

"Eula!"

"Please, C. Please. Why don't you come over early and we can have a glass of wine? Tell me about Walter Reed."

Then Henry got on the phone, "Come on, C! You and me. It'll be fun."

Mostly out of curiosity, Calli agreed. She had heard about this Halloween party, but Audrey had been too little to take when they'd lived here.

Before the party, she reminded herself that she was the same person she'd been when she lived there. Maybe the fact that she had to convince herself should have told her that she'd changed, but she wanted to believe that she could still fit into the Baltimore scene. The move to northern New York hadn't erased her affinity for parties. She was looking forward to seeing Baltimore people.

When she arrived at Henry and Eula's, their girls, Ellen and Mae Margaret, were primping like teenagers for the prom, even though they were only nine and six years old. They were wearing costumes—Hannah Montana and the Cheetah Girls. "Calli! Calli! Look at us!" Ellen chirped. "This is my friend Ella. She's in my grade."

"You both look so great. I love your costumes."

Mae Margaret said, "I love Hannah Montana. I want to be her when I grow up. What costume are you going to wear, Calli?"

"I don't have a costume, sweetie, but I'll still take you to the party," Calli said.

The three girls giggled in the bedroom while they finished putting on their costumes for the party. Calli and Eula, sipping their wine, eavesdropped on their conversation. The little girls chatted casually about who would be there and how they loved parties at the Maryland Club.

How strange it was to be back.

Eula explained to Calli that the same people she saw at every other social event were going to be there. "It's going to be a mob scene—rambunctious children scrambling all over the place, scouring for candy and loot while the parents sip Mount Gay and tonics and Chardonnay, pretending not to notice all the sugar their little goblins are ingesting."

Since she'd moved away, Calli hadn't been back to the Maryland Club. Luke had been a member when they lived in Baltimore, but when they moved, he decided to give it up, not sure he wanted to continue to pay monthly dues for a grandiose club he might never step foot in again.

When it was about time to go over to the club, Henry called. "Darlin'," he said, "I'm running late from this meeting, so can you drive the girls over and I'll meet you there?"

"Henry, I wouldn't do it for anyone else but you."

"I know. That's why I love you!"

Calli became the designated driver of the three excited girls and their empty bags just waiting to be filled with candy. "Calli! Calli! Let's go! We're going to be late!" They screamed. "The party starts at six o'clock and we need to be on time!"

It was only five o'clock—the club was ten minutes away from Eula and Henry's house. She knew she had plenty of time to get there, but after twenty minutes of listening to them whine about needing to be the first ones at the party, she finally acquiesced, stopped tooling around town, and took them.

Streets lined with stately homes turned into blocks of Georgian, Federal and Greek revival row homes with marble steps, some shabby, some refurbished, and grass gave way to sidewalks bustling with students and professors from Johns Hopkins and University of Baltimore. The bus fumes and restaurant aromas wafting through the air seemed recognizable, but it wasn't the same. There's no Maryland Club in Jefferson County and no one cares where your children go to school, Calli thought. In Sackets Harbor, New York, there wasn't much pretense, and what little existed paled in comparison to the quixotic, insular Baltimore scene they'd left. She wondered what Daphne and Josie would have thought of her. They didn't care about status. Calli realized she didn't care about it much anymore, either.

As she approached the club, she was in such a swivet she could hardly speak. After seeing Richard lying in his hospital bed minus his right arm and leg, her desire to go to this party felt dampened.

The girls were correct that they needed to be there on time. When they arrived, there was only one parking space still available behind the club. The SUV barely made it in between a BMW and a Mercedes sedan.

"Come on, Calli! Let's go in!"

"Okay, okay, just let me grab my purse. Let's go!"

Breathing deeply, her spunk lasted barely a minute when she walked into the party. The girls bolted from her the moment she walked through the door. "Girls. Girls!" she tried in vain. They had slipped through her fingers into a sea of costumed partygoers young and old. Calli looked around. She knew no one.

She walked to one of the makeshift bars and ordered a Chardonnay from the bartender in his country club uniform—pressed white shirt, black necktie, black trousers. Nibbling on salty nuts and sipping her wine, Calli prayed that someone she knew would walk through the door. As she lamented her decision to come while Eula was reading Italian literature in some classroom with hot Italian men who flirted and laughed, Jen Hobbs walked in with her two sons. Relief. Calli smiled and sauntered over, remembering how just a couple of years ago they had been relatively tight friends spending time at each other's houses cooking out.

Jen gushed, "Oh, Calli, you're here. This is such a pleasant surprise. How are you? How is Audrey? Do you love Fort Drum? Oh, and how is Luke? It must be so hard..." The moment was short-lived—Calli barely had a chance to answer, "I'm fine. Audrey's fine, too."

"Calli, I'm so sorry, but I have to run after Mark before he eats too many cookies. I'll catch up with you, okay?" Jen, cocktail in hand, dashed off to find her son, leaving Calli alone at the bar.

A slight void, that place Audrey would fill, stood with her. Calli missed Audrey but was relieved not to have her tethered to her. She realized why Eula hadn't wanted to come to this thing. She started to search for Henry. At least she could talk to him.

In the midst of the hunt, Krista Potter, an acquaintance, stopped her, "Calli! How are you? Oh my gawd, I think about you all the time. Where's Luke? Is he here?"

She wanted to blurt out, "You fake. If you thought about me all the time, you'd probably ask someone where we are living. You'd know that Luke is in Iraq." Instead she demurely smiled. "Hi, Krista. Well, Luke's in Iraq. Has been since August."

Then Krista gave her The Look. The oh-you-poor-thing look, the thank-god-it's-you-and-not-me look. Calli had given it plenty, but never received it until this moment.

The Look announced how cloven her world had become—how isolated she felt. No one in the room tonight knew what she was going through. She gulped her wine, staring at her fingers gripping the glass. Her eyes blurred, her ears rang. Gazing into the wine, she hoped that when she looked up, everything would be different. Luke might reach for her elbow and kiss her cheek, asking her, "Where have you been hiding, my love?"

Tonight was the funeral for the former Calli.

As more and more people gave her The Look and then quickly

found reasons to move away from her, she knew she epitomized what they didn't want to face. In their early twentieth-century Colonial homes, driving fifty-thousand-dollar cars, raising their healthy, intelligent children in a relatively safe environment, they didn't know the anxiety and distress that squeezed the muscles in her chest.

She got another glass of wine and drank for the rest of the night. Henry, clearly waylaid at the men's bar by a phalanx of admirers, forgot to look for her. Ellen, Ella, and Mae Margaret scampered into the haunted house and painted ghoulish faces on pumpkins. With two glasses of wine in hand, she found herself stuck in a corner discussing the war with some sycophant who claimed he knew Luke. But when he introduced her to his friend, he mangled her name, "This is Calli Colton."

She called him out on it saying, "Our last name is Coleman."

He responded, "Close enough."

>>> ⟶ ⟵ <<<

Halloween.

Josie and Daphne insisted that they wanted to spend the night with her and Audrey. Daphne said, "I'll make my famous chili."

"What's in your famous chili?" Calli asked.

"Well, I don't know yet, but I'll let you know. I think I'll do beef and beans."

"You crack me up. I'm making meatloaf."

"It'll be a ground beef feast then!"

When Josie called, she said, "I hear we're spendin' Halloween at your house? I'm so excited. I just can't bear the idea of being here alone, handin' out candy to kids. I love Halloween, but this year it seems different. Maybe I'll put on my flamingo costume."

"Flamingo costume?"

Josie giggled, "Tristan and I went to a costume ball our senior year of college, and I bought this outrageous flamingo costume. It's all covered in sequins and pink feathers. I love it!"

"You know Audrey is going to want to wear it."

"Well, maybe I'll let her try it on after Halloween."

That afternoon, when Calli went to walk with Audrey at her preschool Halloween parade, she started chatting with the mother of a boy in Audrey's class. "Hi, I'm Calli Coleman. Audrey's mom."

"I'm Rachel. Nice to meet you. I'm Timothy's mom. And this is Miller. He's one. Is your husband deployed? Mine is."

"Yes, how did you know?"

"I've seen you in the mornings. I'm a little shy so I don't go out of my way to introduce myself. You don't look like a Watertown person."

"A Watertown person?"

"Oh no!" Rachel sighed. While the teachers were organizing the children for the parade, Timothy climbed under the library bookcase and pulled out a long fluorescent bulb while Rachel balanced Miller on her hip, pleading with Timothy to stop.

"I'm so glad my child is not the only one who does things like that," Calli told her.

She smiled at Calli. "I'm new to Fort Drum. My husband deployed about two months after we got here."

"Mine, too!" Calli said.

"I am not a very good military wife," she told Calli.

Calli thought, That's my line.

Rachel's hair was dyed the color of a Japanese maple. She had tragically pale Irish skin, which Calli suspected probably prompted her to see the dermatologist regularly. Calli noticed Rachel's right thumb unconsciously gnawing against the outer cuticle of her right index finger, the skin peeled like tiny white curlicue ribbons. Upon further survey, Calli noticed that most of Rachel's cuticles appeared compulsively ravaged. Rachel caught her and nonchalantly admitted, "Don't mind my OCD. Had it since I was in college. Anxiety."

As the children gathered, the mothers and fathers lingered on the sidelines. One of the teachers bellowed, "When the teachers give the go-ahead, everyone march outside for the parade around the block."

Calli stuck near Rachel. "This is so organized," Calli giggled.

"Much like the Army, I guess," Rachel laughed with her. "Although, I really don't know what I'm talking about. I see those young know-it-all wives who like to boast how they helped their husbands rise through the ranks. And I'm thinking the whole time, who cares?"

"Me, too!" Calli agreed.

"Do you like Tia Maria? I love Alice in Wonderlands. Do you like them?"

"Alice in Wonderlands?" Calli guffawed.

"It's so good. It's Tia Maria, Grand Marnier, and tequila. You should try it. I'll make you one sometime."

"I'm more of a wino myself, but I'm willing to give it a try. Grand Marnier reminds me of my grandmother—she used to bake the best Grand Marnier orange Bundt cake. Oh, it was so good." The moment Calli met her, she knew that Rachel would fit into their little sorority. The thought of Rachel spending the holiday evening alone with her kids suddenly disturbed her.

"Hey, would you like to come over tonight? With your boys? Go trick or treating with Audrey and me? I'm going to make meatloaf. My two other friends—they don't have kids, but they love them—are coming, too. Daphne and Josie. They're Army wives, too. Does five work?"

"Yes! Yes, I'd love that. Thank you. I was feeling a little lonely thinking about going out with just the boys."

"Oh, that's wonderful."

"Sure. That's perfect. Thanks so much. I'll bring some Alice in Wonderlands, ok?"

"Oh yes!" Calli said.

Calli made everyone mummy meatloaf, shaping the meatloaf into a mummy form and covering it with white American cheese fashioned as the mummy wraps and two black sliced olives for the eyes. The weather was mild for October and it wasn't raining. It had been pouring at four. Audrey and Calli sang, "Rain, Rain, Go Away" the whole way home from school. As the sun set over Sackets Harbor, Calli lit the toothy jack-o-lantern and set a large bowl of chocolate bar miniatures on her front porch with a note, "Be kind, just take one."

With a bit of buzz from the Alice in Wonderlands, Calli said, "Okay, ladies, ghouls, goblins, flamingos, and superheroes, let's go get some candy!"

"Yay!" all the kids squealed.

"Cal, to-go cups? For our drinks?" Daphne chimed. She'd already filled a red plastic cup to the rim with red wine for Calli.

With her camera, Calli snapped away at Audrey. At the boys. At her friends. Audrey was delectable dressed as Wonder Woman. Timothy was Mr. Incredible and Miller was Superman.

After trick-or-treating, the women migrated back to Calli's house. While the kids ripped open their candy, Calli opened another bottle of red wine and poured everyone a glass. Rachel fit in immediately, as if she had been friends with the Divas from day one. Calli opened up to Rachel. "This is the second Halloween Luke's missed. Last year, he was training at NTC. What other holidays and events will be just words on a page for him? I feel like Audrey's growing up without him. His emails and a letter here and there are the only proof of his existence," Calli said. "I'm so jealous when I hear other women talk about their daily calls from their soldiers in Iraq or Afghanistan. But it makes no sense to get upset. My focus is on the positive. On Audrey. Keeping her healthy and happy."

"I know," Rachel said. "Aidan, my husband, took a medical school scholarship in exchange for active duty. I don't have a clue about any of this."

"A medical school scholarship? I don't know what that is."

"It means we are obligated to the Army for each year Aidan was in medical school. And we're not attached to a unit, so I don't even have an FRG to call."

"Calli's an FRG leader," Daphne chuckled.

"Well, maybe you can help me. Aidan was given only one month's notice about his deployment with a unit out of Fort Hood, in Texas. A thirteen-month deployment. Aidan left without any fresh uniforms and had to pay out of his pocket to ship his gear down to Fort Hood. The Army agreed to reimburse him, but there's still a pile of paperwork to complete, and it's confusing."

Josie said, "That's bullshit. I've got some handbooks others have passed on to me. I'll give them to ya, for what's it's worth. We'll help ya."

"Hey," Calli said, "we get together on Tuesday nights for dinner. It's really casual. You can get a sitter or bring the boys. We all pitch in. And drink lots of wine!"

"Sold!" Rachel said.

"On one condition," Daphne said. "You have to call yourself a Diva War Bride."

"Diva War Bride?"

"Yeah, it's our nickname."

"I love it! I definitely want to be a Diva War Bride."

November 2006

My dearest love,

It's funny how so many things over here (much like Panama) become very black-white issues. I am convinced that if every one of us had to suck it up and deal with forced privation, 90% of our stress and worries would be erased. But I wish this on no one, that's for sure. We are delusional if we think these knuckleheads are ever going to live together in peace. The bad guys here are evil, which does give credence to this deployment, and I am quite confident they're related to terrorists in some way, shape, or form. That part is easy to comprehend, it's the next step—when we'll be able to leave—that is puzzling. Of course, and it's probably valid, the Vietnam comparison looms. How are we going to ever pull out without someone sticking "defeated" or "lost" to the tail end? I don't know, Cal, it's a very confusing battlefield, far more so than Panama. There are plenty of enemies here to keep us gainfully employed for quite some time. But the sectarian violence, that's almost impossible for the US to solve, at least from where I stand.

I miss you so much, Cal, and I can't wait to get home. You've been so good with the FRG and all the things you do for Audrey and me. Give Auds a huge squeeze from me. I miss her desperately. Off to breakfast for now, but know this comes with a whole lot of love. More soon.
Love,
Luke

Thanksgiving 2006
Dear Immortal Wives and Mothers,
I've heard the adage "no news is good news" a lot these days. More often than not, I do not find it a charming or comforting phrase but a bitter reminder of the dreadful year I must endure away from my husband. However, for the first time in months, I am honestly using the phrase, as austere as it may be. We are coming up on the one-third mark of deployment, and I know that I am so thankful that the last several weeks have been without incident.

As Americans, we are blessed in many ways. We are blessed that we have our soldiers who have answered the call of duty to serve our great nation. Over the past few months, I have had the honor to learn what a sacrifice the soldier makes, and it is a tribute to their glory and their devotion to duty that I am thankful this year. Additionally, I am also blessed and thankful to have my Army family: all of you. I must thank you for supporting Audrey, Luke, and me.

As we are thrust into Christmas and the end of 2006,

many of us will be traveling. I will be in the area until December 21, and then I will be taking a temporary leave of absence as one of the FRG leaders. Veronica McLeod has graciously offered to step in while I take a much-needed break for a month. I know she will carry the mantle well while I am away. I will also forward her information to everyone once that time approaches.

Also, please remember to keep us up to speed on your whereabouts in the unlikely and unfortunate situation that we must do a call-out. Our FRG advisors have asked us not to email incident reports, so if we cannot reach you on the phone, then the information can't be disseminated. While we are aware that sometimes there are people who don't get the information (their numbers are disconnected or changed and we weren't notified), we've also created a system to help us get in touch with everyone on the list. Devastating news takes a long time to recover from, and continuing to try and call people several days after the fact sometimes gets lost in the grief.

On a happier note, all the men are well, and as I alluded to above, it seems that life in Yusufiyah is relatively calm. Please remember to utilize the FRG website for updates on 4-31 and Alpha Company.

As always, please feel free to contact me if you need anything or have any concerns.
Best,
Calli

The last time Calli spent Thanksgiving away from her family was the year after she graduated from Juilliard. Working in the West Indies as a cook on a Sparkman Stephens mega-yacht called the *Sea Angel*, she cried from the end of November through the end of the year because she was so homesick. She'd never worked so hard in her life—and during holidays. Most of her friends and family thought it was adventurous of her to live and work on a sailboat.

But the work, on a tiny floating boutique hotel with only three staff to serve and wait on up to eight guests, was tiresome. Up at six-thirty to cook breakfast, clean, and be ready to wait on guests by eight. She waited on and cooked for loathsome nouveau riche guests who thought that class started with *K*. For eighteen hours a day, seven days a week when they were on board, she worked ensuring that they had food and drink for their every whim. The guests expected—and paid for—five-star service with gourmet meals and top-shelf liquor. From the moment they awoke until they slipped into their bunks at night, the crew was their slaves. Calli's only oasis: a coffin-sized bunk next to the engine room where the generator would roar so loudly she often opted to sleep up in the cockpit under the stars.

The highlight of her year was the job offer she got from one of the guests, a kind gentleman by the name of Alberto Fiumano, who asked Calli if she would go work on his newly acquired mega-yacht in Italy. Fiumano, a cabinetmaker's son from Taranto, was making millions from his global furniture empire. The captain of the *Sea Angel*, Hunter, and his wife, Agnes, who was the stewardess, were also offered positions.

"I'm going to Italy!" she screamed on the phone to Lucy and Haines.

A bit skeptically, Lucy said, "Are you ever coming home again, Calliope darling? We'd like to see you."

"Of course you have our blessing," Haines chimed in quickly. "I'd like to know more about these people, though."

"I have to come home for Ann's wedding. Remember Ann? From Juilliard?"

"Yes, of course. When is she getting married?"

"Sometime this spring."

The Fiumano party left the *Sea Angel* after two weeks of sailing in the Lesser Antilles and French West Indies to head back to Rome.

For a week, Calli and her crewmates had a respite before the next group of charter guests arrived. One Sunday night, while they were anchored in English Harbour, Antigua, Calli suggested to Hunter and Agnes that they get off the boat. "Let's go onshore to the jump-up at Shirley Heights. Steel drums, the sunset over the island, jerk chicken, and rum punch. What could be better?"

Agnes declined, "Nah, I'm not really up for that." Often she stayed behind, as she seemed content to read romance novels and eat leftovers. After a final plea, Hunter and Calli left Agnes lying on the settee with one of her Danielle Steeles and a bowl of mint chocolate chip ice cream.

It was not unusual for Hunter and Calli to go off at night to explore whatever local island they happened to anchor near. His South African charm kept Calli laughing throughout their arduous days when guests were on board.

"What kind of pig slop are you going to feed them today, Calli-o?"

"Pig slop? Seriously?"

"Yeah, where'd you learn to cook?"

"I'm self-taught. And you know what. You don't have to eat it. Agnes and I will. The guests will. You can go off and smoke your lungs out. Drink your rum—alone. Bad boy."

"You Yanks, you're all alike. Indignant and spoiled."

Technically, Hunter was her boss, so Calli tried to keep him happy by making the coffee the way he liked it. Calli always made sure he had a pack of cigarettes near his coffee mug. His breakfast: caffeine and nicotine—stimulants to kill his daily hangovers from his love affair with rum straight up with only a squeeze of fresh lime. Calli poked fun at him, calling him Old Man and Saffer, inquiring about his life in Durban and how he ended up a boat captain. Calli would often go ashore in the mornings to scout out a local bakery and bring back some fresh-baked croissants or a loaf of bread they would share.

Agnes always said, "I'm on a diet, Calli. I can't eat that stuff."

Calli loved Agnes, too. She just seemed not to notice or care that

Hunter was flirting with Calli. Calli, not wanting to stick her nose in their business, romped around the boat like a puppy when she wasn't in the galley preparing food. They were all the best of friends.

That night, after partying with the natives, tourists, and band members, Calli, quite tipsy, said, "I think I have to go to sleep, Hunter. I'm done for tonight."

"You're a lightweight."

"Shut up, Saffer. You can barely stand up, either."

Drunk from punch, they stumbled into the *Sea Angel's* dinghy. He revved the engine into gear. Speeding across English Harbor, luxuriating in the Caribbean ambiance, Calli felt a little less homesick. Her friendship with Hunter and Agnes was wrapped around her like a worn childhood blanket.

"Calli. I have something I, er, I need to say."

Sober enough to realize he was trying to be serious, she stopped beaming out over the salt water to listen.

"I don't love Agnes. You know. She's gotten fat. I'm not in love with her."

"Oh. I'm sorry. Does she know?"

"No. She doesn't know. I haven't told her. Well, you're going to Italy, right?"

"I already told my parents."

"I was hoping we could go together, Calli."

Wham.

She couldn't go work with this man—he was confused, thinking he loved her, not Agnes. She wasn't sure now how she was even going to continue working with him on the *Sea Angel* with this knowledge.

"Hunter, but I don't love you."

"You don't?"

"No. And I like Agnes. I can't do this to her. Even if you don't take her and you and I go. It will be awkward. I don't have feelings for you. You're my boss. Why did you tell me this? I can't do this to Agnes."

She jumped off the dinghy onto the deck without saying good-night. She was mortified. Drunk enough, she passed out immediately on her bunk in her suffocating, febrile cabin, deaf to the roaring generator.

The next morning, still soggy from sugarcane and yeast pumping through her blood, she tiptoed anxiously into the galley to make coffee for the two of them and to turn on the tea kettle for Agnes. Agnes's ice cream bowl, still in the sink, was sticky with green sludge. Even through the fog of the residual rum, she tried to will away the final moments of the night before. She ran through breakfast menus for the next week's guests: toasted pecan pancakes with pure maple syrup. Homemade granola with fresh fruit. Fresh grapefruit and assorted homemade muffins with jam. Bagels with cream cheese, smoked salmon, sliced tomato, cucumber, red onion, and capers. Eggs Florentine.

She knew what she had to do.

Later that week, she called the owner of the *Sea Angel* and told him that her mother was dying.

***

Thanksgiving without Luke, without her family. She only had to show up, with Audrey, at Kelly and Roger's house, roasted onions and parsley pesto in hand. Kelly and Roger had so much family in Sackets and Watertown. More than twenty-five of them sat down at two tables. Kelly and Roger had also invited Daphne, Rachel, and Josie. Rachel, though, had gone home to see her family in northern Virginia and Daphne went to spend Thanksgiving with her eighteen-year-old son in Tempe, where he was living with her stepfather and going to community college. But like Calli, Josie had decided that spending Thanksgiving with family was too onerous. Calli said, "I'm so happy you're going to be with us."

"Me, too. I literally cannot imagine goin' home."

Kelly and Roger may have been from small-town USA, but they were worldly. They used Roger's grandmother's silver for the turkey. Monogrammed white linen napkins and pressed tablecloths dressed the tables. Candelabras with white tapers glowed. Kelly's cousin arranged tantalizing mixes of lush hydrangea, fall lotus pod, a variety of fall pompoms, alstroemeria, carnations, texture focals, and lush greens. Bountiful helpings presented themselves on Kelly's wedding china: salt-roasted turkey. Giblet pan gravy. Wild rice stuffing with pine nuts. Maple-braised butternut squash. Roasted cranberry sauce with herb-candied walnuts. Homemade braided bread. Room-temperature butter in a polished silver dish. Calli's roasted onions with parsley pesto. Josie's golden brown butter and pecan praline tart. Pumpkin pie. Caramelized apple pie. Hand-churned vanilla ice cream. Kelly, accomplished in the kitchen, showcased her best effort for her family. For Josie, Audrey, and her.

Eula had sent Audrey a Black Watch party dress outfitted with tulle, a wide swath of black velvet ribbon to tie around Audrey's waist into a bow, and exquisite smocked embroidery on the bodice. Calli squeezed Audrey's chubby legs into the white tights and black patent leather Mary Janes, then added a matching Black Watch bow-barrette to her hair. Although Eula and Calli weren't in constant communication, she continued to be extraordinarily generous to Audrey, sending her elaborately wrapped care packages stuffed with the latest children's books, toys, Swiss chocolate, and trendy girls' clothes that Calli had no chance of finding in Sackets or Watertown. Calli didn't have too many occasions to get dressed up the way they had in Baltimore, so she was eager for Audrey to wear the outfit—a small glimpse of the past, or perhaps the future.

Appreciative of the invitation, she tried to speak to all the people at dinner. With the aid of Chardonnay, her gregarious former self rose out of her for a few hours. She engaged the family with anecdotal tales of life in Baltimore, the West Indies, and Arenzano. She asked them about themselves: hobbies, schools, careers. Trying always to steer the conversation away from the Army. War. Politics. Luke. She melted into the family as if she was a long-lost cousin who'd been living in Hong Kong, finally home for the holidays. The wine flowed, Josie and she happily acquiescing to each generous pour. High on wine—and the reprieve—they giggled together, sitting on the floor after dinner, relaxing by the warmth of the wood burning in the fireplace. Audrey tottered around. Her bow-barrette dangled at the ends of her hair, Mary Janes forgotten somewhere in the house. Kelly had put on a *Thomas the Tank Engine* video for her in the den. It amused her but didn't keep her from getting up and coming into the living room where the live action was taking place.

The only mention of Luke or Tristan was during the Grace, when everyone prayed for their safety. Their safe return at the end of the deployment. Otherwise, Josie and Calli were left to inject them into conversation. She knew that these glaring omissions weren't meant to be hurtful, but rather, purposeful. Clemency.

Calli drank too much. When she went out to the car to drive home, fortunately Roger, a gentleman, followed her out. He'd stopped drinking a few years ago and must have realized that she was not in a sober enough position to get them home. "Calli," Roger called out, "Let me drive you and Audrey home. Okay?" She acquiesced. She had a very important person to get home safely.

Patrol Base Yusufiyah
Thanksgiving 2006
Dear family and friends of the Alpha Company Immortals,
It is such an honor and privilege for me to be in the position to write this note. A simple thank you hardly seems adequate. I wish I could convey the joy, happiness, and excitement that follow the packages and goods that arrive from the families and loved ones, but no adjectives seem to fit. When those boxes arrive and I distribute them to the men, we very briefly are able to forget about life in Iraq and remember the goodness and love at home. It will be impossible to repay you all in kind, but please know that your support means so much to the soldiers.

As you settle in for Thanksgiving with your families and

dear friends, please remember all that you are thankful for this year. We all are blessed in so many ways despite all of our hardships. Whether in a desolate patrol base in Iraq or on the beautiful shores of the Chesapeake Bay or at Fort Drum, we all must take a moment and remember what makes this country of ours so great. Your generous support is something that I am certainly thankful for this year. That you are free to drive to a big city or catch a train to New York or even just take a drive to the local store with no fear of assault is worth an extra prayer of thanks.

Thank you all so much for your generosity and kindness. The Immortals are committed to victory over here, and with your support, we will be that much closer to reaching our objective. We wish you all the best for this holiday. Safe travels and Godspeed.

Luke Coleman
Master Sergeant
The Immortals

Eula called Calli.

"Why didn't you come home for Thanksgiving?"

"What do you mean?"

"I thought you were coming home. Henry and I wanted to see you."

"Eula, I told you I was going to stay up here with Josie."

"Well, when are you coming down? You know I just can't stand the cold, otherwise I'd come to see you."

"I know. I know. I hate the cold, too. I don't blame you. I'll be back at Christmas, promise. It just felt like it was too much to go home for Thanksgiving. I had such a weird time at Halloween. Everyone ignoring me or staring at me. I got stuck with that obnoxious shithead at the Maryland Club, who claimed to be such good friends with Luke and then didn't know our last name. I was so pissed."

"I'm glad you've made friends up there, but I miss you. Henry and I want to have a party for you over Christmas."

"Eula, no! Don't do that. It's really thoughtful but not necessary. I just want to see you guys, okay?"

There were times, not many, when Calli felt as if Eula thought she was her toy. Something to be tossed about. At times, she seemed to forget that Calli wasn't in the same economic situation, couldn't just fly down to Baltimore for parties. Calli wondered if Eula might be jealous of Josie.

The thought took Calli back to her college days, when Calli had introduced Gwynne Smith, her roommate and a viola player from London, to Lawrence Woody, aka Woody, one night early in her freshman year. Gwynne and Calli had been friends from day one of orientation. Woody was a sophomore who went to Columbia. His best friends, Will and Sasha, lived next door to Gwynne and Calli, so she'd often see him going in and out of their room. One night when she'd had way too much beer at a party and wobbled home alone, she stumbled across Woody in the elevator of the Rose Building as he was heading up to their floor. Brazenly she said, "I know you. You're Woody. I see you all the time. Why don't you ever say hello to me?"

"What's your name?"

"Come on. Don't you know? Calli Wendover."

"Bendover?"

"Bendover? WEN-dover. Calli. Calliope. I know, it's lame. My parents are professors."

"Well, well, Miss Calliope Bendover, it's my pleasure to meet you. Do you want to come to my friends' room for a beer?"

Although Calli was pretty lush with beer, she had admired these three sophomore boys, thought they were so cool and cute. Will and Sasha hadn't invited Gwynne and Calli into their clandestine world, so she was elated when Woody gave her a pass.

"Sure!"

From that night on, Woody and Calli would run into each other all over the Upper West Side. He called her "C-Bear." Sometimes "Bendover." Will and Sasha warmed up to her, too. She'd wander into their room late at night after long hours of practice and classes while they watched Mr. Spock and Captain Kirk catapult the Enterprise from one galaxy to the next, sit down on their lopsided, tattered gray sofa that sank in the middle of each cushion, and blend in with the wall. Eventually, they started to talk to her.

"C-Bear," they'd say, "how's that French horn of yours?"

"Oh, it's just dandy," she'd reply earnestly.

"I like a girl who blows a horn," Sasha flirted with her. Calli's face went crimson, and she fantasized about Sasha naked in her bed.

Secretly, she had a crush on Sasha, but she did her best to hide it since he already had a girlfriend. She'd be patient. Wait it out. Let him see her as a friend first.

Soon, Gwynne realized that the boy she liked in a different dorm wasn't such a good guy and started to follow Calli to Sasha and Will's room for the late-night post-practice routine of watching *Star Trek*. One night, as they were strolling around the corner from their room to Sasha and Will's, Woody appeared.

"C-Bear!"

"Woody! This is my roommate, Gwynne Smith."

And thus began her group at college. Gwynne and Calli were the only non-girlfriend girls in a gang of about eight sophomore guys. For the rest of their freshman year, they felt loved and included, privy to the best parties, and escorted to bars that served underage students. The guys became big brothers.

Sasha never did fall for Calli.

When they arrived back at 60 Lincoln Center Plaza for their sophomore year, Gwynne and Calli roomed together again. They had seen Woody over the summer. Several of them from school had met up in Nantucket at her parents' house for a week of lying on Nobadeer Beach and partying all night at the Chicken Box. Back at school, they fell into the previous year's pattern. Practice. Practice. Practice. Will, Sasha, and Woody had rented the infamous "Bud

House," a dilapidated Victorian brownstone about five blocks away from campus. The parquet floors, peeling wallpaper, and wood paneling resembled a fusty Victorian interior, like some old person had lived there a long time and just let the boys rent it for cheap. Ikea sofas and a gigantic TV were the only furnishings. It looked more like a camp out than a home. There were always students there. Kids saying things like, "When I get out of school, I'm going to start my own music school back in Hannibal." Or "I've just heard from Steven Sampson...you know, the conductor of Stamford's choir? He wants me to audition!" They were Juilliard and Columbia kids who all needed to let off steam from the hours and hours of practice and study. At the Bud House, everyone seemed like a rising star.

What Calli hadn't seen, and what really surprised her when they revealed it to her, was that Gwynne and Woody had fallen in love. They claimed it happened in Nantucket. She was wild with jealousy, lurking in corners, spying on them as they walked from her apartment on West End Ave or sitting in Café Luxembourg. She hated herself because she couldn't understand why she felt jealous. She didn't have feelings for Woody beyond friendship. He was an older-brother figure. And Gwynne was her best friend. Why wouldn't she be happy for her?

She spent an entire semester seething inside. She hid from them, claiming the need to practice her horn more than she had been. She was jealous, not of them per se, but that they seemed so in love with each other. The closest thing she'd ever had to a boyfriend was a short-lived relationship with a Nantucket lifeguard one summer. She longed for the boys who seemed too elusive to really be interested in her. The gorgeous junior who played the lead in *Equus*. The rugged drummer who played in a band called Sister Judy. The cute boy in her music theory and ear training class with the most glorious blue eyes, shaggy blond hair, and J. Crew khakis.

She awoke one morning in March, alone in her room—Gwynne was off with Woody—and a switch turned on for her. She could manipulate her feelings. She was the director of her own play. She'd had enough of being jealous. *Enough.* She felt stupid for wasting so much time begrudging their relationship, so much so that when they broke up a few months later, she was genuinely sad.

Now, she sensed that Eula was jealous of Josie and her. Vowing that she would never let rivalry interfere with any relationship again, she tried to email Eula as much as she could.

Eula's feelings were important to her.

⫸ 18 ⫷

"What do you think about a Christmas party?" Calli asked at the Divas' weekly dinner get-together.

"Ooo, I love that idea," Josie chimed in.

"That's a perfect idea. We definitely need some cheer," Daphne said. Rachel nodded in agreement.

Rachel had seamlessly joined in with the women. She came to every Tuesday night dinner. The first Tuesday she attended, she brought tequila and homemade French onion soup with Parmesan croutons. Each week she made another soup for them to try, but always brought her Alice in Wonderland cocktails. When they decided to throw a party, Rachel said, "I have the best Christmas decorations and ornaments! I'm sure my in-laws will ship me some BBQ from North Carolina—both kinds: tomato and mustard—and I'll make cocktails." Calli loved her slightly bucktoothed smile. A physician's wife, she knew much about the inner workings of the Army medical system. With Audrey fighting off her third ear infection since September, Rachel suggested some medication that would help ease the pain and lower her fevers so that Calli didn't have to keep driving over to Fort Drum to see the pediatrician. Rachel called one of the PAs she knew and even delivered meds to Calli at home, ensuring that Audrey was comfortable.

Her Virginia charm reminded Calli of Eula.

>>>>>> <<<<<<

One week before the Divas' Christmas party, Calli had bronchitis and a bacterial infection in her lungs. For days, she'd been in denial and kept thinking that it was just a cold and a scratchy throat. She pushed and pushed herself. Audrey had had so many ear infections that Calli was bound to end up with some kind of illness.

When she finally admitted she was sick, it was too late. She couldn't move. The receptionist at Fort Drum told her she'd have to come in for an appointment before they'd give her any medication. By that point, her head felt so heavy that she couldn't even stand up and had to crawl to the bathroom to get a thermometer. Her fever was 103 degrees. Wheezing like an asthmatic, Calli lay listless in bed while Audrey watched Noggin for hours on the floor, surrounded by cookie crumbs and half-drunk juice boxes with sticky straws.

She called Josie. "Hey, Jose. I'm not feeling so hot. Any chance you can come help me with Audrey? I hate to bother you, but I'm really feeling shitty. I've got to drive to Fort Drum to see the doctor."

Josie must have called Daphne, because before Calli knew it, they were both at the house.

"You are not driving to Fort Drum," Daphne said.

"Calli, you look awful. I'll drive you. Daphne can stay here with Audrey."

Gingerly, they helped her get into the backseat of Josie's car, where she lay down, flat across the seats. Daphne said, "I'll make Audrey dinner and put her to bed if you aren't back in time."

She didn't remember much after that until late the next morning, when, for the first time in days, her head didn't feel like the flowing lava driving down a volcano's side. The antibiotics had reduced the pain of the infection, and Daphne had made Calli some broth to sip. Both Josie and Daphne had spent the night. They took turns nursing her and entertaining Audrey.

Within a few days, her throat was still raw, but her head had cleared out.

>>> <<<

The Christmas party was a huge success.

Josie had been at the house with Calli since noon the day before. She vacuumed and decorated the banister and windows with simple white twinkle lights, set the tables and the bar, and played with Audrey while Calli polished silver, temporarily rejoicing in the chill of the air and the excitement of the season. Rachel and Daphne had been cooking and baking, calling Calli every other hour to make sure she didn't need help, giving her updates on their progress with their dishes.

Calli dressed Audrey in her Black Watch party dress again. She'd already gotten taller since Thanksgiving. Calli wasn't sure how many more wears she would get out of it. Calli planned to pack it for her to wear on Christmas Day when they went down to see her parents. Rachel had Timothy and Miller dressed in matching red wool sweaters with plaid bow ties and khaki pants. Daphne found a wide red velvet ribbon to tie around Satchmo's neck. He wasn't pleased with his necktie. In her closet, Calli found a black silk cocktail dress that she had worn the first New Year's Eve after Audrey was born. Luke and she had gone out to dinner with Henry and Eula. She loved the dress because it had a confetti pattern with explosions of color splattered across the black. It reminded her of champagne.

They had invited about forty people of all ages, congenial locals who had been so generous with their words and good deeds since Luke left. Friends and neighbors arrived in Christmas tops and festive moods. Several of the civilian ladies from their book club came, like Kelly Mumford and her sister-in-law, Freddie Mosely. Their husbands. Catherine Lansing, Violet Holmes, Sherry Weiss, Sara Path, Sierra Putnam—more civilian friends—and their husbands. The Divas all took turns playing bartender and passing hors d'oeuvres. They had food for twice the number of people who attended and blasted Christmas carols. The gas fireplace and flowing cocktails kept everyone warm. For an evening, the war was not forgotten, but it wasn't center stage.

Rachel and her boys left at midnight to drive home to Watertown. Calli suggested that they stay over, but Rachel said she wanted to sleep in her own bed. She also was leaving the next day to drive south to spend a month visiting family in North Carolina.

Josie, Daphne, and Calli stayed up most of the night. Calli kept sitting down, her mind momentarily blanking out. The stubborn remnants of her bronchitis lingered. She probably should have taken it easy, but she loved parties. Josie and Daphne spent the night, staying up to talk and drink one more bottle of wine. When Calli couldn't keep her eyes open—she told the others to go to bed, too—Daphne cleaned up the entire party by herself. By the next morning, almost every platter and piece of silver had been washed, the tables and bar torn down. She claimed insomnia drove her to stay up and finish. For breakfast, they reheated leftover ham and cheese tea sandwiches and drank steaming mugs of black coffee to cut through the cobwebs.

>>> <<<

A few days after the party, Calli drove around town to say good-bye to her friends. "Have a great Christmas. Happy New Year," she told them. "See you when we all get back. More diva dinners to come."

"I'll call ya everyday," Josie whispered as tears inched down her caramel cheeks.

"I know, I know you will. We're going to get through this," Calli assured her.

With renewed optimism about her family, she fondly remembered all the Christmases past in the Baltimore house. Tchaikovsky's *Nutcracker Suite*, Handel's *Messiah*, and Dave Brubeck's deft take on the sounds of the holiday played in her head as she drove south. Her shoulders loosened from the yoke and plow she'd pulled since Luke left. In a few hours, she'd see Lucy, Haines, Dinah, Charles,

Adelaide, and Petula, and everyone else Lucy had invited from the family to sing carols, drink spiced eggnog, binge on an enormous Christmas feast, and tear open gifts that she'd started buying last June. Calli didn't buy anyone anything. Only Audrey. Santa had to deliver something.

Eula and Henry didn't give up on the idea of hosting a dinner party for her while she was back for Christmas. "I don't give a damn if you keep saying no because I've already arranged it, and you can't not show up because you are the guest of honor," Eula said.

Eula had invited several of Luke and Calli's friends, people Calli hadn't seen for years. Eula had been kind to Luke. She continued to send him monthly care packages filled with gourmet snacks, caramels, dried fruit, and Virginia boiled peanuts. In a letter to Calli, Luke wrote, "Eula sent me a new iPod and several gift cards to buy music. There was a small Christmas tree and little ornaments, too. There is no way Christmas here will be celebrated, but in some small way, I feel as if I won't have been forgotten."

Calli sent Luke's Christmas presents over a month ago. They'd been told not to send Christmas trees because it would offend the Muslims in Yusufiyah. Lucy and Haines very generously sent him some Army boots he'd requested that Calli couldn't afford. Madelon sent him presents, too. She'd knitted him a blanket and bought him some new boxer shorts.

As Christmas Day got closer, Calli's light attitude waned as Lucy flitted about. Her nostalgia for English traditions strained Calli's nerves. She'd say things like "Father Christmas" instead of Santa Claus. It struck Calli as pretentious.

Lucy had her halls decked with armfuls of spruce, magnolia, and holly. Her talent was winding branches into gently tamed boughs and decorating them with dried twigs, fresh limes, pinecones, long cinnamon sticks, and tiny white lights. She'd decorated in the not-so-subtle hues of a British expat who grew up in old houses in Europe, surrounded by antiques. She enjoyed her journey back to Christmases long ago with candles burning in sconces, candelabras, and a chandelier. Her crystal sparkled and her arsenal of silver glittered. Haines played bartender—pouring wine, refreshing glasses. He loved buying and giving presents, never seeming to want anything in return but love. With each successive cocktail, Lucy disclosed more and more intimate details about her current classes of students and regaled Calli with the literary talk she longed for in northern New York.

Dinah was Dinah—self-absorbed, her narcissism countered by Charles's effervescent curiosity about life in Sackets, Luke, and Audrey. Adelaide and Petula ran circles through the rooms, eventually scampering off to the playroom with Audrey.

>>> <<<

Luke's absence grew more apparent each hour. Thanksgiving was easier—there was an escape plan. At Christmas, everyone was excessively joyous.

The days before Christmas were festive and bulged with cheer, singing, eating, and laughing as if they were immune to bad news. Calli hadn't received an email from Luke in several days.

There's another blackout. I'm sure of it, she thought.

Two days earlier, they'd learned that a soldier from Huey Hollis's company had been blown up by an IED, causing him to lose most of his right arm and leg. He had two little girls and a wife who was in the Army also. Something had happened. Calli's cell phone was charged and on her person always.

She'd written an email to Veronica giving her Lucy and Haines's address down in Baltimore. The protocol was to make sure that the Rear Detachment and the FRG knew how to reach her at any time in case of an emergency. Every time she left Sackets, she made sure to give her exact whereabouts and how she could be reached, emailing a detailed timeline from the moment she knew she'd be pulling out of her driveway. She didn't want to hear about Luke being wounded from anyone but the Rear Detachment Commander. Today, she felt sure that they all knew she was in Baltimore for Christmas.

Lucy and Calli took the dogs for a walk, strolling through Mt. Vernon with a clear sky and cold, crisp air that shot up into Calli's nose. Satchmo was with them, too, his black square head bobbing and his tail swinging from side to side. His unwavering love for Calli was helping her far more than she expected. Their human-animal bond provided a sense of solace and relief and helped her to cope. Satchmo was a powerful ally against the constant slideshow of disaster that played in Calli's head, Lucy's barbs, and the incident calls. She needed him.

With the dogs on leashes, the two women chatted about the plan for the day, lunch, naps, and attending the early church service so they could be back at the house for a celebration. It should have been such a normal conversation except for the nagging feeling that she hadn't heard from Luke. It felt like walking through a frontier town knowing a double-barreled shotgun lurked around the corner.

When she got back, she immediately went to the computer. There, like a muscular, thick-bodied viper, was an email. The subject line said it all:

Incident in 4-31.
One soldier killed. Seven wounded. Burned.
They were driving in a Humvee when they rolled over an IED.

⇛ 19 ⇚

Calli couldn't pinpoint the exact moment when she stopped dwelling on how awful her life was because Luke was deployed, but it happened almost without her noticing.

The invitation read, *Black-tie "in-between" party*—as in between Christmas and New Year's—sent by some friends in Baltimore. She needed a reminder that life was still good and not filled with nightmares about soldiers being blown up and killed.

Calli accepted the invitation more as a diversion from her situation. She didn't often have an excuse to get dressed up, and this party seemed as good as any—even though she had no idea who would be there.

"Hey, lady. Let's take the kids to Towson Mall," Eula called. Calli agreed. The mall's bright lights and sterile floors would distract her. When they finished eating lunch at Chick-fil-A, Eula said, "Do you mind if I slide into Nordstrom, alone, to pick up something?"

"Ahh, like a new pair of Manolos, perhaps?"

"You know me, Cal, yes you do."

Calli agreed and took the kids to the Stride Rite shoe store. An enthusiastic Audrey announced, "I'm gonna try on every shoe in the store—too big, too small—it doesn't matter." She was like a miniature Imelda Marcos hoarding all the shoes. "Mama, help me," she called to Calli wrestling a pair of miniature cowboy boots down from the shelves. As Calli pulled off her sock, she noticed that Audrey had a lacy red rash on her ankle. She pulled up Audrey's shirt. Her other pant leg. The rash covered her body.

Calli hurriedly started to put the shoes back on the shelves, trying to get three kids to cooperate with her. "Come on, girls. Help me now. Eula—your mama—will be here in a second." Quick. Quick. Quick. Calli raced to replace all the sneakers and sandals while the three girls chattered, "I like the pink sequined ones." "I want those boots." "Next Christmas, I'm gonna ask Santa for those pink ones with the Velcro."

"Girls, please! Now!" Calli pleaded. Finally, they left Stride Rite and went to find Eula.

"Audrey has a red rash over her entire body. What should I do?"

"Let me call Mama." Eula's mother was a trained RN, so Calli trusted her opinion. "We need to take her to the Emergency Room," Eula reported.

Eula drove them all back to her house. "Here, take this," Eula said and gave Calli a portable DVD player. "So you can watch a movie while you wait. Also, here are some snacks and bottles of water. You're off. She's going to be okay, Cal. I promise."

"Why do I feel like everyone keeps telling me it's going to be okay?"

"Listen. Listen to me now. Pull up your bootstraps and be strong. You can do this. I believe in you." And with that, Calli sped off to the hospital, the same hospital where she'd had Audrey three-plus years earlier.

Their wait wasn't very long, and a pediatric ER doctor saw Audrey and her within minutes of their arrival. Back in the exam room, though, the atmosphere turned to frustration when the admitting nurse kept telling Calli that her military ID wasn't proof of insurance.

"I'm sorry, but this doesn't prove anything."

"What? What are you talking about? Yes, it does. Here, let me call Fort Drum."

The crabby nurse suggested, "Why don't you just pay out of pocket for the visit and then submit the paperwork to Tricare." The nurse didn't want to deal with Tricare, and if she paid out of pocket, Calli knew it would be months and months and several phone calls and explanatory letters before she would be reimbursed.

Calli said sternly, "I'm going to call up to Fort Drum and speak to one of the nurses. To find out exactly what I need to do." After speaking with Fort Drum, she explained unflinchingly to the crabby nurse, "Please submit the paperwork to Tricare. We do have insurance. My husband is in Iraq, for God's sake." The Crab raised an eyebrow at Calli, conceding and embarrassed, then hurried off to fetch the pediatrician. Having free health care was one of the perks of being a dependent of an active-duty soldier, but it wasn't always easy to see doctors, visit the Emergency Room, or get medicine off post.

Fortunately, Audrey and Calli were at the hospital on a Thursday afternoon, not late Saturday night. The attending pediatrician, a young intellectual-looking woman with a nose like an ibis who spoke without emotion as if she was reading a list of ingredients off the back of a cereal box, took one look at Audrey and Calli and said, "Mrs. Coleman, I've never seen this before. I'll have to go back to my office and look through my books."

"Look through your books? Yikes, how long will that take?" she said. "You've never seen this?"

"Mrs. Coleman, rashes appear for many reasons. Your daughter has a bright red diffuse rash covering most of her body and cheeks. I want to make an accurate diagnosis. The upshot is that your daughter doesn't have a fever."

At least Audrey had the portable DVD player and was contently and quietly watching *Madagascar* for the hundredth time. Calli sat and stared at the antiseptic white walls and wondered how she was going to get a Red Cross message to Luke explaining that Audrey had some life-threatening rash and he needed to come home. Her mind raced as she tried to remember where the party invitation was.

She was going to call the hosts and explain to them that she was in the ER and Audrey had a mysterious rash no doctor in Baltimore could diagnose. Several minutes later, the pediatrician returned. In her hand was the heavy desk reference, with a Post-it note jutting off one of the pages. She placed the book in front of Calli and opened to the page with a picture of two little girls—both of whom had the same lacy rash as Audrey. She said to Calli, "Now, doesn't this look familiar?"

Fifth's disease. The kissing cousin of measles, mumps, and chicken pox. Why had Calli not heard of it if it was so contagious? And for that matter, why hadn't the pediatrician heard of it? No, it wasn't serious and Audrey would be fine in ten days or so. They were free to go.

Free to go. No waiting interminably in a pharmacy. No follow-up. Just free to go. So they went. Calli signed some paperwork and they packed up the portable DVD player, the snacks, drinks, and other comforts, and away they went. *I dodged a bullet*, she thought triumphantly on the car ride back to Eula's house in Guilford. There was still time to shower and go to the party, where she would know no one. Her daughter wasn't going to be ravaged by some flesh-eating rash. She wouldn't have to call Luke. Taking a very deep breath, Calli rolled down the car window to let in a raw, winter whiff and blew all her worry out into the air.

Thinking about a huge glass of red wine, Calli pulled into Henry and Eula's driveway. Henry was outside playing with the kids in their backyard. For an instant, she despised all of them because she wanted what they had. Quickly, she boxed up the resentment. Fortune had just sprinkled her dust on Audrey and her at the hospital.

Audrey unbuckled herself and ran to the swings and was relaying the hospital story to Ellen as Calli told the story to Henry. She beamed.

"Hey, C! Good news, darlin'. How about I pour you a glass of wine?"

"You read my mind, my friend. I can't wait to sit down for a minute and relax."

Her cell phone rang.

Just as surely as she'd known that the pediatrician didn't know what was wrong with Audrey, she knew that this call was a death knell. She glanced a her cell phone's caller ID, registered the number, and said, "I'm going to take this inside." All the relief and happiness from Audrey's non-illness slipped through her hands like fine sand. She retreated to the quiet of the living room and answered—reluctantly—the call from Veronica.

"Calli. It's Veronica. I'm so sorry to bother you, but there's been an incident."

"Jesus, Veronica. When is going to end? It's Christmas, for god's sake."

Two soldiers in Luke's unit had been killed when their vehicle struck an IED. Two more soldiers, only two days after Christmas. Now, three soldiers had died within five days and seven had been wounded. When would this Hell end?

Laughter and squeals permeated the glass window, Henry's deep voice joining the cacophony, evoking an alternate universe where Luke wasn't a soldier at war but rather a businessman who wore a necktie and lace-up shoes. Calli envisioned herself out there swinging with them, the smooth, curving motion, swaying back and forth; she wanted to be three years old again. She remembered a colossal oak tree next to a small lake at her grandparents' farm where her grandfather had tied a swing, a stout wooden seat that little knees could lock onto, with a thick manila rope suspended from sturdy tree branches. The swing was fastened so high that the rope disappeared into the canopy of a huge laurel oak. Pumping hard, she could swing fifteen feet above the water, miming wings and taking off in flight. Besides riding her grandmother's gray Welsh ponies, swinging on that swing on hot, sticky days filled her young heart with ruckus and mayhem. Haines and her grandfather sipped beer and fished for spotted sunfish with worms Calli and Dinah dug up outside the stallion barn. Always there was a glycerin aroma of saddle soap from the tack room and freshly mowed pastures of switch grass and tall fescue. The ponies whinnied at Dinah and her as they ran past them to the swing by the lake. If she had sugar cubes stuffed into her small fists, she'd stop and feed the ponies off her palms, then scamper down to the lake. She wanted to fly.

The ephemeral image vanished, and soon she was sobbing on the sofa. It was Christmas, for goodness' sake. Why? Why now? Why ever?

Calli walked outside and explained to Henry, sighing and gently nodding. "There's been another incident."

"Oh, darlin', I'm sorry. Are you okay?" He hugged her and she rested her ear against his chest. His heart beat loudly through his jacket. His warmth shattered her strength as she acceded to his embrace, collapsing into him.

"Two KIAs."

"I know this is hard, but we have to be grateful that Lukey isn't one of them."

"It's just awful. It's Christmas, Henry. It will never be the same."

"No. No it won't."

"I probably won't be long at the party but I need to go. I already RSVP'd, and I'm not going to renege on my word.I'm not going to let the Bad Guys win. I won't."

That evening Calli turned the corner. For months, she had allowed herself to be the victim. The war tried to devour her, to prey on her vulnerabilities. Now was time to break out her sling and five stones.

Calli arrived in her long black silk gown, with squeaky-clean hair and perfect lipstick. After pulling into the Baltimore Country Club, she handed her car keys over to the valet. A ghost of the life she used to have before they'd moved to New York haunted the porte cochere. The cold night fostered a breath from earlier days. She pretended to be one of them, one of the civilians who'd just celebrated Christmas or Hanukah. She pretended that the afternoon in the hospital with her daughter's strange rash never happened. She pretended that the phone call only a couple of hours earlier had been happy news. She pretended that she was fine, just a woman out on the town celebrating the season.

Of the two hundred fifty people there, Calli knew only the host and hostess. She sauntered over to one of the bars, ordered a glass of Chardonnay, and slowly but intently walked around the grand ballroom and smaller side areas in the wings. Clenching her teeth and taking a deep breath, Calli stopped staring out the window. Go introduce yourself to someone, she said to herself. I didn't come here to look out a window. I'm going to walk straight up to a group of people, feign interest in their conversation, and introduce myself. Force yourself, Calli! Meet people and ask them about themselves. After a hefty swig of wine, she put on her autopilot as she had learned to do so well over the last months.

Just keep moving forward.

A small group of three women on the other side of the ballroom looked friendly enough. Bull's-eye. Her mind raced through its arsenal of conversation starters: What do you like to do for a hobby? or Are you from Baltimore originally? or Where do your children go to school? Her laundry list of topics sprouted at a rapid rate, from Christmas adventures to geese flight patterns, anything but who she was. Tomorrow she was driving down to Walter Reed again to see more wounded soldiers. Tonight, she was Cinderella.

Dear Immortal Wives and Mothers,
As I look into the sunset of 2006 and think back on all that I've learned, seen, heard, accomplished, forgotten, cried about, and laughed about, I am stunned at the range of emotions. It seems like eons ago that Luke and I were on block leave, savoring each day knowing that we would be separated for so long. We are ending this cruel year on a sad note, leaving behind six Immortals, but we must keep up our morale for 2007. We must continue to pray for our

men, as well as their wives and their children. Please take care of yourselves and give yourselves time each day to pamper yourselves with a nap, a good book, a phone call with a friend, your children or parents, or just take a nice walk and get a snoot of fresh air.

I was at Walter Reed again yesterday and was not able to see Richard Strong because he had a pass to go away. However, that is the good news since it means that he is doing well. Additionally, one of the Immortal Mothers, Ande Prather—mother of Chad Pritchet—flew in from Ohio to visit our wounded warriors and I got to meet her as well. We were so impressed when we watched a video of Richard WALKING! Yes, I saw it with my own eyes! Plus, we can dub him Lee Majors because his new prosthetic arm looks just like the Bionic Man's hand. AMAZING how far we've come in that technology.

Let's pray that 2007 brings us peace.

Best,

Calli

Christmas week was Hell for Calli. She received an incident call almost daily. She attempted to be jolly for everyone else's sake; for Christmas's sake. Yet, inside all she could focus on were the families who would never be able to celebrate Christmas or New Year's in quite the same way ever again. A monstrous cloud hung over the homes of the families visited by the Trifecta that week. The same week, she learned of a young boy—a family friend's son—who was driving on Christmas Eve after he'd been drinking. He drove off a country lane, missing his turn on a poorly illuminated street, and flipped his car. Both of his arms and legs were broken. Calli felt little about the boy, thinking, That's not so bad.

She supposed it was her mind's way of coping: We're losing men at a terrifying frequency. I can no longer spend days crying in agony for the soldier who stepped on an IED and instantly lost a leg and an arm. I don't even cry at the memorial services anymore. I still have a dreadful feeling before the memorial services begin, but even the words to "Amazing Grace" no longer push me into the emotional puddle.

The ringing phone continued to make her pause, but an aggressive resilience shrouded her. She asked Daphne, "Did this happen to you? This numbness? Is this what soldiers go through in war?"

Several of her mother's friends and people from Baltimore said to her, "Oh, you are fortunate to have email and constant communication. It was a catch-22, though, because access to the Internet, cell phones, and instant messaging had changed everything. If she didn't receive an email from Luke every day, she envisioned the worst.

Calli thought of Rose, a fifteen-year-old babysitter they'd had for a few months when they first moved Sackets. Rose's father, Colonel Frank Rexel, had deployed to Iraq with First Brigade Combat Team in August 2005, a few months before the Colemans moved to Sackets Harbor. Rose would relay to Calli stories of her father and how this was his final deployment before retiring.

"Where do you think you'll move when your father retires?" Calli said.

"We don't like cold weather. We've been stationed at Fort Drum for seven years. My mom wants to return to North Carolina or Kentucky. You know, someplace warmer! My dad said he'd let my mom decide since she's followed him around for twenty years. It'll be great. I'm kinda sick of this place."

Rose had a certain sturdiness that must have been the result of being the eldest of three daughters and the child of a man who had deployed three times in six years. At fifteen, she was more seasoned in surviving deployments than Calli would ever be. She and her mother were also quite close and were the glue that kept the family together during her father's long absences. One afternoon when Rose was scheduled to babysit, she didn't show up. It was strange, so unlike reliable Rose. Calli tried to call her, but there was no answer.

Two days later, Rose called Calli. Her voice, unwavering, very casually said, "I'm sorry that I didn't show up, Mrs. Coleman, but something beyond my control has happened. I have to go out of town for a while. I'm not sure when I'll be back."

Calli said, "Rose, is everything okay?"

Rose, evenly, said, "I'll tell you when I get back. Okay? Bye."

A bit angry and very confused, Calli hung up the phone. Calli didn't like Rose's cryptic tone. These teenagers. They just don't care that people depended on them sometimes, Calli thought.

Later that day, Louise, who had referred Rose, called Calli.

"Calli, yeah, it's Louise. Listen, hon, Colonel Rexel is in critical condition at Walter Reed Army Medical Center."

"What?"

"Yeah. He and two other soldiers were in a vehicle that drove over a roadside bomb in Baghdad. The other guys were killed instantly. Colonel Rexel has serious head trauma. Prognosis isn't good."

"Oh my god. Poor Rose. Oh, poor, poor Rose."

Rose had mentioned none of this on the phone to Calli; not even a hint that something dismal had just happened to her beloved father. He died five days later with Rose and Mrs. Rexel at his side.

Calli never asked her to babysit for them afterward. Calli couldn't even look at her for several months. Sometimes when she was driving she would see Rose walking in the village and pretend that she hadn't seen her.

>>> <<<

On a dingy, drizzly morning Calli announced, "Mother, I'm going home today." Her time in Baltimore had been filled with raw emotions. The Divas had returned to northern New York and Calli missed them. She was ready to be back in her own home, sleeping in her bed.

"Why? I thought you were going to stay until the middle of January?"

"Mother, I'm exhausted. I just want to be in my house."

"Okay, if that's how you feel."

"Yes, it is how I feel. Why do you make me feel guilty?"

"I'm not making you feel guilty. If you feel guilty, then that's because you must be guilty."

"Guilty of what?"

"I don't know Calli, you tell me."

"Seriously, Mother. What are you talking about? Sometimes I feel like you want me to be here because it makes *you* feel better about Luke, like you can pawn off all your fear on me. I know you're worried. I get it, but I can't help you. Being here isn't my reality. I don't know what reality is anymore. But this is not it. I can't pretend my life is the way it used to be. I can't pretend anymore. I'm so sick and tired of this Baltimore bullshit. People being stupid."

"Are you saying your father and I are stupid, Calliope?"

"No! No Mother, I'm not. I'm sorry. I know you sort of get it. But only my friends up there get the war the way I do. It's barely even headline news unless a soldier's been killed. How are we going to get out of this? I mean it."

"I don't know."

"I don't know, either. But I do know this. People down here don't get it. My friends up there, they get it."

"Okay, I just don't want you to be alone. You and Audrey all the way up there."

"Mother, I'm okay. I promise. I love you. I know you're worried about me, but I'll be okay. Just please, please understand that I'm not doing this to hurt you. I've got to be there for my own sanity."

"Your father and I would buy you a house here if you wanted."

"Mother! We have been over this. I really, really appreciate your offer, but no. I have a house. I'm going back to that house."

Lucy sighed. "I've loved having you here. It's been great."

"Thanks. I've had a great time, too."

When Calli got back to Sackets Harbor, she had barely gotten Audrey settled and herself unpacked when Lisa Herbie, one of the Army wives, called: "Calli. It's Lisa. Remember we met at Veronica's? And you had on that really cool necklace, the one with the antler, and when you brought the chocolate chip cookies over—which I loved by the way—and you said I could ask you anything?"

Calli didn't remember saying anything to Lisa like that. "Oh yes, hi Lisa. How are you?"

"You see, well, I just don't want to move to California. With Howard. My brother. It's a long story, but I need to stay with you; you seemed so nice when you came over to deliver the cookies, and I just don't want to move to California with Howard; he's a bit, well, strange, and his wife doesn't particularly like me because she thinks I told Howard that she's a shoplifter—which she is—but I didn't tell him that."

"Hmm, I'm sorry about that—"

"I saw her do it, and she pretended that she'd already bought the makeup, when I know she put it in her purse."

"Oh, okay. Are you and your brother—"

"Howard."

"Howard. Are you close?"

"Howard's a policeman, and that Veronica McLeod is, I don't know, kind of a bitch, and she looks at me funny when I go to the FRG meetings, and the other wives all seem so young but you; you're probably my age—thirty-six, right? —And we know more about life than these younger wives, we've seen more than they have, and my neighbor, I just know she's going to call that cunt Veronica McLeod and tell her that I was the one who knocked over her gnome, like I'd even step foot on that cunt's yard, and Joseph says Master Sergeant Luke is such a great guy, a great leader and inspiration and a movie star from Panama who knows all the famous people in Hollywood, even though most of them are Democrats and I'm not—I'm a Republican, but I think Master Sergeant Luke is a good person and that you're probably good, too, even though you have blond hair, the same color as my mother's—"

"Lisa are you okay?" Calli was confounded by this irrational call.

"Well, yes, yes, and it's just that well, I really need a place to stay, and you always send those nice emails to all of us, encouraging everyone to reach out to you if they need something—so I'm asking if I can stay with you a few weeks until Joseph comes home on leave."

There were no words that could help Lisa. Holding the phone away from her ear, she knew she was getting acquainted—too acquainted—with schizophrenia in the form of Lisa Herbie. She hardly knew Lisa Herbie. She and her husband had arrived at Fort Drum about the same time as the Colemans. They'd met at Veronica's. A few days later, Veronica asked Calli if she'd mind stopping by Lisa's to welcome her to the unit, "You know, because you're Luke's wife and there's the whole movie business. Lisa might like that."

Reluctantly, Calli made Lisa some chocolate chip cookies and took them to her apartment at Fort Drum. When Lisa invited her into her on-post apartment, Calli immediately noticed at least six prescription bottles sitting out on her coffee table. Lisa quickly said matter-of-factly, "I injured my back bending over to stock the shelves at the supermarket where I worked in Seattle, where we were stationed before Joseph was moved to Fort Drum."

"Oh, I'm sorry to hear that. I have back pain sometimes, too."

"You don't know pain like this, trust me—I can barely take care of myself and I'll never have children. Every move is violently excruciating, and I know the prick who was my manager planned for everyone else to be busy and made me stock the shelves even though he knew—he knew because I'd told him when he hired me and the neighbor across the street, that cunt, she watches me out her window. I see her stare at me when I get the mail."

Calli nodded pleasantly. Lisa's hair was greasy and there was a sallowness about her complexion, like someone who hadn't eaten well in a long time. It was odd that Lisa never really changed her tone except when she used words like prick and cunt.

"I'm in pain, Calli. Can you help me find someone to drive me around? Maybe you could help me find someone to come pick me up for my physical therapy sessions. Could you help me find friends, because the only people I've met so far are young military wives, who are morons, and some ladies from a born-again, right-wing, zealot church who don't know that I can hear what they are saying about me behind my back. I need you to drive me around because you're Master Sergeant Luke's Hollywood wife and we need to stick together, you know what I mean, because those other cunts, well, I just think they don't realize I can hear what they are saying. Can I call you if I need a friend?"

In Calli's mind, Lisa had used up her quota of favors within the first ten minutes of Calli being in her home.

A few months into the deployment and Lisa was zeroing in on Calli again. This situation was beyond Calli's capabilities. Lisa's deteriorated mental state frightened her a bit, like the time she'd witnessed a teenage boy have an epileptic seizure at the mall when she was a young girl. There was no help Calli could provide. When Lisa finally finished going on and on about needing a place to live, Calli calmly deliberated with her for an hour, trying to negotiate a way off the phone.

"Lisa, I have to go. I promise I'll look into something for you."

"Calli, listen I need to move in with you—"

"Lisa. Listen to me. I live in Sackets. You don't want to live out here—"

"That cunt sister-in-law of mine thinks she doesn't know that I know what she's saying about me to Howard—"

"Lisa, my daughter is calling me. I really have to go. I'll help you, but I have to go now. Bye." Calli practically hung up on her.

Dearest Calli,

Happy New Year! I am so in love with you it hurts. There is nothing more in the world more important to me than your love. I hope you always remember that. I'm ecstatic that you are playing guitar again, and I love the lyrics you've sent so far. You're really onto something. This deployment absolutely sucks, but the thought of spending the rest of my life with you is what helps me get through each day.

I finally finished the last of my care package thank-you notes. So many kind people, it's hard to be timely. I am writing this letter with a beautiful fountain pen from Eula and Henry. They have been so kind.

How are you feeling? I know the travel over the holidays was stressful, and I think you made the right decision heading back to Sackets.

I just saw Huey. He was out last night with his boys. He is doing a very good job here despite the complexity of this fight. In some ways it's like Panama—armed thugs, militia, etc. In many ways, it is completely different. We see the Sunni-versus-Shia struggle here daily—not always fighting—but we hear the local mosque sermons denouncing the other side. All that "don't do this or that to offend the Muslims" is crap. Other than the fact that they pray five times a day, they are no different than any other religion. There are devout Muslims and there are asshole Muslims. Looking back on everything post 9/11, the fact that none of the peace-loving Muslims clerics in America denounced the attacks shows what hypocrites they are—not ALL of them by any means—but we are so afraid of offending them. If there is any group of people that should be asking us to stay in Iraq, it is them. But where are they? They sure as shit aren't here helping to preserve the Holy Land of Allah. It would be like Christians allowing Bethlehem to be surrounded by the Palestinians.

Sorry about that rant, my love! It's 1430 and the mail arrived! Thankfully the DVD players arrived safe and sound. I was so afraid that they had been stolen. They are very nice DVD players. I will pass several out here and there

*for the boys. You have done an excellent job, once again!
Thank you from the bottom of my heart. I plan on continuing Operation Morale next year and want to expand it to
include the kids at Walter Reed and the burn center in San
Antonio.*

*I love you so much and hope you are smiling while you
read this. I know I am all over the map, there is always just
so much to write and nowhere to begin. I love you and can't
wait until May when I come home for leave. It will be so
great to come home, then by the time I return to Iraq, we'll
literally be packing to come home.*

*You are doing a wonderful job, my love. Be safe and know
my heart belongs to you always.*
Love,
Luke

Calli sat down to write Luke a letter with more lyrics of some
of the songs she'd been working on. Audrey was still asleep. It was
early in the morning. These were her coffee moments. The aroma of
fresh coffee filled their house, and while she drank a steaming mug
at her desk underneath a window, she'd look out at their backyard
to the derelict barn across the pasture that abutted their property as
it stood like a very old man trying desperately to stand up against
the wind and weather of northern New York. Vines crept up its
side and invaded the gaps. The roof, semi-collapsed, might not be
there tomorrow. Every morning Calli checked on it. Played a game
with herself: If the remaining roof is still there tomorrow then that
means Luke is okay.

As she pulled out her favorite pen and notepaper, her phone
rang.

Ring, ring, ring...

Calli bristled. No. Not again. It was early morning, and she had
planned on spending the day playing with Audrey. She had been
so busy with her own life, the FRG, the wives, the casualties, the

phone calls, the email, that she felt like she'd neglected Audrey. It was Veronica.

There was no way she couldn't answer. These calls chased her wherever she went. There was no escape.

"Hi, Calli. Listen, it's not an incident—"

"Oh, thank god!"

"It's about Brittany Lunderman." Brittany was the very young wife of one of Luke's privates, Rick. "She just called me in tears. She's pregnant from her ex-boyfriend and Rick knows."

"Why didn't she call me?"

"She said she's afraid that you'll tell Luke. I'd help, but I have to deal with my eighteen-year-old who got caught smoking pot behind school."

"Okay, okay. What a mess. These poor guys have enough to worry about and now she's gone and gotten herself pregnant—with her ex-boyfriend? I'll call her. I won't tell Luke. She's so young, Veronica. I mean, what is she, eighteen, nineteen?"

"Something like that. Brittany called me to tell me that she thought she was having a miscarriage and was on her way to Planned Parenthood. When she was in Ohio over the holidays, she went out one night to a party. Her ex-boyfriend was there, and Brittany told me that she remembers nothing except that the next morning she woke up in the ex-boyfriend's bed. Now she is claiming that she was raped by this guy, but she never reported it or had an examination at the hospital."

Calli hung up with Veronica and immediately dialed Brittany's cell phone.

"Hi, Calli. I'm about to go into to the exam room. I'll call you back."

Calli should have realized that there were some red flags the moment she hung up, but thinking Brittany had been raped, she didn't stop and think.

Calli initially met Brittany and Rick soon after the birth of their child, Hannah, at the first incident briefing that fall. Brittany was eighteen and had a pierced tongue. Rick, nineteen, was short and had dodgy black eyes. They had gathered in the chapel at Fort Drum to hear about the first incident, a soldier who'd been killed in Iraq. Most of the wives sat close to the back of the chapel, as if shielding themselves against the severe news and all its details.

Brittany and Rick and their one-week-old baby, Hannah, sat behind Calli. Everyone sat rigidly in the pews, as shocked as she was to hear the details of Specialist Taylor's incident. Calli leaned over and asked Veronica, "Who are they?"

"Oh, he's with Luke over there at the same FOB. He's home on leave to be with Brittany." Veronica said, "Rick is trouble. I heard he lied to Luke to get home earlier for his leave."

Calli went over and introduced herself. "Hi, Brittany. Hi, Rick. I'm Luke's wife, Calli Coleman. It's nice to meet you."

Brittany held the baby, awkwardly rocking her side to side, while Rick stood up and shook Calli's hand, but looked over her shoulder into the distance. "Hi. Nice to meet you."

Awkwardly, Calli said, "Well, I just wanted to introduce myself." A month later Calli saw Brittany again. She had called Calli, crying. "Can I please come over to your house? Please?"

Brittany arrived with tiny Hannah in tow. Attached to the hip of her tight jeans was a pink sequined cell phone, the kind Calli had seen teenagers at the mall carrying on their hips. Brittany had probably been one of those teenagers just last year. Now she lugged a baby in a car seat, a large diaper bag, her own purse, and the garish cell phone. Brittany's face looked care-worn at eighteen with a wanness that evoked exhaustion. Her body was still plump, bulging in her jeans from pregnancy like a satiated tick; it was evident that this girl had not had an easy time of it, ever. Hannah, bundled in a fuzzy white bunting, innocent and unassuming, was strapped into the car seat. As Brittany started to take her out, the ringtone on her phone, an animated version of some pop song Calli didn't recognize, started. "Yeah, lemme call you back," she said to someone.

With her, Brittany brought a stack of printed email—proof that Rick was cheating on her, if not physically, at least emotionally, with another girl. "Look at these. Like, like she doesn't even care about me. It's like I'm not here."

"Let me see," Calli said. Who was this girl who brazenly wrote, *I want to hold your cock in my mouth* and *I touch myself when I think of you* knowing full well he was married and a father?

"I've been instant messaging Rick. Like, I told him, 'I know about the email.' He told me he doesn't write her back. Liar." This worried Calli. How was she instant messaging Rick? No matter how justified Brittany's fears may have been, their troubles were distracting Rick from his job as a soldier, potentially endangering not only his life but also the lives of the other men with him.

The vulgar pink sequined phone rang again. Without excusing herself, Brittany answered. She must have known who it was because of the caller ID on the phone. As she walked outside coatless onto the deck, leaving Hannah, Calli heard "Yeah, what?...Shut up, bitch."

Audrey said, "Who is that girl, Mama?"

Calli explained to her, "Mommy was just helping Hannah's mommy," then ushered Audrey down to her playroom. Calli held Hannah in her arms while she sat on the sofa waiting for Brittany to return. Holding Hannah suddenly aroused Calli's attention. Would Audrey have a sibling someday? she thought. It amused her to consider another baby, but she was soon interrupted. There was a muffled shout and then Brittany walked in, crying. Soon, the ringtone went off again.

The girl on the other end, Spike, was the woman her husband was chasing. "Brittany, let me have the phone." Taking the phone, Calli said, "Spike. I am a friend of Brittany's. My husband is Brittany's husband's boss. Listen, it's just not a good idea to be writing sexy, provocative emails to Rick in Iraq."

"Who the Hell are you, bitch?" Spike screamed at Calli.

Calli took a big breath. "Spike, try to understand my point of view."

Not backing down, Spike replied, "I'll do whatever the fuck I want, you fat bitch." Calli calmly handed the phone back to Brittany.

"I don't think your calling her is going to make this situation better. Really, Brittany. Stop calling her. Don't answer if she calls you," Calli told Brittany when she hung up. But Brittany stared at the floor, her total indifference to Calli's words summed up in a shrug.

>>>> <<<<

Now, months later, when Brittany called Calli back, she explained, "Planned Parenthood told me to go to the hospital and to take another person with me to help me with Hannah. Could you come?"

Calli paused before answering, thinking about Audrey, about her marriage with Luke, and about how even though the seams in her own life had unraveled in one sense, she never questioned Luke's loyalty. "Yes, I'll take you. But Brittany, would it be okay with you if I call JAG to find out exactly what to do about the rape? We need to make sure we know the protocol. I'd feel better if we had some information. Is that okay with you?"

"Yeah, I guess. Sure." Brittany's voice was sluggish, like someone who'd just woken up from a long night's sleep.

Calli called JAG. "Hi, I'm Calli Coleman. I'm an FRG Leader. My husband is deployed. He's attached to one of the infantry units. Anyway, one of my husband's soldier's spouses has been date-raped. She's pregnant. She hasn't had a gynecological exam or reported the rape yet." The whole time Calli was explaining the situation, though, she kept hearing this little voice saying, "You know she is lying to you, Calli. She is taking you for a ride, and you are letting her because you want some kind of accolade. You want to save the day."

But regardless of this voice, Calli appeased Brittany. She left Audrey with Josie and took Brittany to Samaritan Hospital in Watertown. Calli still wasn't clear why they were going to the hospital.

In the car, Calli said, "All right, you don't have to answer me if you don't want to because it's none of my business, but what happened?"

"What do you mean?"

"Like, when did this happen?"

"I'm trying to figure out how pregnant I am. Maybe the baby is Rick's from when he was home on leave."

"But he was home several months ago."

"It might be his."

"Then when was the, the incident?" Calli shuttered at the word, but it popped out before she could think of a better one. "It's January. I thought you said you saw your ex-boyfriend at Christmas. I'm just trying to help, Brittany. It's really none of my business, but do you think you're one month pregnant or three months pregnant?" Calli said and then thought, I may not be a math genius, but I can figure out how many months have passed since Rick was home. Was the miscarriage a ruse? Had she really been raped? Calli drove.

"When I spoke to Rick, I told him I was pregnant. Now he wants me out of the house, saying Hannah's not his child. I'm thinking I'm going to get an abortion."

Abortion? I thought she was having a miscarriage, Calli thought.

>>> <<<

She had taken someone to get an abortion before. When Calli was in her junior year at Juilliard, she befriended a likable, winsome girl named Sylvie Perez-Padilla who also played the French horn. Sylvie had grown up in Barcelona in a prim Catholic family and wore faded blue Chucks with every outfit she owned—even in the snow. Her father loved the US so she spent her summers on Fishers Island on her parents' estate, where they'd arrive each June. The first time Calli visited Sylvie there, she was awed. Sylvie was the best slalom water skier Calli had ever witnessed.

Sylvie, Calli, and Calli's friend Gwynne became the closest of friends. They were always together, ate lunch every day, partied together at the same bars, and borrowed each other's clothes. The guys all fell for Sylvie's luscious black curly hair, startling deep-azure eyes, and Spanish accent. The summer after their junior year, Sylvie—back on Fishers Island—met and fell in love with a Benjamin Caspar; a guy who'd attended Yale briefly before dropping out to become a bartender on Fishers Island. She wrote Calli a beachy postcard: *I am smitten. XOXO - Sylvie*

Calli didn't hear from Sylvie again until the day before they were supposed to be back at school, when they were both back in the city. Sylvie called and said, "I think I, I . . . might be pregnant. Will you go to the store and buy a pregnancy test for me?"

Calli had heard of girls in high school who'd gotten pregnant, but she thought Sylvie was wiser in the contraception department. Calli bought the test for her. Sylvie was positive. Positively pregnant.

"Does Benjamin know?"

"No . . . no one knows."

"You should tell Benjamin. He's your boyfriend."

"I'm not sure I'm in love with him anymore. He doesn't have any ambition. You have to take me, Calli. You're my best friend."

"Take you?"

"You know. I can't have the baby. I'm only twenty. My family would flip. I really need you to help me."

In the end it was Calli who took her, watched her quietly go into the room at some clinic in the East Village. It still didn't sit well with Calli that Benjamin wasn't there. She expected Sylvie to be teary and emotional when she came out.

But when she did, she said with a crooked smile, "Okay, let's go." Never looked at Calli while she tucked a thin brown paper bag under her arm.

"Are you all right? How do you feel?"

"I'm fine. Let's just go."

On the ride home, she said to Calli, "I'm definitely going to break up with Benjamin tonight."

"Really? Are you going to tell him?"

"Why? Why should I tell him? It's over. He doesn't need to know."

"I don't know. I think I'd tell him."

"Calli. It was my mistake. Why ruin his life? No. It's my secret. It's just something I'll have to live with."

Calli walked Sylvie to her room, again asking if she needed anything. "No thanks."

Sylvie and Calli were close all through the rest of college, but for some reason they lost touch a few years after graduation. Her Christmas card was a single composition, usually of her three raven-haired kids on their sloop in Fishers Island or at her manse in Barcelona, her beguiling husband squeezing her while she stared out at the photographer with her gorgeous hair and deep eyes twinkling. Calli always wondered, Does he know?

⋙ ⋘

Calli dropped Brittany off at the front doors of the Emergency Room while she parked her car. After searching for ten minutes for a place to park, Calli finally pulled into a spot on the far side of the lot and unbuckled Hannah. Poor Hannah. Her parents were a mess.

Inside the waiting room, the white antiseptic walls and uncomfortable chairs depressed Calli. It was eleven o'clock in the morning. A larger woman in jeans squeezed into one of the chairs across from her. She feigned interest in the show on the TV hanging in the corner above the piggy woman's head. There were soldiers there, too. Fort Drum didn't have its own hospital so the military used Samaritan. It was a far cry from the hospitals Calli was used to in Baltimore. Here, there was a little girl who'd super-glued her eyes shut because her mother hadn't put it away somewhere safe, and the sluggish receptionist seemed more interested in the Internet than in helping them.

Shortly thereafter, a paramedic rolled a wheelchair into the room. In it was a woman with a pinched red face and squinty eyes that didn't concentrate on anything. She retched into a metal bowl in her lap. The paramedic helped her out of the wheelchair and laid her sideways on a row of chairs. Calli looked down at Hannah, who smiled at her. At four months old, she'd begun to develop her emotions. Brittany and Calli watched sitcoms, maybe three to four hours of laugh tracks, until finally Brittany was called into the exam room for a sonogram. Calli waited with Hannah for another two hours. The skin on her face grew hot as her anger rose.

At four o'clock, a nurse called to Calli, "Brittany would like to see you, come on back." She gathered Hannah in her arms and went back into the exam rooms. Brittany was lying on her side in a white, backless hospital gown on a bed in a small room. Calli noticed her cell phone glued to her hand. "Rick called me four times already today." Then she said, "The sonogram says I'm pregnant."

"Are you okay? You didn't have a miscarriage?" Calli said, all the while concluding that Rick must have his own mobile phone. No one was supposed to have his own phone. They were verboten. At a pre-deployment meeting Colonel Capslock clearly spelled that out. "No soldier will be permitted a personal cell phone. In the event a soldier is captured, a cell phone becomes a tool for the enemy."

"Yeah. Um, no. I went to Planned Parenthood thinking I was going to get an abortion, but when I got there I chickened out. But then Rick said he wouldn't support me. Or Hannah. So I figured I had to get an abortion. But I really didn't know how pregnant I was. I really thought maybe it was Rick's. It's not. I'm going to stay here and have an abortion. Can you watch Hannah for me?"

"Of course. But what happened. Were you really date raped?"

"No. I just thought you'd be mad at me if I told you I cheated."

Calli shook her head, unable to disguise her frustration. Confused and grumpy, she had wasted an entire day sitting in this foul hospital waiting room with a girl who had lied to her, watching her baby. Calli had wanted to be with Audrey today. She didn't know how to respond. "I'm not in a position where I can advise you one way or the other. The decision is yours," Calli said. "Listen, Brittany, I'll take Hannah back to my house. Once you can come home, call me and I'll come get you. But will you do me a favor? Just make sure you talk to the doctor about getting some contraception. Okay?"

"Yeah. I will. Thanks, Calli."

When Calli got home, she called Veronica and told her, "I am through with FRG. Sorry to leave you hanging, but I've had enough."

"What? Why? What's going on?"

"Between Lisa, Brittany, the call-outs, and the incidents, I'm falling apart."

"Oh, Calli."

"It's okay, I'll be okay. I can't take on these wives' problems. I'm sorry. Someone else will need to step in."

≫≫ 20 ≪≪

Patrol Base Yusufiyah
January 19, 2007

Dear friends and families of the Immortals,
Happy New Year and warm wishes from your men in Iraq!
I apologize for the very late report. Time has passed quickly
since my last update. I will ensure that we get our updates
out in a much timelier manner in 2007. We thank you all
for all your prayers and support over the past few months.
Each day that passes brings us one day closer to returning
home.

The men are doing an outstanding job with their assigned
missions. This is a very complicated environment to say
the least, yet your soldiers are undaunted in their pur-
suit of victory. We have made steady progress in our area
of operation (AO) and continue to push the enemy away
from the local population. We, like all of you, are trying to
read the tea leaves as to the future of Iraq. I will tell you
that each day is different as so many outside factors influ-
ence the battlefield daily. In the end, though, whatever the

atmosphere of the environment, the Immortals continue to do what they do best: SOLDIER.

Your men are spread from Baghdad to the Euphrates River, and several spots in between. Though I do not see each of the men regularly, someone from any particular platoon is in touch with another soldier at least weekly. Our phones have been installed at the Patrol Base in Yusufiyah, so voice messages should be somewhat more regular depending on the tempo. The men at the river have access to a satellite phone every few days; again, it is all depends on the particular operations that are being executed. We are in the middle of a big move of platoons across the area, so some of you may be out of contact with your soldier for a week or so. Please be patient with the system.

One of the observations I have made over the course of the deployment, and certainly something I am very proud of, is the resilience of the men in Alpha Company. Though we are separated from each other as a company, with three completely different missions, the men have reacted to these challenges with positive attitudes. They responded with the tenacity and dedication necessary to win, anywhere, anytime. Four months into this soup and these men, YOUR men, are as poised and ready as they were on the first day. I wish that I could take some credit for this, but the truth is that this success is because of each of you. You are the ones who set the values that guide these men. You are the ones who taught them how to be men. It is no stretch to say that you each hold a piece of the victory trophy at the end of this deployment. It certainly makes the commander's and my job much easier. Your soldiers have opened previously impassible roads that we took from the enemy. Your soldiers have captured wanted enemy personnel. Your soldiers have helped provide safety for schools so local children could go back to school. Your soldiers are right in the middle of enforcing foreign policy and doing it very well. You should all be proud of the men and the job they are doing. There is so much more to say, but again, due to the OPSEC restrictions I am obligated to wait until we get home.

I also want to thank all the ladies of the FRG. Often I think that the job of the spouse at home is more difficult that the job we have here. Information is always too slow to disseminate; that is a given in the deployment world. Please take a moment to thank the wives who make up the FRG team. They all work so hard to ensure that the spouses are as informed as possible. We have several very generous support groups who routinely provide the men with wonderful gifts and goods from the US. We have received DVDs, books, magazines, food—you name it! It must seem odd back home to try and understand the living conditions of your soldiers. We run the spectrum from almost extravagant (in Baghdad) to primitive (at the river). But, all in all, our men are hanging tough each and every day. We are trying our best to ensure that their needs are met so that they can focus on their mission. As we have said time and time again, this is a marathon and not a sprint. So, anything that I can do to help make the tour here a little more bearable for the men is my goal. Thank you all for your love and support.

This particular holiday was very difficult for all of us. But the good news is that we are all in this together. We have been through some very dramatic and sad events here but have also responded with some overwhelmingly positive actions and events that have shown the true spirit of these great patriots. We must be relentless in both our path to victory and our obligation to mutually support each other. We will take care of the former. We need you to continue to help with the latter. I look back on the events of 2006 *and count so many blessings. They are often disguised, but when I look hard enough I am thankful for the opportunity to be associated with such brave and noble men. They live right here with me 24/7.*

We wish you all the best for a safe and healthy 2007. We'll be heading down the backstretch before you know it. We will look forward to the reunion at the airfield! God bless you all.

Luke Coleman
Master Sergeant
The Immortals

The northern New York winter toiled on. The war continued in the Middle East. Calli and the Divas continued to have their Tuesday night dinners and monthly book club meetings with the local women from Sackets Harbor. Her guitar and songwriting kept her creativity plump and diverted from the status quo. Some days the temperatures outside were in the negatives. And with the wind chill, it wasn't uncommon to see minus twenty on the thermometer. The tree swing had vanished beneath the white quilt of snow, leaving two long ropes plunging into the powder. Just south of them, the snowdrifts piled more than ten feet high on the sides of the roads. Calli had never seen snow like that before or felt such cold. It was cold in Iraq and Afghanistan now, too. Such extremes.

Rachel reported that her husband Aidan's brigade's stay had been extended in Afghanistan until late June. The Divas had a morale booster dinner for Rachel. Calli ordered a bunch of sex toys—vibrators of varying sizes and colors, edible lotions, faux-fur-lined-handcuffs, fruity lubricants, black feather nipple clamps, sex position cards, Ben Wa balls, and erotic lingerie—and for a few minutes, Rachel and the rest of them howled with laughter. They never talked about how she and Aidan would be separated for eighteen months by the time he got back.

After the Divas had gone through several bottles of wine, they analyzed the sex toys, the lingerie, the lacy bras. "Have you had a mammogram?" said Daphne.

"Not yet, why?" Calli said.

"Well, get ready. When you turn forty, you get to have your boobs squished."

"Daphne!" Rachel screeched.

"It's true. They flatten them out like pancakes."

"I have a phobia about mammograms," Rachel said.

"Why?" Josie asked.

"Do you know where the emergency switch is to turn the machine off? What if the technician faints and your boob is stuck between the plates? What do you do?"

"What?!?" Calli roared.

"It could happen. And no one would hear you screaming for help because the room is soundproofed. I'm short enough that I'd be dangling there with my boob stuck while I tried to locate the off switch!"

"Only you, Rachel. Being married to a doctor has fried your brain," Josie cried.

They discussed how and when they would ever use these toys when their husbands returned. Calli modeled some of lingerie—her breasts showing through the bubble-gum pink sheer organza, her thong underwear barely covered by the lacy hem. Prancing around her living room like a pole dancer with her guitar over her shoulder, she used a multi-colored dildo as a microphone, bellowing Tom Petty's "American Girl" to her friends. Everyone agreed that if her music career didn't take off, she should go into the sex toy business.

Before his tour had been extended, Aidan was due to be home the following Saturday. He and Rachel were planning on getting out of the Army and moving away by March. This is going to happen to us, Calli thought immediately when she heard the news. Luke is going to be extended, too. He won't be home this summer.

A plane filled with soldiers from third brigade combat team

had landed at Fort Drum the previous Wednesday. Calli heard that the soldiers had sat on the plane, waiting to get off and greet their families and friends who had come to welcome them home. While they were sitting there, they learned that the plane was re-fueling and they were heading back to Afghanistan for another five months. They never even got off the plane.

Josie said, "I heard another group of soldiers who got home last weekend had the welcome home ceremony at Fort Drum but will be headin' back to Iraq today and tomorrow. The wives and families were furious, shoutin' and yellin' at their Rear D colonel."

Calli thought, I'm preparing for the worst.

>>> <<<

One of Josie's talents, besides baking, was skiing—really, really fast. She was an avid downhill skier who told Calli that she'd once clocked herself at 85 MPH. Calli didn't think she'd ever want to go that fast on skis—or in her car for that matter. Josie did, she assured Calli, wear a helmet.

Not far from Calli's house in Sackets was a tiny ski resort called Dry Hill, and Josie and Calli took Audrey up there to learn how to ski. Calli bundled her up in a miniature pink ski suit and fleece snow hat that had pastel tassels flopping off the top sides. Josie took over after Calli got Audrey fitted with rental skis since Calli didn't think she'd be a good teacher. She stayed in the lodge and watched out the large bay window as Josie took Audrey's little hand and pulled her along in the snow, acclimating her to the motion of skis. They headed over toward the lift, where people were waiting in line to be taken up the hill. As they edged closer and closer to the chairs, Calli began to wonder if Audrey was crying or what they were chatting about.

She ran outside with her camera to capture them getting onto the lift. As they inched closer and closer to the lift, her heart beat louder and louder. Calli thought, A three-year-old on skis is a cute picture. *Your* three-year-old on skis is nerve-racking.

Finally, the lift approached. Calli watched as the bench turned, Josie coaching Audrey to turn to look behind her shoulder to ready herself to be scooped up by the conveyor belt, and then—whoa, they had lift-off. Calli snapped picture after picture for Luke. Another first he would miss, just like her first swim and her first ballet recital. "Audrey! Hi! Audrey!" Calli called out and they waved to her. Audrey was smiling, laughing. Josie was laughing, too. Although it was bitter cold out, she waited outside for them to slide down the tiny hill. For a moment, they were out of sight, but within minutes Calli saw Audrey cruising down the hill with her skis in a pizza pie position, Josie trailing behind her. She seemed to have no fear of falling down.

About every three weeks, Calli recorded on the Dictaphone, telling Luke everything as if he were sitting in her kitchen while she made breakfast. It was important to Calli that he heard her voice. Recording a message about Audrey skiing with Josie would be a treat.

The sun shone on their faces. Audrey's face, mostly obscured by the large goggles and her fleece hat, was rosy and healthy. Calli couldn't believe Audrey conquered the hill on her first try. "Josie, Josie, can we go again? Again? Please!" Audrey was relentless with Josie, knowing that Josie would give her whatever she wanted. "Yeah, come on!" And they were off.

After several runs, Josie brought Audrey back into the lodge for hot chocolate. Josie's phone rang.

"It's Daphne," Josie mouthed to Calli.

Calli took Audrey to the bathroom and then to get a snack.

When Calli and Audrey returned to the picnic table inside the lodge, Josie was crying. "There was a fire last night. Huey and Tristan's building in Iraq burned down."

"No. Is he okay? What happened?"

"Yes, he's okay. It was the new Command Center built on the site of a previous Army building that had burned down during an earlier deployment. Bad juju. Electrical malfunction. Computers, ammunition, maps, weapons—everything went up in smoke. Our wedding pictures. The quilt I knit him for Christmas. It's all gone."

The ad-hoc barracks were made out of creosote-soaked plywood from Kuwait that burned quickly. The Army was already over their budget. Housing on the front lines seemed ancillary.

"But he's ok, right? Huey's all right? No one is hurt?"

"Yes, yes, he's all right," Josie said, crying but clearly happy. "He's all right. Oh my god, he could have died Calli. He's all right. He's okay."

Calli got up and moved to Josie's side. Hugged her hard and let Josie cry into her hair. The men were always close to death, but the wives presumed it would be the enemy that would get them. The idea that they could die while they were inside the wire added another dimension. Another worry.

>>> <<<

Snow from the low-slung gray canopy pumped in sideways for five weeks straight. The thundering scrape of snowplows every three hours rumbling down Mill Creek Lane didn't even stop at night. Satchmo had pooped a ring around the outside of Calli's house; she forged a small path for them to walk to the driveway from their front door. Louise's son, Herbie, owned a plow and plowed Calli out about twice a day. Snow piled up so high on the deck that it was hard to tell where the deck ended and the yard began. When Calli pushed the sliding glass doors open, snow tumbled into the kitchen. She shoveled a tiny path on the deck to find the wrought-iron furniture that she had left out. She imagined the deck falling off from the weight of the iron and snow. For an hour she dug through heavy, wet snow to locate the chairs and table. One by one, she uncovered the pieces and pulled them up and over her head, tossing them over the railing of the deck into their snow-blanketed yard below. It was minus twenty-two with the wind chill, but she was sweating.

She'd been working on a song that wouldn't let her go. Playing her guitar eased her muscles and quieted her mind. Writing music quieted the annoying tone of war. It was cathartic to jot down her thoughts in her leather journal with her Montblanc, the pen Luke found for her in a pawnshop. The crinkly paper felt thick with ink, her thoughts and desires, what became her music. Playing guitar liberated her stubborn soul, creating an outlet where she felt free from the constraints of life. Her guitar was an extension of her. Strumming her guitar provided her with an escape that appealed to her bewildered view of things. More and more mothers and wives had started to write her. They were attuned to her information from Luke and perhaps felt that she was their connection, regardless of the fact that she had quit the FRG. She thought someday her song would be played for these women, the wives and mothers who stayed behind craving the moment their soldiers stepped off the plane, back on US soil. Like Satchmo, Audrey, and the Divas, her guitar kept her afloat. In the afternoons when Audrey got home from school, Calli would play songs and they'd sing together: "Crocodile Rock," "On Top of Old Smokey," "Edelweiss," "Great Green Gobs," "The Muffin Man," and her favorite, "You Are My Sunshine." Most of the songs made Audrey laugh. Audrey had stopped talking about Luke or asking when he was coming home. Calli hadn't told Luke this. Perhaps it's for the best for her not to remember him or think of him. We have to live in the present—just Audrey and me. Luke is the past—the future—but he's not here.

Calli and the Divas continued to make trips to Walter Reed, to see more of Luke's men. Calli brought her guitar with her. Sometimes she didn't know what to say to these severely broken young men, so she'd play songs for them, her guitar bridging the gap between their wounds and their hopeful exits from this place. Many people trod through Walter Reed bringing brownies, cookies, books, magazines. Celebrities made guest appearances. But Calli believed in her heart that when she sang to them, offered little bits of her songs for them to hear, she felt their moods lift, the blood wash away, the agony dissipate, the tragedy of reality suspend. Her years in high school and college, struggling against herself to perform, to be the best, vanished. The notion that she had spent all those years auditioning for orchestras, vomiting before each and every one of them, auditioning to get into Juilliard, and practicing for hours just to end up playing a guitar for wounded soldiers in the hospital seemed comical. At the same time, it was transcendent. Sometimes she'd weep, not sure what the emotional force was because simultaneously she'd feel happiness and grief. Joy and sorrow. Tears rolled across her face as her fingers strummed and her voice carried melodies into the hospital wards.

Josie, Daphne, and Rachel never spoke to her about her tears. They accepted Calli's new essence, her process of filtering the war, Luke's deployment, the endless possible outcomes of her husband's future, her shift out of darkness and away from fear. All who knew her well saw her transformation. She had changed. Her previous idleness, even in college, her stagnation with life, sloughed off, jettisoned like a disease that had vanished.

Her visits to Walter Reed guided her spirit. She had never been devout about religion, but she felt confident that God or the Universe, whatever divine energy existed, was cooperating with her now, acting as her docent down the path.

After her most recent visit, she'd had an epiphany. Pulling over to the side of the road, she rummaged through her purse to find a pen. Piles of songs—mostly bad ones—were scribbled in her notebook. Titles hadn't hatched but choruses, poetry, beats, lived in ink in that notebook. The lyrics of the one song that really stuck with her, that wouldn't let her go, were there. As she read them, the title "Blue Star" pushed itself forward like an eager child in a candy store. "Blue Star" after the Blue Star mothers' custom of hanging the rectangular banner, the Service flag, in the window. A blue star with a red border waited in her window. She'd hung it on the window latch the day Luke deployed. This service flag had a blue star for each member in the family who was serving. A gold star for a service member who had lost his life.

The Blue Star mothers began in 1942. They banded together,

volunteering in hospitals and train stations, and packing care packages. Their official banner, which had been designed during WWI,
became the unofficial symbol of a child in service. At that time, most
flags were handmade by mothers across the nation. During WWII,
the practice of hanging flag became much more widespread. The
Department of Defense now specified that all family members of a
deployed service member were authorized to display the banner in
their windows.

Calli's song spoke to the women affected by war, the melody lilt-
ing, rising, falling, and rising again. It was a triumph of eclecticism
stemming from her classical training, guitar-driven pop covers, and
alt-country. She'd let go of the rules that made rigid music. The song
was authentic Calli.

⟫⟫ 21 ⟪⟪

One afternoon in early spring, when the snow had mostly melted but the temperature was still chilly, Calli and Audrey returned from a long meeting at Fort Drum after being gone most of the day. Major Rob Whitney, the executive officer for Luke's battalion, was home on leave and attended the meeting to discuss how the deployment was going. August didn't seem that far away for a moment.

She met Rob before the deployment. His boyish good looks and charm struck her immediately. She liked him. He didn't feel Army to her. Even with his high and tight haircut and Army uniform, she joked around with him. "Are you ready to spend twelve months with Luke's snoring in your ear every night?"

"Is he ready for me to snore in his ear every night?"

"It's be good medicine for him since he doesn't think he snores."

"I don't think I snore, but Mellie swears I do." He didn't take himself so seriously. His wife, Mellie, charming also, was one of the head FRG leaders of the battalion. She always said kind things and asked Calli about Audrey. Rob mentioned how there was a chance the brigade would be extended—but it was a very small chance. This wispy assurance was enough for Calli. Luke's coming home in September, she thought. We're more than halfway through the deployment!

Madelon, Luke's delightful mother, was up for an extended visit. Madelon reminded Calli of Aunt Bee from the Andy Griffin show. She was always a picture of gracefulness, except when she catnapped on the sofa with her embroidery in her hands before dinner and a small, yet distinct snort would escape her mouth. Her presence was welcome since she not only shared in but also took over most of the cleaning and cooking duties for the three weeks she was staying. Madelon mentioned, "Your cell phone rang several times while you were out. I forget it sometimes, too. Your friend Henry called, dear," she said. "I answered. He asked if you'd call him back when you got home. How was Fort Drum?"

"Oh fine. I ate too much pizza but Audrey had fun playing with the other kiddos." She retrieved her phone from the kitchen counter where she'd accidentally left it. Her voicemail held a jarring message.

"Calli. It's Henry. Call me as soon as you get this message."

Henry never called her Calli.

She called Henry right away. "Hi Calli, how are you? How is Audrey?" His tone was deflated, hollow. Something was wrong. Sometimes she wished they could put their manners aside and say what needed to be said right off the bat. Do away with the "How-are-you-today" provisos. Finally he cried, "I have some bad news..."

"Henry! What happened?"

"Eula is gone," he choked. Time hiccupped. Calli slid onto a chair next to the fireplace, thankful that Audrey was playing quietly somewhere other than here next to her. Madelon quietly unplugged the iron and left the room.

Surely she had not heard him correctly. A dream—a nightmare. Eula couldn't be gone, as Henry said, because Eula was the future, Calli's most passionate champion, someone who transformed simple, dry experiences into transcendental seascapes. Without Eula, life lost its color.

"What did you say?"

"She died last night."

"Henry, NO! Henry, I know you are kidding me."

"It happened last night after dinner. I went up to the bedroom when she didn't come down to watch the movie and found her on our bed. She had a heart attack. My beautiful Eula. She's gone."

Calli froze. Grappling, she thought, How do I call Luke when I am six thousand miles away from him? How do I hug him and hold him? How do I tell him that one of our best friends is gone? How will I get in touch with him now?

Hastily, she wrote three emails to Luke, all with the same subject line: URGENT. CALL ME AS SOON AS YOU GET THIS!

Calli called Rob Whitney. Please answer, please answer, she prayed. It was about ten o'clock at night in Iraq. Rob must know how to reach someone who was still awake. Mellie, his gentle wife, answered. Calli sobbed into the phone, "There's been an accident and I need to speak to Rob."

"Calli, what's wrong? Are you crying?" Without hesitating or waiting to hear, Mellie handed the phone to him.

Calli asked him, "I need a huge favor. Please have Luke call me as soon as he can. Can you please call someone to wake up Luke? I need him to call me before he does anything else. A great friend of ours died. One of Luke's fraternity brothers already sent out an email about her, and I pray that Luke hasn't read it before I speak to him. I want Luke to hear it from me, not from an email."

⟫ ⟪

At two o'clock in the morning, she was up watching a M.A.S.H. marathon on TV, still waiting for Luke to call her. Henry's exquisite wife, one of their closest friends, was dead. Luke would be devastated.

Calli's heart broke for Henry. For herself. For Luke. Luke had missed so many of his friends' weddings because of his work in the Army. Now, one of his best friends had died, and he wouldn't be able to go to the funeral. Everyone Calli had spoken to tonight was in disbelief. At least, Calli consoled herself, Eula died peacefully and quickly. One minute she was alive, and then she wasn't.

The phone rang. She knew it was Luke, and for a second she prepared herself. He spoke first: "Hi, my love. Is everything okay?"

She'd rarely heard his voice since October.

"No. Did you get my email?"

"Yes. Is this about Eula?"

"Yes. You know then."

"Yes."

"Oh Luke, it's so awful. I am so sorry! I tried and tried to reach you before you read the emails."

"It's okay. I know it's late. I'll call you later when you are awake."

"Okay, I love you. Please call me tomorrow."

"I will. I love you, too."

>>> <<<

Calli hid in her bedroom crying for most of the next day. Eula's death didn't sit like the other deaths she'd experienced since Luke deployed. With them she'd rest in a chair, stare out the window, and let the news settle like dust in an old house. With Eula, pangs of anguish vibrated from her feet to her head, and a hole punctured her soul. Sitting still was impossible because when she sat still the infinite place where Eula went struck her as impossible. Closets were purged and reorganized, then the cupboards. Calli walked up to the bedroom and forgot why she had gone up there. A mutual acquaintance called. The viewing would be on Tuesday. The funeral: Wednesday. It was Sunday, and she had to get to Oxford, Eula's hometown, by Tuesday afternoon. It was happening so fast.

When she called Henry, he cried, "This is not a good time, okay?" She called and emailed him a few more times.

Henry, I don't know what to say or what I can do to ease your suffering. Please know that I am here for you.

Henry, my dear friend, Eula was, well, extraordinary. Of course she was, that's why you married her. She represented a light for all of us—a light so natural yet so charged with meaning. She opened up an inner experience, a complete and mystical experience. She drew life with pen and ink like Rembrandt's drawing of Saskia— flowers in her hand, dreamy-eyed. Her spirit will be absorbed into all of you. I miss her. I am here if you need me.

Henry, it's C. I know Luke has written you, but in his email today he told me to tell you he's so sorry not to be here for you. We love you. Call me if you want.

He didn't answer and she didn't expect him to. Eula's sister, Belle, called Calli to tell her the news. Too composed, she said, "Hello Calli. We have some horrible news to share."

Before Belle had to say the words again, Calli butt in, "I know, Belle. I know."

"It's been hard, but we're all fine here." Calli recognized Belle's shock.

"Belle, I'll be there. At the funeral. No matter what." When Belle called back a day later, Eula's father asked to speak to her. He cried "Oh Calli, our Eula, our Eula has gone to heaven." This was the same man she'd heard so much about—the larger-than-life legend, who'd won the Heisman trophy, who was a Rhodes Scholar, an Army Brigadier General, who ran for Senate, and who now was the president of United Mississippi Bank.

He asked, "Calli, will you give the eulogy?" The request seemed natural when he asked her, but when she hung up the phone after agreeing to speak, the weight of the appeal struck her. She had just agreed to eulogize her closest friend. Could she could stand up in front of the hundreds of people? Eula would do it for her—and what an honor it was that they had asked her. Calli had one day to compose and practice a eulogy for a woman who had lived an extraordinary life, a woman who was one of her best friends, a woman who knew thousands of people and made friends wherever she went. Eula's family had asked her to do this.

Calli dove in headfirst and started to compose her first, and maybe only, eulogy. She had been to many memorials and knew that people wanted to hear the nuances, the idiosyncrasies, the triumphs, and the peccadilloes of the person.

Beautiful Eula—my champion, my friend, exuberant Eula— she bound us together even when she'd fallen asleep after a glass or two of wine...

Madelon would watch Audrey while Calli was at the funeral. She had her plane ticket and a room to sleep in when she got there. She wrote Luke an email and explained that she was ready to represent them both at the funeral. She knew he'd be happy that she was going for both of them. When it was all over, she wrote him again.

My Dearest Love,
I am home again after quite an eventful forty-eight hours in Oxford celebrating Eula's life. It's still so strange to me that she is dead, but there is no doubt in my mind that you have the best guardian angel around.

For starters, I have had about six hours of sleep since I left here Tuesday—up at three a.m. to catch my flight. I arrived in Oxford to a balmy eighty-degree sunny day, which was most welcome to this northern New Yorker.

I arrived at the funeral home and waited in line for two hours. Someone later told me that at least two thousand people came. Since Eula was Catholic, it was open casket. I've never seen a dead person before, and to see Eula dead was really creepy. She looked like a wax figure. I just reminded myself—that's just her body, not her. There were millions of flowers and pictures of Eula all over the place. Henry collapsed in my arms. I don't know how the family did it. They stood there chatting with people for hours and hours. Henry made me promise that we will be there for him and the kids and that we have to keep Eula alive for the kids. I told him we will definitely do so and that the first thing we are going to do when you come home is visit.

Everyone was sad and shocked. Strangely, because of the deployment, I am a bit desensitized. I certainly was sad and cried a lot before I got there, but I seemed more focused than everyone else. Does that make sense? Anyway, I finally met Belle and her husband Rick—both are fantastic. It was incredible. I have to think that Eula must have talked about us to them all the time. They kept saying, "Eula loved Luke and you, Eula loved Luke and you!" It was really beautiful and I was so honored to be there for both of us. I kept thinking, I know Luke is here in spirit.

At nine, we finally went back to the hotel and started partying in the lobby until one. It was mostly Baltimore people, your fraternity brothers, and me. All your fraternity brothers were asking about you. I have to admit, I was pissed that some of them said, "I think of Luke all the time, how is he doing?"—he's in a fucking war zone, you idiot. They don't get it, though, so I can't be too harsh. I told everyone how you were and that you were excited to come home.

At two o'clock, I turned the light off. I think I slept for about three hours because then I was up and starting to get nervous about the eulogy. I ended up getting out of bed and going down to the lobby to meditate and try to get a grip. The last thing the priest said to me before I left the funeral home was that he didn't really like having people get up and do eulogies so we had to keep mine short.

I had to be to the funeral home at ten a.m. I wasn't the only one who looked tired. I also began regretting my choice of attire: a white eyelet cocktail dress. When I had made the decision to wear it, I was thinking back on Granny's funeral and how she didn't want anyone to wear black. She only wanted people to celebrate her life. When I was packing, the thought made sense to me, but as we were driving to the funeral home in the cold rain, I really thought I'd made a dreadful choice. It was too late to turn back and change, so I just hoped no one would notice I was dressed in white.

When I arrived, only the pallbearers, family, and Henry's friends were there. It was so bizarre to see him bring the kids in and tell them, "Now everyone, say one final thing to Mommy." Mae Margaret looked up at the casket and said, "Thanks for being my mommy." I lost it! I had to walk out of the room. I kept thinking, What if this was Luke's funeral? Then we all gathered together and said a nice prayer. I felt so displaced, appallingly dressed, tired, and worried about the eulogy. Fortunately, Henry introduced me to his friend Elliot Vernon, who ended up as my escort. Elliot's about sixty-five and told me that he's married to a woman who is forty and they have two small kids who are six and four. His wife is from Colombia, where they live. He's a great guy, and I am hopeful you will get to meet him. I really didn't think I should have been there, but Elliot just kept telling me about himself and calmed me with his gentleman's grace.

The Oxford Police Department was there to escort the entourage. I needed you there with me, and yet once again I was forced to stand alone and be brave. Since it was raining and I had neglected to pack a raincoat, one of the policemen loaned me his. Finally, we got into one of the four stretch Lincoln limos to go to the church. Elliot sat next to me in the way back of the limo that was also hauling several of the pallbearers. It was so surreal. The police escort stopped traffic as we passed by. Eula would have been proud.

When we arrived at the church, it was pouring rain, so we ran into the lobby and then the pallbearers brought Eula's casket in. Most everyone was inside the church, but those of us still with Eula said another prayer, and then we walked into the church behind the casket and the family. There were so many people there. Easily a thousand people! There was standing room only. Elliot and I sat in the second row on the right in the pew behind the pallbearers. There was a man in the pew behind us who looked just like Geraldo Rivera. There was a beautiful picture of Eula on the cover of the program. I'll send it to you. During the entire beginning of the service, all I could think of was how to shorten my eulogy. I didn't know what I was going to do. I don't think I heard one word the priest said except that it was clear to me that he didn't know Eula very well. Then it was time for the eulogies—first it was Belle. Poor wretch could barely speak and was up there for about ninety seconds. At this point I am whispering to Elliot, "What I should do?" Then Todd, Eula's brother, spoke. He did a really fitting job, but his was only five minutes. THEN, me . . . I walked up to the pulpit and still didn't know what I was going to do. I turned around and looked out at a sea of people staring at me. I said—but I didn't realize that I had until afterward when someone told me—"It's really difficult to sum up Eula's life in three minutes." And then I just heard you say to me, "Go man, go!" and I went for the gusto—the whole kit and caboodle.

I have to admit, I don't remember much about being up there after that. I made it through the entire thing, until the last paragraph, without crying at all. Then it was over, and we left the church to go back out to the cars. As we were processing out, Elliot whispered, "Look, Ross Perot is here. And did you see Geraldo Rivera sitting right behind us?" I thought, "Good god, no, because there would have been no way I would have been able to speak up there."

While the casket was being loaded up, people came up to

tell me that they loved my eulogy. One older woman told me that it was the best eulogy she'd ever heard. Many people came up and thanked me and thanked you, too!

Then we got back into the cars, and with all the pomp and circumstance, the police escort, and hundreds of cars, we went to the gravesite.

There was a brief ceremony, and some woman played Pachelbel's Canon. I sobbed. And every time I looked up, I was looking right at Ross Perot, who was directly across from me on the other side of Eula's casket.

Afterward, we went to their country club for a luncheon. Everyone said, "Eula talked about you all the time...Eula was so proud of Luke...Eula totally looked up to you...Eula thought the world of Luke...Eula LOVED you!"
I love you!
Calli

Although Calli detailed Eula's funeral to Luke, she neglected to write him everything.

The night of the funeral, she found herself drunk at a bar with Henry. His warmth drew her to him, warmth that had been lacking in her life since Luke deployed. His fresh sweat coupled with his Polo cologne created a recipe that she could not resist. She prided herself, as did the other Divas, on not being the spoofed wife who goes out to bars and picks up men while her husband is deployed. In Sackets Harbor, even appearing at a bar could garner suspicion. If another soldier was at the pub, he could start a rumor that could reach Iraq or Afghanistan with an email.

But on that inebriated Wednesday night at a bar in Oxford, with Eula gone and Luke in Iraq, the rules vanished. There weren't any clean-shaven privates or sergeants or captains from Fort Drum, no one who knew her. She danced like a whirling dervish, jumping up on tables, playing the air guitar, and singing loudly and off key to earsplitting eighties music. The bartender paid her bail from a self-imposed sentence with every additional drink, and the excessive alcohol supplied the permission to let loose.

Henry drunkenly flirted with her and sometimes accidentally, sometimes on purpose, bumped into her, a kind of foreplay that had persisted since they met. "You don't have a bra on," he noticed.

"This dress is a halter top, I can't wear a bra."

"Are you commando, too?"

"Wouldn't you like to know?"

She was slippery after a few stolen seconds of frottage at the bar. All her measured inhibitions, the shrewd clamp on her reputation, and her relationship with Luke felt distant and foggy. Her brain shut off as the delicate dance between them escalated. But Henry and she had sometimes fallen into this routine before. And Eula and Luke had flirted with each other, too. A cloying romantic comedy that never amounted to anything because they all loved each other and were just playing around. Calli never doubted that she'd go home—alone—even if it was fun to be letting loose with Henry after all the sadness, all the months of hurt, the shock of Eula's heart attack.

By three a.m., when the bar shut down, Calli sounded like she had marbles in her mouth. Henry offered to give her a ride back to her hotel in his rental car. Agreeing, she hopped in the front seat of his sedan and sang songs to him on the way. Her body, warm with grabby desire, craved touch. Six months of celibacy left her wanton after this strange day. The alcohol was driving her, like a diabolic power, to contemplate lewd sex with Henry. Where were the Divas to pull her out of this situation? No one would ever know. "Do you want to get another drink at the hotel?" she asked.

"Darlin', I'm up for anything." As they stopped in front of the hotel, the pavement gave way, cracked, and she moved toward him. And as she leaned over to kiss him—a shift in aromatics brought her back. His breath, laden with beer and cigarettes, sickened her. "We can't do this. I love Luke. You love Eula," she said, slurring. Briefly she thought of Brittany, the eighteen-year-old wife who'd cheated at Christmas. Henry stared at her. Through her murk, she saw Brittany and some boy who wasn't her husband in someone's basement fucking while Rick was in Iraq. She wasn't Brittany. But maybe she was.

Henry said, "Darlin', no one will ever know. I need you. You looked so hot today." He slid his hand under the top of her dress to hold her breast.

And with that fetching overture, the wine cheering on her hormones, her loins aroused, she leaned in and kissed him. They were both nude and in the back seat of the sedan within minutes. Suspended in time, she let him run his hands all over her. She contorted herself so he could lick her, dancing his tongue in and out of her while his finger glided gently in and out of her pussy. "Oh my god, Calli, you're fucking hot! I need you. I need you," he cried.

Her back arched and she grabbed his hard penis. Her breasts heaved up and she felt herself close to orgasm. She just wanted him to fuck her. Just wanted carnal pleasure. "Let me get on top. I want to feel you inside me. Come on!" He maneuvered himself underneath her. She felt his skin; his chest was hairier than Luke's, but not fuzzy. His cock was shorter and wider, and as she slid him into her, she felt immediate ecstasy, riding him. He grabbed one of her nipples with his mouth while he cupped her other breast with his hand. She clawed his back in a frenzy, driving him deeper into her, pumping her body harder and harder on top of him as if she wanted to eradicate the last six months and start over again. "I've always loved you. Always. Since that day in Nantucket," Henry whispered. The humidity in the air and their fervor to wipe away the outside made them sweat and stick together.

"Don't talk," she said. "Please, don't say anything." She only wanted to be transported. He climaxed first and then she did, her body writhing with rapture, crying a slow and tender drawing up of guilt.

She collapsed.

⟫⟫ ⟪⟪

"C! C! You've got to get up. The alarm is going off!" Henry said.

Her eyes blinked open, the tiles on the bathroom floor warmed by her cheek. For a few brief, blissful moments, she didn't know where she was. The after effect of the alcohol weighed down her head. As she pushed herself off the bathroom floor, she noticed that her dress was on inside out. No bra or underwear. A violent stab slammed into her temples. Oh my god, what have I done? What have I done? She didn't recognize the bathroom as hers.

A vomit stench hit her nose as a rogue section of her hair hung down her face. Henry pushed open the door. "Your cab is going to be here soon. You've got to get up." On the verge of tears, she tried to stand up. A plane to catch. A crooked back from passing out on the bathroom floor. A tsunami of memory smacked into her.

Henry reached for her to keep her stable. Keep her with him. He pulled her close to him. She fought him. "Get off of me," she screamed. "Henry, what have we done? I have to find my shoes." Sneaking a glimpse of herself in the mirror, she shuddered and threw her hands over her eyes. Calli tried to pull off her face. Tears streamed down her cheeks. How she wished she could climb out of her body and float away. If only there was a rewind button. Push it and they could be back seventy-two hours ago when Eula was still alive and Luke was still married to his faithful wife.

"I love you both," he said. Calli didn't know who "both" was. Eula and her? Luke and her? "Let me help you." She fumbled with a toothbrush—Henry's, she hoped—her hands trembling as the tooth-paste tube squirted three times as much as she needed, falling onto the floor.

"No!" Calli said.

"Please, C. We have to talk about this. You can't leave like this."

"No—no. I can't. I think I'm going to throw up." But her defenses were still down. Calli dropped the toothbrush, dropped back down to her knees, and leaned toward the toilet where she let go of whatever was left in her stomach. She cried, grieving her lost friend.

Henry, awkwardly, propped her up. "Calli, listen. I'm sorry. I'm so, so sorry. I'm just . . . just confused and sad."

Calli laid there, her inebriation slowly fading. A serious cramp in her stomach lurched around. "I don't know what to say."

"You don't have to."

"I just cheated on Luke. We—"

"He'll never know."

"He'll hate me. He'll leave me. I hate me. I don't deserve Luke. I hate myself. What have I done?"

"Calli, we're both suffering."

"What!?"

"I know it doesn't make it right, but it's not as if you don't know me."

"How the hell does that qualify anything?"

"Don't tell him. Don't tell him, C. It'll kill him."

She did not respond, but flushed the toilet. Not sure if her legs would support her, she used the sink to pull herself up off the floor, not looking at Henry.

"There's always been something...a passion that, that, I think has always been there. For me, anyway." He leaned in to kiss her forehead, but she pulled back, glaring at herself in the mirror, and grabbed a towel to wipe off her face. Then she just stood there and waited for him to leave. "I'll go look for your shoes."

Calli felt ripe with blame, drenched in remorse and stale sex. Her abrupt ecstasy, now foggy, disappointing, as if it'd been a prize she'd desired from a milk can carnival game that she realized, away from the carnival lights, was cheap. How could Henry be so ignorant of the pain they'd created? What if she never saw Henry again? Could she get used to that? She was still grappling with never seeing Eula again—had barely gotten used to Luke's absence.

Henry knocked on the door. "C?"

Silence.

"Are you ok?"

22

Audrey and Calli are in the tornado room. It's a gray metal box. The bolts keeping the room together are as large as her fist. There is nothing else in the tornado room. The storm will be here in a few minutes. They only have a few minutes to get out of its path. All she sees is the tornado and the debris flying in the air, random projectiles of wood, metal, glass, and farm animals.

When she knows the storm has passed, they climb out of the shelter into what was their home. It's a pile of large splinters and nothing else. All of their material goods—vanished. Her first reaction is shock; but then, in another instant, she realizes that Audrey and she are alive and okay. She can replace everything else—she realizes Audrey and she have survived the tornado and she feels peaceful.

This was the dream she had the night she returned from Eula's funeral. She'd read an article saying she should take stock in her dreams, so she believed that this one was a sign. For months, her grip had been like an anchor in a tug-of-war contest.

The best thing she'd done since moving to Sackets was to surround herself with people who got it. There was an unspoken language among military wives that unless someone had been through it, no amount of empathy even came close. The only other people she knew who had had a somewhat similar understanding were people who'd lost a loved one—which clearly was far worse. Henry was in much more pain than she'd ever known, yet she knew this vulnerability. She'd let this vulnerability encapsulate her, them.

Friendship with Henry, well, that was fuzzy. Supporting him felt right in some far-flung way, but her gnawing shame, teetered like a bulging water balloon on the edge of an open windowsill, prevented her from extending continued sympathy so instead she ignored him. No one would understand. But she and Henry would. He would know why. Sylvie's words from almost twenty years earlier surfaced: It was *my* mistake. Why ruin his life? Calli would never tell Luke about the affair with Henry. Never in a million years could she have predicted that the well of strength she now had—and needed—was possible. She had taken chances that she would never have taken if Luke hadn't left. But she'd also made a huge mistake.

Never could she have predicted that while Luke's deployment was the worst thing to happen to her, it was also the best. She'd returned to music. The lyrics and notes for "Blue Star" were almost complete. She'd found passion working with the wounded veterans. For all the fear, anxiety, depression, and sadness, there had been abundance, clarity, purposefulness, and extreme strength.

And the night with Henry. A slipup. A transgression. Remorse. Embarrassment. Confined only to her mind. A lifelong prison sentence.

23

Calli looked at her calendar. Luke would be home in a month for his fifteen-day leave. She hadn't seen him in over nine months. It doesn't feel as if he's going to be here, where I can touch him, hear his voice, and look into his beautiful brown eyes, she thought. They were getting much closer to the end of this thing; once Luke went back to Iraq, they would only have about two more months. Two more months of Luke being away.

In the meantime, she'd been perusing cookbooks searching for something to indulge his appetite. Huey Hollis would arrive home about a week before Luke, and Daphne and Calli had been discussing their plans. They shopped together for new lacy bras and underwear. Started to iron sheets. Calli said, "I have an idea. I think I'm going to rent a stretch limo to pick up Luke at the airport in Syracuse."

"Calli, brilliant! Can I steal your idea? Huey will flip!" Daphne was so excited. "Luke has no idea that I am going to do this. It'll give us a chance to have some alone time. I've written to him that I am going to leave Audrey at home so we can be 'alone' in the car—perhaps we'll stop next to some woods on the side of I-81!"

April 2007

WASHINGTON (CNN)—Tours of duty for members of the US Army will be extended from twelve months to fifteen months effective immediately, Defense Secretary Robert Gates announced Wednesday.

"What we're trying to do here is provide some long-term predictability to our soldiers and their families," Gates told reporters at the Pentagon.

In exchange for the extension, Gates said the service will be able to give all units a year at home between deployments. He denied that the order was a sign that the Army has passed its breaking point under the stresses of the wars in Iraq and Afghanistan, saying the service has met or passed its recruiting and retention goals.

But he added that the military has been "stretched" by the conflicts. He blasted Tuesday's leak of the extension proposal to the media, saying the Defense Department had hoped to give the troops forty-eight hours' advance notice of the decision.

Some petulant vermin in the Pentagon leaked the story, and the wives and soldiers were some of the last to know. Calli screamed at Josie on the phone, "Washington has NO FUCKING CLUE! And predictability—there's nothing predictable about this for me or for any of us. They are in a fucking war zone with BAD GUYS."

In the subject line of an email, Calli wrote to Luke, *I guess we're really only halfway . . .*

>>> ‹‹‹

Calli called Dinah. "Yes, it's officially happened; Luke's deployment has been extended. He'll spend an additional ninety days in Iraq. The worst part: Luke found out from me. It's bad news—certainly— but I don't want to be angry anymore. I want to rise above this and create something positive."

"What do you mean, he found out from you?"

"The story was leaked before the commanders even knew."

"Oh, Cal. That sucks. So what does that mean?"

"It means that instead of a twelve-month deployment, he'll be gone for fifteen months total. Fortunately, he's coming home for leave soon. I've made it this far. I'll just keep going. I can't wait to see him. It might be weird, but I think we both know that. I don't think there are any expectations that things will be the way they were before. But Luke is so grounded. I can't imagine that it will be too weird."

"Nine and half months is a long time to be separated. Just don't set yourself up for, for, well, don't put too much pressure on him. Or yourself."

"I'm not. Really. I just want to see him. I need to see him. One more month, and he'll be home. With us."

>>> <<<

A late-spring snow. Coconut flakes rushed sideways, frosting the landscape. Audrey's fourth birthday, Calli thought as she peered out her bedroom window. Audrey was surprised when Calli presented her with strawberry ice cream and chocolate-covered cupcakes for breakfast. Calli got out her guitar and sang "Happy Birthday" and "You Are My Sunshine"—Audrey's favorite—and climbed into Audrey's bed. Snuggling together under Audrey's down comforter, they ate the birthday treats.

It was the middle of April, and someone was holding spring hostage. She thought, It's almost comical that we are still in winter here. The longest year of my life with the worst winter in recorded history. Satchmo hadn't been walked in months. Calli was almost unable to button her jeans. The Divas and her cooking and eating and drinking incessantly had begun to show on Calli's hips and thighs. Some wives lost a lot of weight and exercised manically while their husbands deployed. Many got boob jobs since the Army only charged for the implants. Some got pregnant while their husbands were home on leave. Not Calli. She just ate her way through the time. And since she didn't own a scale and it was too cold to exercise outside, she settled on the idea that she'd gotten a little rounder in Luke's absence. Luke was the kind of man who would tell her—convincingly—that she looked gorgeous even if she had gained some weight. He would tell her that she'd been too skinny and that he loved her bigger boobs and wider ass. The blistering wind and perpetual snow were such a great excuse to gain weight. Calli decided that she didn't want to buy new jeans, so she'd just have to continue to squeeze into the pairs she already owned and perhaps not eat dessert every night. But she couldn't start tonight, because it was Audrey's birthday. Daphne, Josie, Rachel and her boys, and some of the neighbors were invited over for cake and presents. Luke would understand, Calli thought. A few extra pounds won't make a difference to him.

Calli's mood lifted thinking about how she would be able to have a conversation with Luke. In person. She would pick his brain about what was really going on abroad. So far, she had had to rely on his cryptic emails and a half dozen letters to determine what the truth was. Soon enough, he could tell her face to face.

When Calli got out of bed with Audrey, she said, "Auds, this is going to be the best day. Ever. I'm the luckiest mommy in the entire world. I love you, birthday girl. We have so much to be thankful for."

"I love you, too, Mama. Can I have cupcakes for lunch, too?"

"I guess, yes. Won't you be tired of them?"

"Noooo. I love cupcakes. And dinner, too? Please?"

"I guess, if you really..."

"Yes, mama, yes. And can we watch Noggin all day, too?"

"Sure, my beautiful Angel. Let's go."

⤜⤜⤜ ⤛⤛⤛

The good news about blizzards in April was that the snow didn't last long. It was Mother Nature's annual fight to unfurl her spring wings and whisper good night to winter. Calli opened the sliding glass doors and was met by the cacophony of crickets singing to her in the cool night. The tree swing undulated beneath nascent birch leaves. The first sign of summer. A summer filled with the Divas. Perhaps Calli would take them to Nantucket with her. She had tossed out the idea to Lucy and Haines, who surprised her and said yes, she could invite the Divas for a visit to the Nantucket place. Originally she had planned for Luke, Audrey, and her to celebrate the end of the deployment in Nantucket. The extension ruined that plan. Calli knew better now: Don't make a plan.

As Calli sat down getting ready to relax and watch a movie with Josie, something on the dining-room floor caught her attention. She got up, and upon inspection, she saw it was dog shit—an assortment of large, smelly turds under the window. How did I miss this? she thought. I cleaned the whole house.

Some days were just filled with piss and poop. Earlier that day, Audrey had wet her underpants in the car. She'd been doing this more frequently, holding it until she was about to burst. There were times when Calli had to stop on the sides of interstates and let Audrey out to tinkle on the side of the car. The roaring eighteen-wheelers buzzing by at seventy miles an hour were terrifying. "*Mommy!* I have to *tinkle*! Please!" This, of course, fifteen minutes after they had just stopped at the rest stop.

But today, they had just left her preschool, New Day, and were on their way to the Thompson Park playground, maybe five minutes away. "Mommy! I have to *tinkle*! It's coming out!" The next thing she knew, Calli watched her pee all over the beautiful pink smocked dress Eula had sent months back—and the car seat. "Oh mommy, I'm sorry!"

"It's okay, everyone wets her pants sometimes. Just take off your wet underwear and your dress will dry."

Audrey had no panties on. It didn't seem to bother her. Playing at the playground was far more important than wearing underpants. Calli hoped that she wouldn't lift up her dress and show the world what a bad mother she was to let her out without underpants.

This had happened more than once. Last month, they'd been at a birthday party, and suddenly Calli realized she'd neglected to check if Audrey had on underwear before leaving the house. The party was at the YMCA, where they had a huge gymnastics room replete with the soft, squishy pit to land in after double flipping off the bars. The kids were running and jumping in. Audrey followed suit, and as she jumped, her dress went out like Mary Poppins' umbrella. No underpants! And of course all the parents were there, watching at the precise moment when she jumped in.

Today Audrey's lack of panties caught someone's eye. The woman had a direct shot of Audrey as she slid down the slide. Audrey was still in the au naturel phase, and Calli figured there was plenty of time for her to have body image issues. The woman got up and gingerly approached Calli, and before she sat down, Calli said, "I know, I know, she doesn't have on underwear, she wet them on the way here."

Calli imagined the woman criticizing her choices and some snarky comeback she could belt back. The woman pulled something out of her bag—a pair of little girl panties. "Hi. I always carry an extra pair because one of my young daughters wets her pants, too. You can have them for your little girl. My name is Grazia," she said in an Italian accent, an accent that Calli recognized from her time with Gigi. "Minna needs these sometimes too."

"You are my new best friend, Grazia. Thank you so much." She didn't make Calli feel embarrassed or ashamed. Calli was just another Mom with a four-year-old who wet her pants, not a freak who let her daughter go out in public half-naked. Audrey came running over and, without even thinking it was strange, put on the panties.

"I'm from Italy. Veneto. My husband is in the military." Ah ha! A military wife. Her husband had gotten up to push his daughter and now Audrey on the swings. "We love to bring the girls to Thompson Park. Do you come here often?" Grazia's English was perfect.

"Now that the weather is better, I try to bring Audrey, my

daughter, after school a few days a week. I know the Veneto. I lived in Arenzano briefly, in Liguria. My Italian is really rusty, though. Sorry."

"No, no, no. Don't worry. What did you do in Arenzano?"

"It's a long story, but I was dating this crazy guy, who was a chef in a restaurant there. He was really nuts, so I didn't stay for too long. About a year or so. But I love Italy! When my husband gets back from Iraq, I want to take him. He's never been. I miss Italian food. Oh, my god. The wine. The pesto. The best!"

"Oh, so your husband is deployed?"

"Yes. He's in Iraq, in Yusufiyah, south of Baghdad. He's attached to 4-31, an infantry unit. He's a master sergeant."

"My husband is in Triple Deuce. Why is a master sergeant attached to 4-31?"

"I'm not sure. He volunteered, he told me. Is Triple Deuce an infantry unit?"

"Yes. He's the executive officer. Your husband volunteered? That's interesting. I suppose anything is possible in this war."

Calli briefly remembered when she'd arrived at Fort Drum. When she knew nothing and no one and couldn't converse with other wives about unit names or ranks without having to pretend she knew what was being said. Now the words flowed out of her mouth.

"You might be familiar with my husband, Luke Coleman. The main character in *Rio Hato* was based on him." Calli surged with pride as she admitted this to Grazia.

"Really? Of course I know the movie. I loved the book. Hey, Ritchie, mi amore," Grazia said, calling out to her husband, who was pushing Audrey on the swing. "Do you know Luke Coleman?"

"Yeah. I mean, I don't know him, but I know of him."

"He's her husband."

"It's absurd and I don't usually tell people right away. I hope you don't think I'm boasting, but for some reason I just thought you'd understand," Calli said.

"No, no. I think that's neat." Calli and Grazia sat and talked about Italy, literature, and feeling like outsiders compared to the other Army wives for close to an hour while the children scampered around the playground. Ritchie played tag with them, keeping Audrey busy while Grazia and Calli conversed.

"I know we've just met, but we're going to take the girls to that diner off Arsenal Street. Do you want to join us?"

Without hesitating Calli said, "I'd love to. Thank you. Grazie mille. See, I remember a little Italian!"

》》》 《《《

Some days Calli waited. For the phone to ring. For another casualty. For an email from Luke. For a letter from Luke. For Luke to come home. For Luke to come home from the war for good. She waited. The entire US isn't going through this like we are, she thought. The deployment felt like that bitchy month February—the shortest month of the year that took the longest to get through because of storms and ice and snow. Gray days and delays.

Audrey reminded Calli of Tinker Bell, inquisitive, reflecting light. It was impossible to imagine a child more robust with enthusiasm and spontaneity who teetered between real and imaginary worlds. Theirs was a simple relationship with simple boundaries but deeply rooted in love that amplified every day. Sackets Harbor would have been like the beginning of the movie *Wizard of Oz*, a gray tumbleweed landscape, without Audrey. Audrey was like finding the perfect, delicate, exotic pink conch shell on the beach that hadn't worn with time.

My Dearest Love,
Spent some time with some local children, ages 3–10, this morning. Seeing them smile and happy in this torn land reminds me not only of Audrey but of why we must protect these kids from the evil here. 105 at 1000 this morning—having a pool is sounding better and better. Much like road

*marching and rucking for twenty years, spending extended
periods of time in the heat makes me never want to be hot
again. The resupply convoy that Gen Anderson says we
don't need just arrived so I better run.*
All my love,
Luke

Whenever Calli walked into the village from her house, a small
garden where peonies grew first caught her nose, then her eyes.
Last week when they passed by, Audrey started pulling at one of
the voluptuous pink blooms. The owner had come running out.
Thinking he was going to scold Calli for letting her curious four-
year-old pull on his prize flowers, Calli grabbed her and said, "We
don't pick other people's flowers." The owner of the house, with a
huge smile, said, "Please take some. Pick as many as you'd like."

Audrey said, "I'm gonna pick three flowers, one for Daddy, one
for Audrey, and one for Mama."

The fragrant aroma of fresh peonies perfumed the kitchen for
about a week afterward, but what lingered much longer was the
sense of generosity the man had when he came bounding out of his
house to share his flowers with them. Whenever she walked by, she
thought of that moment.

Besides Gus Pepys, who was resting in a mental hospital near
Syracuse, Calli had fallen in love with the people of Sackets Harbor.
How could she not, when there were people like Kelly and Roger
Mumford, who insisted that Audrey and she join them for dinner
at least once a week? Calli felt part of the community. Her mixed
supper club (half military wives, half local women) had blazed a
path for her friendships with a bevy of fascinating women who'd
ended up in Sackets for various reasons. Marriage. Familial obligation. Natives. Love of the weather (Calli never understood that one).
Homesteaders who'd stayed after the military. Job opportunities.
For the same reasons anyone would end up anywhere. There wasn't
a magic formula. They had started to ask if she and Luke would

settle there when he got home from Iraq. Sometimes Calli thought that perhaps she could raise Audrey there. A surprise, since she had been completely anti-everything less than a year before. Her reply: "Let's get Luke home and then we'll decide."

>>> <<<

Luke was scheduled to arrive in Syracuse at noon.

The limo will be here in forty-five minutes to pick me up! thought Calli. She'd bought a new dress and made him a ham and cheese sandwich, chocolate chip cookies, and packed him a cold Heineken in a cooler. She loved her dress—a halter-top A-line, black with white polka dots. She felt gorgeous in it, with nothing on underneath. For two weeks, Luke would be able to touch her, her body. She danced a little while she made his sandwich. I haven't made him a sandwich in nine months, she thought. Ham and American cheese was his favorite. An image of him taking a bite—knowing that there was love in the sandwich. She never thought that making a ham and cheese sandwich would be so exciting, so tender, so loving. Last night when she'd made the cookies with Audrey, they giggled, "Daddy loves chocolate chip cookies!"

"I know, just like someone else I know."

"Who, me?" Audrey said with chocolate smears on her cheeks and a bit in her hair.

"Yes, little girl, you. Go look at yourself in the mirror."

What's he going to be like? Is he going to be the same or will have nine months changed him? I wonder if he'll be gaunt and thin like all the soldiers I've seen at Walter Reed? I've changed, Calli thought. A brief montage of the previous nine months flashed in her mind. Military planes flying overhead. Wounded men at Walter Reed. The Divas. Playing guitar again. Eula. Henry. Oh yes, the painful reminder of that insane night that she never allowed herself to dwell on. Still unsure of how she could keep such a secret for the rest of her life. Push it aside. I'm stronger. I'm a better person in other ways, she thought. Had Luke changed? Did any Iraqis care about him? Or hate him? Had he seen mothers and daughters who reminded him of Audrey and her? Had he had to point his rifle at them? Get back in the house! Or duck. Get out of the way. What about rebuilding the mosque where Sunni and Shia alike could worship once again? Did the children in Yusufiyah see him and think he was some sort of Santa Claus bringing them pencils and Beanie Babies while he walked their streets on patrol, searching for Bad Guys? Was it worth it? Henry would say yes, but she pushed him out of her brain along with their affair. Not affair—tryst. A cheat nonetheless. If Luke had killed Iraqis, would that outweigh her adultery on the scale of public opinion? No. Killing in self-defense everyone understood. She had no right to screw his best friend. Luke would not know about Henry.

She climbed into the limo with her cooler, wearing her polka-dot dress, naked underneath to meet Luke. In her mind, the drive south took far longer than fifty minutes. She ran her thumbs over the tops of her freshly painted nails. Her fingers combed her hair while she obsessed over the smudge on her pedicure. A compact mirror crept out of her purse every fifteen minutes, offering Calli the image of cleanliness and pink lipstick, mascara, and lightly dusted rosy cheeks. Finally at the airport, she emerged from the limo to the vapors of jet fuel, which, in the past, had turned her off, but today the smell excited her. Her hands smoothed the skirt of her dress. She walked into his terminal. His flight was on time. Only minutes to go until his eyes were on her, her hand in his. Miniature biplanes soared and rolled in her gut, performing aerobatics and loops at high speeds then dove rapidly only to make a tight turn and soar again. Moments to go, until she spotted his bald head, his uniform, those eyes she'd fallen in love with on the beach in Nantucket. Tick... Tick... Tick... Tick.

Through the emerging passengers, he walked toward her. His smile taut. Tears in his eyes. Calli ran to him. "I can't believe I'm seeing you. You're here. I can't believe it. Oh, I missed you. I missed you so much. You're here. Thank god, you're here."

"You look amazing. You look gorgeous. I love your dress."

"You've lost weight. But you look great."

"Oh my god, I've been waiting for this day since the plane left Fort Drum. Let's go home. I want to see Auds."

The limo sped up I-81 with Calli and Luke in the back reacquainting themselves. The small talk came easier than Calli suspected as she handed him the sandwich and beer.

"I made your favorite. Ham and cheese."

"You're the best. And this beer tastes like, like, I don't know. It's just so damn good to have a beer and a sandwich sitting here next to you. I can't wait to go to Lake Placid."

"I don't have anything on under my dress."

"Really? Aren't you quite the sexy one? Now, this is what I've really been missing for all these months. Come here and let me see how I can make the world right again." With that, Luke quickly took off Calli's dress to admire her breasts, her stomach, her legs as she sat on the limo seat waiting for him to take her in his arms. Soon she was sitting on him, rising and falling gently. Deliberately. She giggled. Now *this* is a homecoming! she thought.

They surprised Audrey. Calli hadn't told her that Luke was coming home, both out of a need to protect Audrey—in case he hadn't—and for the surprise.

When the limo pulled into the driveway, Calli got out first. Audrey's babysitter, in on the surprise, opened the door for Audrey to come out. "Mama, what are you doing in that long car?" And before Calli had a chance to answer her, Luke stepped out. Audrey's eyes widened as she took a moment to focus, "Daddy! Daddy! Daddy! You're home!" Audrey said, running into Luke's arms.

24

Lake Placid Lodge, May 2007
Dearest Didi,

We are at Lake Placid Lodge for a lovers' tryst—far away from Fort Drum, the incidents, the death, the war, the horror. Luke could have been there in Iraq, but he's home with me. It's so easy to escape the ghastliness when I can hold Luke in my arms and forget that he has to go back. I have to forget that he is going back, or else I will be miserable the whole time he is home. But if I've learned anything so far, it's that I must go forward and embrace what I have. I can have compassion for those wives and mothers and children who have lost someone, but it doesn't mean that I have to be overwrought with my own grief. Luke is alive and well; he's here with me now. I can't think about how awful it would be if he had been killed—he wasn't.

Luke had his first manicure today. He loved it! The manicurist kept commenting on his smooth hands. Ha! I had to laugh since I think his skin must be naturally exfoliated in the 110-degree weather over in Mesopotamia. Both of us thoroughly enjoyed our massages, and I still love the "Socra-Tease-Me" coral polish I chose for my pedicure.

The meal we devoured at Artisans—the lodge restaurant—was sublime, starting with calamari, a bean and sausage soup, and Caesar salad. Luke decided on the lamb chops while I went back to our Maryland roots and ordered the crab cakes. Our waiter claimed to have been up the entire night before writing a paper for school and had had way too much coffee. He was so cute when brought out dessert—a sampling of everything they had on offer: crème brûlée—my favorite, a slice of Death by Chocolate pie, some mini fruit tarts, and another sinful chocolatey pie. The platter had "Welcome Home Luke" written around the edges in icing. I think we ate every morsel and licked our fingers afterward!

Dinah, thank you, thank you for putting this together for Luke and me. And thank Charles, please. You both are too generous, but I admit these two days have been blissful. Luke and I have not spoken about Iraq or the war once. It's almost as if the only two people in world who exist are Luke and me. There's no war. There's no deployment. Our country is at peace and we never have to face another phone call or funeral again. It's silly, I know, but I'm sure when we get home to Sackets, I will sit down and ask Luke about the situation in Yusufiyah. I just don't want to deal with these things right now. So again, thank you to Charles and you.

I think you might be interested in these letters that were written by our great-grandmother during WWII. We don't get to study personal letters written during wartime in history classes, and only when someone stumbles across that forgotten chest in the attic where a dusty pile of letters have been saved, wrapped in an old birthday ribbon, are we made aware of the nuances of war, the horrors, the clandestine trysts, the wear on the soul, the harmony of soldiers in arms, the remarkable bravery of fighters and their loved ones. It's more than nostalgia. It's living proof of love, fear, hate, shame, happiness, and all the magic of life. An untuned orchestra reflecting on the times.

Who will write our history? I wonder. Who will speak for us? There are so many variations of war. So many perspectives. Who writes letters today? Who keeps track? What if everything is deleted and sent to a trash file, purged into cyber eternity? Some historian will design our history in a linear fashion that suits his political slant. How would we even know about the Annex if Miep Gies hadn't recovered Anne Frank's strewn pages before the Nazis arrived? It's a miracle that Anne Frank's diary was saved.

We have a small snapshot of our family history, Didi. I photocopied them and meant to send them a few weeks ago but forgot. Forgive me. Enjoy.

x,

C

Partway House. August 28, 1942
Dear Pat,
You are, son, I know, trying to do the thing that will be most useful to your country, and the present bad news is driving you to a decision. If you left Yale at just nineteen and trained to be an officer, you would be too young to lead men, for I saw this in the last war. On the other hand, to go in as a private would waste you and what you have to contribute. Please do not be swayed now by any mass movement in your class, but think of it in longer terms of how much more you will have to offer in two years time. I am not writing as your mother, Pat, but simply to point out to you the common sense of the case. I hope very much that you remember how seldom I feel competent to give advice, but in the case I truly think that I do and want, fully as much as you do, to have you do the thing that helps most . . .
Love, Old Boy,
Mother.

New York. April 14, 1945
Darling Prue,
Last night, Mary Bradley phoned me from California to say that she had just received a grand letter from Pat, dated April 5, in which he said he was to have flak leave in a couple of days. Isn't she an angel to do this? It made us feel pretty fine as we have had no letter this week, and week before last many flying fortresses failed to return from Germany. So he got through that week and all this week has been out of it. We can hope that when he goes back again for his last few missions, it won't be so tough going.

The President's death overshadowed all news yesterday and today on every radio station. When we mourn, we mourn! I do think all our methods are highly comic. After the first staggering regret, we begin to pick up hope about the behavior of our country in the world situation. Of course, the military one is covered and there is no worry there. Then, too, one gathers that Truman, even though he made himself through the Pendergast machine, is personally honest in just the way that Al Smith was, whose rise was through Tammany . . . All that Cabinet at last have their chance to work. The Dictatorship, I think, is over, and a free government will gradually emerge. The lines laid down by the President for the Peace Conference will undoubtedly be followed.

He did a great job, but I really think his part in it is no longer needed and a great deal of suppressed, unused ability of other men will now come to the front. Feel that way, or not?
Much love to you both,
Mother.

Partway House. New York.
August 12, 1945.
Dear Pat,
You are doubtless lying listening to the radio by your bed, and the news, by the time you receive this, may be, may be, well, don't you agree it—MAY be? Atomic bombs dropped on Hiroshima and Nagasaki. Will Japan go by way of Germany? I find it hard to take in, having forgotten what a world is like in peacetime. Prue and I take turns in getting dizzy and sitting down, suddenly . . . This whole summer has been reduced to waiting.
CBP

For fifteen days, the Colemans acted like the rest of America, like people who weren't dealing with a loved one in a war. Breakfasts with hot coffee and newspapers. Conversations around the dining-room table. Trips to the supermarket and drives to school. Impromptu lunch outings or drives up to Kingston, Ontario, to check out a new bistro and shopping. At night, Calli and Luke made love to each other after Audrey went to bed. Calli had been so desperate for his touch that she didn't want to waste a single day while he was home. Luke taught Audrey to ride her bike without training wheels and watched her perform her dances in one of her assorted tutus or Disney costumes. "Daddy, watch me!" He took Audrey to Dunkin' Donuts and to Thompson Park for their daddy-daughter dates. Some afternoons they'd snuggle on the couch and watch a movie. Other wives met their husbands in Germany for ski holidays or in France to see Paris. The Army would have flown Luke wherever he wanted to go for his leave. He decided on home. He decided on his own bed with his own towels and hot shower. Luke only wanted to be with his family for two weeks. Nothing else.

In the two weeks Luke was home, there were moments when she thought she might tell him about what had happened with Henry. Affairs were messy, like war. Did any side really win, and at what cost? Losses could be catastrophic. There was no chance that every-one would come away unscathed, no matter how few people knew. She didn't feel compelled to tell Luke about Henry when they talked about him. Or Eula. And when Henry called the house, Calli let Luke answer, grateful for caller ID. It was much easier to compartmen-talize the affair when Henry's name arose. She could grind on the guilt much better when Luke was in Iraq. She'd never tell him in a letter or email. But with him home, she found herself challenging the notion that it was better to keep it to herself.

Her desire to dump this guilt and admit her egregious insan-ity overwhelmed her, caught her off guard. In the bathroom in the mornings when they brushed their teeth. Driving to fetch Audrey at school as he walked out the door to pick up the paper in the front yard. She wanted to tell him. The guilt oozed out of her like an abscessed boil, exposing her pus, blood, and dead tissue. If she told him, she could clean up the wound. Bandage it. But admitting her breach would damage Luke, crippling his love for her and scarring his morale. Destroying his friendship with Henry. She loved Luke too much to do that. She had to endure her guilt on her own. If she were to tell Luke, it would have to be after his deployment. She didn't want to be responsible for his state of mind. Didn't want any-thing horrible to happen to him. They'd made it this far. She could make it another five months. She knew she could.

The night before Luke had to fly back to Iraq, he and Calli lay in bed staring at each other. His fingers tickled her back. A game they'd played when they were first together.

"Okay, guess this one now," he said as he wrote words on her back with his index finger, gently brushing her skin.

Calli lay there blissfully savoring his voice, his tender touch, the gentle-natured moment. Tomorrow he'd be gone.

"Luke, tell me honestly. What's going on over there?"

"I haven't killed anyone, if that's what you mean."

"No, no, that's not it. Well, I guess that's part of it, but...I'm just trying to make sense of it. Do you think we should be there?"

Luke stopped using his finger as a paintbrush, rested his hand on her back, closed his eyes, and spoke. "It smells like all those shitty places; burning garbage. The heat makes the raw sewage reek, the canals are polluted and smell too. We're not supposed to stare at the women, but they wear burkas, which gives me the creeps. You can never be one hundred percent sure that there isn't a weapon under there or if it really is a woman."

"That's so scary. "

"The bull rushes and reeds grow thicker than bamboo from the canal to the edge of the road—literally—they're the problem. It's so thick that you can't see anything. Perfect for hiding an IED or rocket for ambushes."

"Jesus."

"You wanted to know."

Through the windows, Calli heard the crickets singing and above them the tame drone of the ceiling fan. Her toes rested in between Luke's legs by his ankles, and her eyes, adjusted to the dark, stared at his silhouette, curiously searching for emotion.

"Mahmoudiyah is more populated than Yusufiyah, so there's more civilian traffic on the roads. More traffic means we move more slowly, which makes it easier for the terrorists to ambush us. Once we leave the hardball in Mahmoudiyah, the road into Baghdad looks like any road, two lanes each way with overpasses and big green signs like we have here. We drive faster on these roads, but also it's dangerous because the overpasses are perfect hiding spots for snipers and bomb droppers."

Calli said nothing but now turned on her back to look up at the ceiling.

"You said you wanted to know everything."

He went on to tell her that Yusufiyah was all cinderblock and tin. Most of the buildings were in some state of disrepair from the years of fighting and lack of maintenance. No skyscrapers. Baghdad was more developed, with Sadaam's palaces and commercial infrastructure but not modern like in Dubai. "And yes," he said, "they pray.

Many of the Iraqi soldiers are very pious and pray five times a day. There was a mosque near our FOB, and the imam broadcasts the call to prayer five times a day."

Calli propped herself up on her elbow. "Do you think the locals are happy we are there?"

"I think so. I mean, I think there is a general acceptance of Americans. It was really bad at the beginning. Any success we have is always more difficult since Al Qaeda's charge is to disrupt American success and fuel sectarian violence. Many Iraqis are very thankful, though. We pushed Aqiz out of the area west of the Euphrates and opened up the entire AO. We've stopped sectarian violence. We've provided economic support for small businesses with micro-grants."

"Aqiz?"

"They're an Iraqi terror group that pledged allegiance to Al Qaeda."

"Are you still being attacked?"

"Yes," he said, explaining that mortars and rockets were the weapons of choice for attacking the patrol base. "Every time we opened a new patrol base we had a gun fight, but they wouldn't stay too long; IEDs and indirect fire work better for them."

"Do locals carry guns?"

"No, although each family is allowed to have one for security. I'm sure they have more. One day—are you sure you want to hear this?"

"Yes."

"One day, I was driving on a patrol. There was a little five-year-old boy, barefoot, walking next to a mule, holding the bridle while the mother sat on the cart with the bed full of reeds. It was about 115 degrees and the kid was barefoot walking on the street. *Tough little bastard*, was all I could think...and I hope there isn't a bomb in the back of the cart."

"Do you see a lot of children?"

"Yeah, especially around towns and villages. They love pencils and candy, so much that if you make the mistake of not stopping, you get mobbed by kids trying to get something. We smile, but we don't play with them."

"Do you ever talk politics with people there?"

"Sometimes, with some of the Iraqis we work with. They know that sooner or later the Americans will leave, and they'll have to start all over again. They're concerned about the US leaving too soon."

"Do you think that you are making a difference?"

"Yes. Both Sunni and Shia prayers are being broadcast in Yusufiyah now. Before we got there, that would have been unthinkable." Luke paused and was quiet for a moment "Listen, Cal, I don't want to talk about this anymore. I want to talk about you. How's your playing? I loved the last song you sent me."

Calli squeezed her eyes shut, wondering if she was ready to play for him now that he was leaving again.

"Hold on." As she climbed out of bed, it hit her how tomorrow night she'd be alone in the bed again, bewildered by the images of Iraq and the war that he'd shared with her, but she'd abandoned the girl who gave up, the woman in the shadow, the intimidated wife. She would miss him—deeply—but it now it all added up to something, an unanticipated upshot. Her marriage to Luke had been the time and space she needed to figure out who she was. She'd surprised herself in the last nine months. Ambition held Calli in the crook of her arm and carried her to a new land where she felt equal to Luke, a land where, in addition to being a wife, mother, and friend, she was Calliope Wendover Coleman. No more. No less.

With Black Beauty in her lap, she said, "So, here goes: 'Blue Star.'"

You are the author of your life
A girl, a woman, then a wife
Love is the reason
Women in every season
Hang the blue star banner
We send our husbands to war

Even when we're not sure what for
In our hearts and in our windows
Love is the reason
Women in every season
Hang the blue star banner...

Luke whispered, "You're so beautiful. And brave."

⇶ ⇷

Luke flies back today, Calli thought as she fought to open her eyes. Five months isn't as long as fifteen months, but it's still over one hundred and fifty days.

Last night she'd wept on the sofa thinking about him leaving again. She'd read somewhere that grief was the experience of not having anywhere to place love, and that while we grieve, we must pay attention to the most minute details to be more in tune with ourselves so we can somehow find our way back into the rhythm of life. Loving Luke was easy when he was here. Loving Luke the phantom husband made her feel like she had to harness her love, corral it in a paddock, and keep it confined until he came home again. She had to learn to place it elsewhere. She had learned to filter her love for Luke into the Divas, her music, and Audrey.

Compared to when he deployed last August, she didn't feel empty and confused. Audrey and she would be fine even though they would miss him. She would miss him when she smelled the sand and the waves, when she smelled a cigar or heard Johnny Cash, when she saw a soldier in uniform or a tall, attractive bald man, when she made Audrey pancakes or added cinnamon to her coffee, when she went to bed each night and woke up each morning seeing that the other side of the bed was still perfectly made. She would miss him when she went to his favorite places, when anyone asked her about him, when she needed to pick up the phone and hear his voice. She would miss him when she was tired of being Audrey's sole parent and she wanted to sip a glass of wine and eat Stilton and oatmeal biscuits with him in their backyard. I'll miss him, she thought, but I don't need him—there's a difference.

At the airport, Audrey and Calli were allowed to go down to the concourse where Luke's plane to Atlanta and eventually Iraq would take off. Calli started to cry, but Audrey and Luke seemed to take all this in stride. Luke had on his uniform and carried his backpack. They held hands with each other and Audrey.

Walking down to his gate, Calli was surprised how quickly the last fifteen days had passed. It certainly wasn't enough time to get used to Luke being home. In fact, she thought, if he was home any longer, this good-bye would be more difficult. Finally, his flight was called and inevitably his section. Luke was already in Army mode: rip off the Band-Aid, let's get the show on the road, the sooner I leave, the sooner I can return.

The three hugged. Calli cried more. Luke hugged Audrey. She seemed oblivious, or maybe she knew something Calli didn't know. They walked up to the ticket agent with him. Calli squeezed him again with her whole body. In five months, he'd be home for good. "I know you're coming back to us. But, damn, I love you so much. I'm really going to miss you," she said. And without a pause, he turned to walk away.

Audrey and Calli stayed to watch him walk down the jetway and eventually out of sight as he boarded the plane. They stayed until the bitter end, watching the plane taxi away from the gate, onto the runway, and eventually take off. "There he goes, Auds!"

There was no reason to linger in the airport, so they walked back to the car hand in hand. Audrey handled the separation from Luke better than expected. Calli had heard horror stories of children yelling and screaming, clinging desperately to their fathers as they headed back out to war. Audrey was calm. As they walked into the garage, Calli said tearily, "Auds, I miss Daddy."

She turned to Calli and said, "Mama, you're going to be alright."

>>>> <<<<

A woman named Jenny Kelly from David Hess's office called.

"Calli, I work for David Hess here at Hess Studios, and we want to help you get your music published. I think, actually, we met at the premier of *Rio Hato*."

Calli was stunned. "What? How did you know about my music?" Then Calli remembered that she had written an email to one of the interns in Hess's office who had been working with Calli to send care packages to Luke and his men. At the time of the email, she wrote that she was dealing with the deployment by writing songs. "Wow, I don't know what to say. Thank you so much."

"You're so welcome. We want to help in any way we can, to thank Luke and you for your service to our country. There's no guarantee that anything will come of it, but the first step is to get your music registered for copyright protection. Have you done that yet?"

"No, no I haven't done anything. I've been going down to Walter Reed to see the wounded guys, and I play for them. I'm writing music and, and...I just can't believe I'm having this conversation. I must sound like an idiot."

The woman laughed graciously. "You're fine, Calli. You're great. Get in touch with the United States Copyright Office for starters. Once you have that worked out, call me and we'll go from there. We have people we work with in all different capacities to help find music for our movies. We'd love to see if we can pair you up with someone. Okay? Sound good?"

"Sound good? Yes! Thank you."

That night, Calli invited the Divas over to eat cake and drink Prosecco. "We're celebrating!" she said. "I baked all afternoon—a five-layer coconut rum cake."

When the women arrived, they pumped Calli for the details.

"I was so overwhelmed. I had completely forgotten that I had even mentioned I was writing songs to the intern. They might want to use my music in a movie. But who knows..."

"Calli! That's amazing," Josie said.

"See, I told you, you could do it," Daphne said.

"I don't want to get too excited, because there's always the chance that it could be rejected or not picked up..."

"Stop it!" Daphne said. "You are so talented. I've watched you sing in front of those guys at Walter Reed. When that guitar is in your hands, you're a rock star. Luke is going to be so proud of you. Have you told him yet?"

"Yeah, I wrote him an email as soon as I got off the phone. I haven't heard back from him, but I know he'll be thrilled."

"We're going to know a famous singer-songwriter!" Josie said.

"You have to take us to the Grammys with you," said Rachel, smiling. "Ooh, we can go buy dresses together."

"You rock, sista! Viva la diva!" Daphne said.

"Viva la diva," they said all together, clinking their champagne flutes together.

My Dearest Love,

Happy news! Happy news! I'm beyond thrilled to read your latest news about your song. David Hess's gang is first class, and I know they will treat you will the utmost respect. You deserve this. I'm so proud of you and excited for all our adventures together. I'm behind you one hundred percent

Things have quieted a bit here. Soon enough, I'll be on a plane heading back to Audrey and you. You're an awesome mother, wife, and songwriter. Please give Audrey a huge kiss and hug from her dad. I miss you both and love you a googol.

Enjoy today but know you are my miracle every day.
All my love,
L

⇶ 25 ⇷

June 14, 2007
Immortals Patrol Attacked Near Baghdad, One Soldier Missing
By Col. Edward Browne

FORT DRUM - Just before dawn on the morning of June 12, an Immortals' patrol was attacked by Iraqi insurgents. The patrol's mission was to prevent the enemy from emplacing roadside bombs in an area known for its improvised explosive device (IED) activity. The attack was coordinated and well planned. By the time fellow soldiers could reach the scene, four Iraqi soldiers fighting alongside US soldiers had been killed. One soldier from the patrol was taken prisoner and is believed to be in the custody of an al-Qaeda-allied group called the Islamic State of Iraq. The military is using helicopters and fixed-wing aviation support, unmanned aerial vehicles, tactical river boats, tracking dogs, Special Operations Forces, and Iraqi soldiers to find the missing soldier. Nearby residents and informants have provided the Commando Brigade with numerous tips. The search will continue until the soldier is found.

Calli heard the news from Colonel Robert Whitney, who pulled into her driveway in a brown sedan. Calli was weeding while Audrey swung on the tree swing singing "You Are My Sunshine." The pancakes Calli had made for breakfast crept up her throat while her heart beat so loudly that she was convinced that it might leap out of her chest. She didn't know it was Rob in the car until the door opened. He was supposed to be in Iraq.

"Luke was on a psy-ops mission," Rob told her.

"What?" Her breath came in gasps as her lungs deflated. She clutched the kitchen counter, having invited Rob in for coffee, too disoriented to be ungracious.

Outside the fizzle of a lawnmower started. A faint laugh-track echoed from Calli's room upstairs where Audrey watched a Disney show. "He's a paramilitary operations officer working for one of the government agencies. He may have been in psy-ops in Panama, too," Rob explained to Calli. "I'm not supposed to tell you this."

Calli's cheeks burned.

"The government will deny any responsibility if you ask questions, but I thought you should know."

She gave a frightful staccato chuckle. He reached to hold her hand, but then checked himself. Instead he went on, "A guy like Luke is invaluable for this kind of mission. He speaks Oghuz, Arabic, Kurdish, French. He blends in well. He—"

"No, no. He only speaks a little Spanish. That's it. I remember him writing me a few months ago that he wanted to learn Arabic."

"I need you to understand, Calli. This is classified."

Calli nodded in agreement. She did not know what to do with her body, holding onto the counter to find a new center of balance.

"If Luke is alive, his position would be compromised if anyone knew."

Calli half-listened. *If Luke is alive.* What if he wasn't alive? "Is he dead? Is Luke dead?" she screamed hysterically.

"Listen to what I'm saying. Luke told you he volunteered to go with 2nd Brigade, right? That he was working at Division and that 4-31 needed a master sergeant?"

The intricacies of Luke's explanations—or lack of them—flooded her brain. How naïve she'd been.

"Actually, he volunteered years ago. He's been training for this mission since after 9/11."

"Why?"

"There was a lack of qualified linguists. He was recruited and trained to be the elite of the elite when he worked in the Ranger Battalion. He's been providing support for the agency's intelligence-gathering operations."

"Oh my god. Are you telling me Luke has always been involved in covert stuff? I'm so confused. I just don't understand. Why didn't he tell me?"

"He couldn't," Rob said. "We are doing everything to find him. The Iraqi soldiers he was working with, well, they think one of them turned on Luke."

"They're torturing him!" Calli whispered. "They're torturing my husband. And what is the Army, the government doing? What the Hell are they doing? Oh my god. Oh my god. Rob. They'll cut him up into pieces." She ached like never before thinking about Luke. The gentle man who tried to save a beached whale. The father who made smiley faces with breakfast food. The husband who adored her.

"Don't think like that. Luke is one of the best-trained soldiers I've ever worked with. He's intelligent. He's going to be all right. You must focus on his rescue. His survival. Don't let yourself think the worst. I'm flying back to Iraq tomorrow, and I'll be in touch and let you know anything as soon as I do. I promise. I promise you, Calli. We'll find him."

>>> <<<

For days, she looked out the window for hours. She expected that someone would call her and tell her that Luke had been found, alive—that he was on a plane coming home. She didn't know what to tell people. The tokens of consolation poured in: letters of sympathy, thoughtfully chosen books, concerned emails, inspirational movies, and food that went uneaten. Henry called and called, and Calli avoided him until finally, one day, she didn't.

> *Dear Henry,*
>
> *I'm hopeful that you are well. I've missed talking to you but, well, after what happened with Eula, then Luke, it's just been too messy for me to think about. Before Luke left, and for the first five or six months into the deployment, I felt like the Army had done something to me personally. I resented that the Army always came first, making me second. I had a lot of anger and frustration with my situation. I tried to help without sometimes knowing why or if I should. It took Luke deploying to the war and me forging ahead with a new life, with new friends, for me to let go of what I thought was the truth—that I needed Luke to buoy me up and that I could escape pain and loss.*
>
> *Loss is a certainty of life. As a friend once preached in his sermon, it is in the search for and the reconciliation with the lost that we are most loved if we allow it. I learned to love my life, my amazing friends—the Diva War Brides— my music, Audrey, my family, Luke, in ways that I never felt or imagined possible. Love is with us in all our losses and with us on our journeys to new findings of restoration, recovery, and hope.*
>
> *I surrendered.*
>
> *But I don't feel defeated. And if I was defeated, whoever I was, I was defeated by a much stronger, more compassionate woman. I used to feel like a victim, waiting for a better life to come along, waiting for something to happen, waiting for the next big deal to come down the pike, waiting for my husband to come home so we could start going out to dinner again as a couple, waiting for the worst to happen,*

waiting to eat dessert until I lost ten pounds, waiting for my child to outgrow perpetual questioning—it's just that: waiting. And when you wait, you aren't living, it's just happening all around you, to you.

I hold myself completely responsible for our affair. I was so thirsty for connection. I mistook my feelings—probably because I was drunk and lonely—for something that I had to have immediately. But it was wrong of me to look to you to provide that for me. Now Eula's gone. Luke is missing. And our friendship, I don't know. Henry, I love you. I always have. But I was never in love with you. You're an amazing man, and I wish I could have been there for you over the last year. I just couldn't. You must understand. It's taken me months to write this letter. Maybe when Luke returns, we can move ahead and forget that night. But I have this nagging feeling that God is punishing me because of that night. He took Luke from me because I cheated. Please forgive me.
Calli

Calli had Luke's Rolex fixed and had several of the links removed so that she could wear it until Luke came home. At first it seemed clunky—heavy on her smaller wrist. The stainless steel amulet wrapped around her. Sometimes she would take it off and realize that she couldn't go long without it. The stupid watch. Seconds ticked. Hours passed. During the deployment, she counted down the days until Luke came home. Now she counted how many days he had been away. Too many.

In August, Calli, Audrey, and the Divas were asked to participate in Sackets Harbor's annual jazz parade. With other local women and children, they danced down Main Street, New Orleans style, dressed as flappers while jazz bands trailed behind them. She wore her best impression of robe de style and Clara Bow black wig, dark makeup, and false eyelashes. Daphne and Josie were unrecognizable in their costumes. Daphne bought multicolored eyelashes that swooped down like wings every time she blinked. Her huge breasts braced against the canary-yellow fabric of her flapper get-up. Josie's long legs in fishnets stretched out below her dress while she pranced down the street. They wiggled their fannies and waved to the crowds on the sidewalk. Audrey wore her Jasmine costume, with its turquoise and sequined bodice and pantaloons.

High from the jazz, bold sunshine, her friends, and Audrey, for about thirty minutes she forgot that Luke was missing.

>>> <<<

The weekend before the brigade was due to return home, the Divas and Calli had a party replete with phallic straws, tequila drinks, and Douglas the pink, blow-up penis with a smiley face, who escorted them to the bars in Sackets Harbor. Josie and Daphne surprised Calli when they arrived wearing hot-pink T-shirts with Viva La Diva inked on them, adorned with large, colorful sequins. They made one for each of the four of them, and then a smaller one for Audrey that read Diva in Training.

"I love it!" She tore off her shirt and immediately put on her Diva T-shirt. "You are the best! I love these. What a great idea."

Earlier in the afternoon, the women started drinking tequila shots at Calli's house while they spray-painted welcome home signs on huge white sheets they would tie up on a fence outside the airfield. Calli swallowed hard when Daphne called her and asked if she wanted to do this with them, but she was glad that the Divas hadn't excluded her—even though Luke wasn't coming home with the men. The women had purchased several cans of neon-pink and blue spray paint. They took the sheets out into her backyard and in enormous letters sprayed, Welcome Home TRIS! or I Love You HUEY! How she longed to have a sheet for Audrey and her that she could spray GOOD JOB LUKE! on, or Luke Coleman ROCKS!

Audrey asked, "Is Daddy coming home, too? Can we make him a sign?"

"Not yet," she said, smiling, trying hard to hold it together.

Inside her heart was broken, but her melancholy, misty mood wasn't going to tarnish the sparkle of her friends' excitement. While Miles Davis's "Miles Ahead" played in her head, reminding her of life before the war, she put on the "I am fine" costume that she had become accustomed to donning.

With Douglas, their Diva T-shirts, and phallic straws, they decided to go traipsing around the village. Louise offered to drive them, which was prudent because toward the end of the night Josie wound up falling face-first into the bar. Calli leaned down to help her up, and *wham*, whacked her own head on the side of the mahogany. Too drunk to notice the ache, she tried again to lean down and help Josie off the floor, all the while laughing. After three bars and many drinks, Daphne pulled the plug on the night and suggested they go back to Calli's house to crash. Like circus clowns, they fell out of the car, laughing and holding each other up. The last time she'd let loose like this was after Eula's funeral. Calli winced at the memory. Her eye was bruised and swollen from bonking it on the bar, but she didn't care—didn't feel it. At one A.M., Rachel asked Louise to take her home. Daphne, the maternal Diva, went into Calli's house to relieve the babysitter while Josie and Calli ended up lying in her backyard on the cool grass near the tree swing, holding hands and looking up at the stars.

"I know Luke is alive," Calli told her. "I feel him."

"Of course he is!" Josie exclaimed. "I feel him, too!" Closing her eyes, Calli squeezed her hand harder. Her grip communicated that she, too, believed that if they said it enough times, it had to be true.

➤➤➤ 26 ⫷⫷⫷

Audrey's bony bottom shifted in Calli's lap as she read *Goodnight Moon*.

"Mama, is Daddy ever coming home again? I want to read *Goodnight Moon* to him."

Without waiting for Calli to say goodnight to the cow jumping over the moon or goodnight to the light or the red balloon, Audrey expected an answer.

Her body went rigid on the floor of Audrey's room, where they were nestled together on her blue and green wool rug. The elephants, tigers, lions, giraffes, alligators, and zebras stitched into her rug weren't going to give her an answer. Stuffed bears, Barbie dolls, and her dollhouse family stood mute. Calli could not look down at her. She stared out the window, thinking of Luke recording stories in this very room into a Dictaphone for Audrey before he deployed so she wouldn't forget his voice. Calli's mind took her back to the day before he left when she watched him pushing Audrey on the tree swing while they laughed and sang, "Five little monkeys swinging in the tree, teasing Mr. Alligator can't catch me."

Calli didn't know what to say to her. How could she answer her after all these months of nothing? Audrey hadn't spoken about him. Neither had Calli. They'd stopped listening to those tapes with the recorded stories. Calli's focus remained solidly on Luke returning—alive. For many families, the worst had happened. People being maimed or killed—or abducted—that was the nature of war, whether people liked it or not. But on some level, Calli had been preparing for Luke's abduction—was prepared for it, actually. She needed to be alive and believe. She had to believe that their love would keep them and guide them when they were lost. She had to believe that she was here for a purpose and to live out that purpose every day. She had to believe in her transgressions as well as her good works, learn from it all, and live.

She believed that Luke would come home to her. She truly did.

>>>> <<<<

One day, out of nowhere, Calli made enough food for sixty people. She hadn't cooked in months—then she cooked because it was the only thing that could make her feel again. To eat the food Luke loved was to bring him back to life. She gorged herself on Stilton, Marcona almonds, dark chocolate squares, blondies, rosemary bread, Tuscan olives, salami, slices of red pepper dipped into hummus, gooey macaroni and cheese. For months, it had seemed wrong to do something so life affirming and self-indulgent as eating.

After months of no news, Lucy Wendover convinced Calli to have some kind of memorial for Luke. "Calli, you are not the only one who misses him. Poor Madelon. His family. And Henry. And us. Calliope, we miss him. Even the Red Cross is saying they can't find him. There's no trace of him. You've got to face this. You must do something."

"Mother, shut up. He's my husband, goddammit."

"Calli. I know you don't like me sometimes, but I want you to listen to me. This isn't just about you. Many, many people loved Luke."

"*Love* Luke, Mother. Love."

"Love him. But you can't move forward unless you accept that he might not come back. Would you please consider, for all who love him, having some kind of memorial? Please, Calliope. Please. For Audrey's sake and yours. Please think about it."

"Trust that I'll make the right decisions, okay? I'll have the memorial service. You're right, I need to do it for everyone else, but don't tell me Luke is dead. Don't tell me he's not coming back. You don't know."

>>> <<<

The entire time people were at her house, she stood at the dining-room table where she'd set up the buffet, eating and drinking. It seemed that the more she drank and ate, the more she began to think that Luke wasn't dead, like the food was sending her a message. She was finally going nuts. When people asked her what she was going to do, she'd say, "I'm staying here until Luke is found. He's not dead."

Rachel and Daphne poured her wine even when her glass wasn't empty. While it would have been so easy to drink and eat herself into oblivion, that responsible person who lived inside her would remind her that she had to take care of her little girl. When she looked at Audrey, she saw Luke. Yes, a beautiful female version of him. When the phone rang, Calli wouldn't let Audrey answer because she didn't want any nosy journalists speaking to her, probing her for answers. The JAG office at Fort Drum had advised her on what to say to these media vultures. How could she explain to a four-year-old what was going on?

It was confusing for Audrey when they'd gone, months ago, to Fort Drum to welcome home the Divas' husbands. They all sat together, Audrey, too—wearing their pink Diva T-shirts—so that when the men came marching into the gym, they could easily spot their women in the crowd.

When the band played the National Anthem and everyone stood, Calli trembled. Inside the enormous gym at Fort Drum, people gathered in the stands with their little American flags, bouquets and presents, preparing to reunite with their soldier who'd been fighting for fifteen months. As the anthem played, the soldiers marched in in formation. The pageantry was stunning, their swallow-tailed guidons bobbing in stride, stoic faces masking their utter relief and happiness to be home, waiting to be dismissed for reunions.

As she watched her friends reunite with their husbands, she resolved that she, too, would have this moment. She would make the Army find Luke.

⟫⟫ 27 ⟪⟪

Summer 2008: One year later

L uke's birthday.
It had been almost two years since he left for Iraq. He was still missing. With the help of David Hess's Hollywood connections, one of Calli's songs, "Blue Star," had been picked up by an agent. She was optimistic that millions would hear the music and her words.

One day, an invitation arrived in the mail. The envelope read *Master Sergeant and Mrs. Luke Baldwin Coleman*. She admired Richard Strong's optimism. It was no doubt part of what helped him get out of Walter Reed in less than a year. Usually she loved weddings, but this was the third wedding she'd have to attend alone.

"Thankfully," Daphne said, "I'll be your date. I'm sure Richard and Danielle won't mind if I come with you."

They drove down to Baltimore and spent the night with Lucy and Haines. No one mentioned Luke or asked Calli about her plans for the future. Haines said, "Why don't you borrow my car. It's got GPS in it, and sometimes driving in DC can be tricky."

They happily climbed into his Cadillac Escalade with all the trimmings and headed for Fort Belvoir. When they arrived, Kathy Strong, Richard's mother, greeted them. "Oh Calli!" she said. "I'm so glad you are here. This is such a special day. Richard is thrilled that you could make it."

"Hi, Kathy." Calli hugged her. "I'm glad to be here, too. It's amazing how far he's come. How's he doing with his prosthetics? I can't wait to see him standing up."

"He's doing well. He's not running yet, which frustrates him, but I know he'll keep at it. I see you have your guitar. Are you playing something for us today? I know Richard loves your music."

"Yes, Richard asked me to play a song during the ceremony."

They walked to their seats. Calli recognized several soldiers she'd met on her trips to Walter Reed and some of the others who'd returned with the rest of the brigade at the end of the deployment. Her heart ached for Luke but swelled with happiness for Richard.

When he walked into the chapel, her composure unraveled. She burst into tears. Daphne took her hand. "You'll be okay."

"I know, thank you. Thank you for being here with me."

When she had visited Richard at Walter Reed, she'd never seen him standing. She hadn't seen his prosthetics. She hadn't watched him walk. His strength had returned and his pallor had faded, but to see him walk into the chapel made her breath catch. His life would be different, of course, but he was alive. Here. About to marry the love of his life.

What was Luke doing as she watched the ceremony? Trembling, she listened to the exchange of vows, remembering her wedding—for better or worse. Calli remembered how it had been raining and forty-five degrees in late May, unseasonably cold for Baltimore. People told her that rain was a good omen on wedding days. Calli and Luke had chosen the chapel at St. David's for their ceremony and the Maryland Club for their reception. The rain wouldn't hinder much. They'd have to have their pictures taken inside—and who looked at their wedding pictures anyway? But Haines, usually the calm family member, stomped around his house furiously slamming doors and cursing the weather.

"Dad, it's okay. Don't be mad. You can't control the weather."

"I just want the day to be perfect for you."

"It is perfect. I'm marrying Luke. And the only thing that matters—the only thing—is that Luke and I and Father Daggers show up. We'll just get out the umbrellas and put on sweaters. Don't be upset. I'm not."

Calli thought about the "for better or worse" vow. How many couples actually pondered the worst? And what was the worst? At what point was a couple experiencing the worst? Or the best? On her wedding day, she couldn't have imagined anything worse than losing her husband. But there was something worse: not knowing. She clenched her teeth and focused on the ceremony.

Richard was standing, holding Danielle's hands with both of his. She'd seen him at his worst. She'd witnessed his recovery. And while his limbs would never grow back, his new life—since his Alive Day—was just beginning.

➤➤➤ 28 ⫷⫷⫷

A new soldier family had moved in on Mill Creek Lane. She'd heard from Louise, her snoopy neighbor, that they were military. "Ya know the house at the end of our lane?" Louise asked. "I heard that he's a captain or something. Come from the South, I think. Paid full price for the house. Got four kids."

It was the nature of places like Sackets—military families moved in and out. Many of the civilians didn't like to become friends with military families—not because they didn't like military, but because the military families were transient. It was easier to ignore them.

One by one, the Divas left Fort Drum. Huey Hollis got stationed at Temple teaching ROTC. "You're going to love it," Calli told him. "A ROTC assignment is a cakewalk compared to this BS."

Tristan Merchant decided that he'd had enough and got out of the Army to start life as a civilian. He and Josie moved to Norfolk, where he got a job working for Maersk in the ship management business. Calli missed Josie the most. Of all the Divas, she and Josie had spent the most time together. She was like a younger sister. Since the move, she still called Calli weekly to check in and make sure Calli was alive.

Rachel and Jed's marriage was crumbling. Jed had cheated on

Rachel as soon as he was back from Iraq—with his nurse—and lied to her for months. She asked Calli what she thought.

"I don't know, Rachel. Do you want my honest opinion?"

"Yes, be honest."

"I don't think it sounds good. I mean, seriously, who goes to Saratoga for a long weekend with his nurse, stays in the same room, but it's platonic? And what about that whole thing with the Cartier purchase on your credit card? Do you think maybe he wanted you to find out? It didn't seem like he was trying all that hard to hide it from you."

Rachel took her boys and moved to Wilmington, North Carolina. Calli didn't hear from her often, but Rachel was always close to her heart.

They had one final Diva dinner at Calli's house while they were all still living in northern New York. Calli polished all her silver and even ironed a pink linen tablecloth. She pulled out her Tiffany plates that she'd received as a wedding gift. Several bottles of Moet & Chandon chilled on ice, and there was sparkling cider for Audrey. For two days, she prepared the closing dinner for the Diva War Brides, not sure when they would be together again. If ever.

On the menu were Cabernet-braised short ribs with Gorgonzola polenta and mixed herb gremolata. She cut the rosemary and thyme out of her own herb garden. Daphne made a pomegranate Champagne punch while Rachel brought cheese and a warm French baguette. Josie, naturally, made a flourless chocolate cake and vanilla ice cream. Rachel also made cocktails—smoky mescal on the rocks with lemon.

"Viva la diva!" they toasted.

"Here's to the greatest women in the world," Calli said. "I'm going to miss you so much."

"Oh honey," Daphne said, "we're going to miss you, too. And Audrey."

Calli thought, This wretched chapter is over—for them.

The Divas had inspired and humbled her. These women whom

she most likely wouldn't have known under other circumstances held her up and brought her along during the most challenging time of her life. They took turns nursing each other but also exposed themselves as grief stripped away their costumes. Calli couldn't imagine surviving without them, but she was resolved to stay put.

The other wives moved as well: Brittany and Rick filed for divorce; Lisa Herbie left to go be with her brother in California. Veronica moved with her husband to Vicenza, Italy, where they would be stationed for three years, renting out their purple house to another military family.

So many people had asked Calli, "How do you do it?" But she didn't have a good answer. The best she could do: love. There was an eighty percent divorce rate in the Army—it wasn't easy making it through.

Audrey stopped talking about Luke. Stopped asking Calli when he would be home. This was a relief.

In an effort to keep Audrey convinced, she would occasionally say, "When Daddy is finished teaching the Bad Guys how to be Good Guys, he'll be back."

"When is that, Mama?"

"I don't know, but soon I hope."

She hadn't told Audrey that the Bad Guys captured him. Or that the International Committee of the Red Cross believed they'd never "locate" him—or his remains. Because Luke's mission was classified, it had been impossible for Calli to gather much more than Rob Whitney had originally told her. Sometimes Calli would giggle thinking about Luke speaking Arabic or French when she'd thought he'd only known a little bit of Spanish. She thought about how she considered herself lucky to have a husband who was honest with her—about everything—but actually, they'd both had secrets from each other. Maybe everybody did. Maybe everybody needed to. Would Calli's admission to Luke about her affair with Henry have bolstered Luke's chances for survival? Would Calli have been better off knowing that Luke was more than just an infantryman? No, not all of life's smudged details were worthy of being known.

＊＊＊ ―― ＜＜＜

Slowly, Calli's resolve to wait for Luke in Sackets eroded. Audrey and she were leaving. She'd been packing. For months, she'd grieved. Written. Worked on her music. She'd finally decided to apply to a music therapy program so she could work with veterans. She'd been accepted to Howard University. She and Audrey were moving to DC in a week. Her father had helped her find a house. Robert Whitney took her to the JAG office and helped her to convince them to pay for her "final move."

Part of her was ready to move on. Grief, she realized, was always a work in progress. She needed to start her new life, a new journey. Music therapy would enable to her to marry her love of music and helping wounded soldiers. She was keeping Luke's things, although her mother had told her to face up to the fact that he wasn't coming home. Lucy was less than pleased with Calli's plan to go back to school.

"Music therapy? Calli, your father and I are so worried about you. You've got to find a job and support the two of you."

"I know!"

"We've helped you with the house, but that's where it ends," Lucy said much too crossly. "We're not paying for Audrey to go to private school."

In a sharp tone Calli said, "Mother, let's face it, you're worried that you're going to have to support me for the rest of my life. That I'll drain your retirement fund. That I'm a quitter, that I give up."

"Not this again. You're the one who quit. You said—"

"You should be happy for me. I'm doing what I want to do. I'm doing something that can help people. And I told you, I don't expect you to pay for Audrey's school. I've applied for financial aid and I'll figure it out."

As Calli packed the house, she struggled with what to do with Luke's things. The previous June, after Rob Whitney showed up, she threw herself into Luke's closet and grasped at his clothes, praying that some lingering scent would hit her. For weeks, her soul ached. She drank at least a bottle of wine every night—she couldn't really take care of Audrey. Her mother showed up; she couldn't mend Calli's broken heart, but she was able to cook and clean. Calli felt like she was in purgatory. Her trips to Walter Reed had helped her to cope with the idea of Luke's dismemberment. Back on her first visit, she had crossed the threshold into Richard Strong's room at Walter Reed immediately. One of the physical therapists told her that she could always tell which marriages would make it or wouldn't depending on how long the wife lingered on the threshold of the hospital room.

>>>>- -<<<<

The Sackets summer sunshine radiated into the kitchen, warming the pine beneath her bare feet. Her windows were thrown wide open. Birds chirped love songs and bugs sang. Breakfast plates clanked and chattered in her neighbors' homes, echoing across the yard. Someone was sweeping his patio.

Calli made Audrey's favorite breakfast, sausage and bagels. She toasted her plain bagel and used the sausage to make a face—like Luke used to do for her. In order to safeguard against forgetting him, she'd adopted some of his rituals. The prospect of a new life in DC gave her strength. She didn't know if this was the path the Universe intended for her, but she knew it was the path that would take her away from the pain of the last three years here in New York. Sackets had been good to her, but she didn't want to live here any longer. The winters were too tough, last summer even tougher.

Josie called. "I just wanted to wish ya luck with the move."

Calli probed. "How are you?"

Josie hedged, "Oh, I'm just fine, ya know, all's good."

She tried again. "How's Norfolk? How's Tristan?"

"I'm pregnant!"

Life inside her. Calli was happy for her. Josie was a natural with Audrey, carefully teaching Audrey to ski or offering to sit for her when Calli needed to go somewhere without a child attached to her. Calli knew she'd wanted a baby for a long time. Crying into the phone, she apologized for her sappiness. "I'm so happy for you, Josie. This is the best news I've heard in such a long time." She thought, Will I have another baby? With Luke? I can't imagine a father better than Luke.

Finally, her house was packed, except for the beds and a few dishes. An obstacle course of boxes in every room. The movers would be there in a few days to pack up and move their things.

As she listened to Josie go over her nursery ideas, Audrey ran into the kitchen. "Mama, there's a man walking up our sidewalk."

She looked through the curtains. An unfamiliar car was parked in the driveway.

The brown sedan. A gaping hole sprouted in her gut.

Rob Whitney was walking purposefully toward the house. At once, she was nauseous and hot. She shut her eyes, praying. Shaking, she told Josie she'd call her back and said, "Audrey, sweet girl, please go to your room."

"Why?"

"Please, Audrey. Please, just go up there for a little bit. Mama needs to talk to Major Whitney. I'll take you to the village to get ice cream afterward. Please go."

She walked to the door and opened it.

"Rob, come in," she said. A twinge of disquiet electrified every molecule in her body. Spontaneously, she grabbed Rob's hand and pulled him into her kitchen. If she spoke enough, then he wouldn't have time to answer her, tell her his news, but maybe—maybe—the news was what she wanted. There are moments in life when you leave behind a trail memories in order to create new ones. There's a moment when the history you've created, the story you've told, is about to change.

Pleasepleasepleasepleasepleasepleaseplease.

Rob took both her hands. Squeezed them. "Luke's been found. He's coming home."

Author's Note

I come from a family that still writes letters—handwritten with envelopes and stamps and delivered by the postal service. While we don't eschew email, it's lovely to open the mailbox, recognize personal handwriting, and tear open the envelope. When Matt, my husband, was fighting in Iraq, we wrote letters—and emailed, of course. It was our only communication for fifteen months minus seven very short phone calls. And while most Americans had cell phones in 2006, the 2BCT (2nd Brigade Combat Team) was not allowed to bring personal phones, as they could prove very dangerous on several levels. Someday, I'll give Molly, our daughter, the letters we wrote so she can read about the events, the love, and the turmoil her parents faced during wartime. Perhaps I had—and have—an irrational fear that our personal histories will be erased: email thrown in the trashcan at the bottom of our screens and deleted into cyber oblivion.

It will be forged and written by only a few people, who will take a narrow lens to the grand and complicated events faced by people in a post–9-11 world. I envision it as looking out at the world through a door's peephole. How many of you have unearthed your grandfather's or grandmother's letters offering a vivid picture of life during their time? Can you imagine a world without Anne Frank's *The Diary of a Young Girl*, Margaret Mitchell's *Gone with the Wind*,

Pearl S. Buck's *The Good Earth*, or Azar Nafisi's *Reading Lolita In Tehran*? And while I certainly would never place *The Immortals* in the same category as these amazing books, I would offer that *The Immortals* also gives the reader a glimpse into one family's life before and during wartime. Galvanized by my own great-grandparents' transcontinental letters during the world wars, and the scant supply of women's literature from other authors about Operation Enduring Freedom and Operation Iraqi Freedom, I decided to jot down the conceit of my time as a war wife in a journal. It was my journal and our letters that roused me to create Calli, Luke, Audrey, the Divas, the denizens of Sackets Harbor, and all the other beloved characters in the *The Immortals*.

Less than one percent of the American population served in Operation Enduring Freedom and Operation Iraqi Freedom from October 2001–present day, compared with the more than twelve percent during World War II. It was during these current wars that wives and mothers, husbands and fathers, sat anxiously back here on the home front while their brave family members were sent to war to face a new type of enemy. Meanwhile, most of America, fortunately, was able to continue life uninterrupted. For most of our friends and family, we were their only real connection to the war. Although this is a work of fiction, I drew much of my inspiration from actual events that occurred in Iraq, Afghanistan, and here at home from 2005–2007.

Fort Drum, New York, is an actual Army base where my husband, (ret.) 1SG Matt Eversmann, was based from 2005–2008. He and I, along with our daughter, lived in the quaint village of Sackets Harbor on Lake Ontario about twenty miles west of Fort Drum. In August 2006, along with the 2BCT, he deployed to a region south of Baghdad dubbed "The Triangle of Death," which I reference in the novel.

On May 12, 2007, a US coalition observation post was attacked in Iraq. Four Americans and one Iraqi soldier were killed. Spc. Alex Jimenez, Pfc. Joseph Anzack, and Pvt. Byron Fouty of the 10th

Mountain Division's 4th Battalion, 31st Infantry Regiment, Fort Drum, NY, were abducted by Iraqi insurgents who were part of the then little-known Islamic State of Iraq within one of the most contested areas of the brigade's territory that ran along the Euphrates River on a stretch of road where insurgents routinely plant improvised explosive devices. The area was rural farmland near a defunct weapons factory, populated by intelligence and Republican Guard officers who were part of Saddam Hussein's regime. After fourteen months of relentless efforts by US and Coalition forces, the remains and equipment of all three soldiers were recovered. Luke Coleman's abduction was based on this tragic event.

People have often heard me say that I wouldn't wish the deployment of 2006–2007 on my worst enemy, but it was the best thing that happened to me. Due in large part to the people I met—wives and mothers of other soldiers at Fort Drum, the generous people of Sackets Harbor, and old family friends in the Thousand Islands—I found a courage I didn't know I had and a fundamental connectedness to my own life. Living life in limbo—as I did for far too long—not moving forward, is debilitating. Viktor Frankl wrote, "What is to give light must endure burning." I am hopeful, that for even one woman, one reader, *The Immortals* is engaging, insightful, and helpful in initiating her to take a step—even a small step—toward living an animated life, toward living with all her passion, fear, and longing. If I accomplished this, then I will feel grateful.

Tori Dukehart Eversmann
West Palm Beach, Florida 2015

Acknowledgements

At the end of working on The Immortals I stumbled across a video with the actor and comedian Jim Carrey speaking about failure, fear, and why you should pursue something that you love. He said, "...you can fail at what you don't want, so you might as well take a chance on doing what you love." I always wanted to write a book, but either was too afraid, didn't think I could produce a worthy opus, or perhaps, didn't have the story to write—until I became an Army wife, 9/11 occurred, and my beloved husband, Matt, went to Iraq to fight the Bad Guys. I dabbled in writing all my life, mostly journaling, but never professionally. So in 2007, I took a chance on doing what I love—writing, and thus The Immortals was born. It was and is extremely important to me that we never forget this time in history. A pen coupled with paper can be a powerful tool. However, I would be extremely remiss if I didn't acknowledge the collective group of people who made up my team to make my dream a reality.

To Halle von Kessler, Susan Shaw, Leah Michaels, Thomas Walter, Ginny Larsen, Whitney Dineen, Wendy Doak, Jamie Seward, Sonja Horoshko, Alicia Fish, and Susan Weiss, my beta readers who offered me invaluable comments. Your insight and thoughts pushed me to write a better story. Thank you.

To my wonderful friends and family who listened to me talk about "my book" for the last eight years as I ebbed and flowed in the different phases of writing The Immortals. Thank you.

To Sahffi Lynne who helped immensely in developing the musician in Calli. Since I know nothing about music, I owe you deep thanks for all your answers to my endless probing questions about being a professional musician.

To Jerry Friends, at Thompson Shore Publishing, thank you for holding my hand during this process.

To Lindsey Alexander, my amazing, steadfast, and talented editor. In addition to working on draft after draft, you challenged me to write better and managed to help me mine the words from that first early draft that shaped the novel today. I am indebted to you.

To the gallant wives and mothers of the 2nd Brigade Combat Team who were left behind with me from August 2006-November 2007 while our men were in Yusifiah. You were such a source of support to me before, during, and after the deployment. No one gets an Army wife better than an Army wife. Thank you.

I'd also like to thank all the valiant women in the military. Your lack of representation in the novel is in no way to ignore your resolute support of our Great Nation. Because there is a layer of autobiographical vérité in The Immortals, I never befriended any women in the Infantry or, thankfully, saw any injured women during my times visiting Walter Reed Army Medical Center. You're doing a job I could never do and I thank you.

To the noble staff at Walter Reed Army Medical Center. Thank you for the work that you do to ensure the health and well-being of our wounded military. And to Mark Hoffberger, who confidently held my hand on those initial visits to see Matt's wounded soldiers. I'll never forget your compassion and friendship during one of the most difficult periods of my life.

To Scott Quilty, Ferris Butler, Greg Cartier, Mike Schlitz, and the other brave men I met and befriended after your accidents. Your heroism inspired me, lifted me up, and made me a more compassionate woman. How could I ever repay you?

To The Diva War Brides: Susan, Laura, Wendy, Nicole, and Megan. There is no doubt in my mind that I would have sunk into an abyss without your love and support. Viva La Diva!

To my parents, Debbie Willse and Ned Dukehart, and my stepfather David Willse – for loving me and the wild child I am.

To Matt, my husband, who never doubted me or stopped believing in me, even though there were many days and months I doubted myself. You sustained my dream even when I thought I had abandoned it. Thank you especially for answering all my Army and deployment questions and helping me shape Luke Coleman. Thank you, thank you My Love.

And last, but not least, to Molly, my wise, beautiful daughter, whom I hope will never have to endure war. War is nasty business but part of our humankindness. We made it through: together. No words can express my love and gratitude for your life. You are my gift, my miracle.

About the Author

Tori Eversmann hails from Baltimore, Maryland. She currently lives in West Palm Beach, Florida with her husband and daughter. This is her first novel.